HOUNDED

THE IRON DRUID CHRONICLES
by Kevin Hearne

Hounded
Hexed
Hammered
Tricked
Trapped
Hunted

Two Ravens and One Crow: An Iron Druid Novella

HOUNDED

THE
IRON
DRUID
CHRONICLES

KEVIN HEARNE

BALLANTINE BOOKS • NEW YORK

Hounded is a work of fiction. Names, places, and incidents either are products of the author's imagination or are used fictitiously.

A Del Rey Mass Market Original

Copyright © 2011 by Kevin Hearne
Excerpt from *Hexed* by Kevin Hearne copyright © 2011 by Kevin Hearne

All rights reserved.

Published in the United States by Del Rey, an imprint of The Random House Publishing Group, a division of Random House, Inc., New York.

DEL REY is a registered trademark and the Del Rey colophon is a trademark of Random House, Inc.

This book contains an excerpt from the forthcoming book *Hexed* by Kevin Hearne. This excerpt has been set for this edition only and may not reflecct the final content for the forthcoming edition.

ISBN 978-0-345-52247-4
eBook ISBN 978-0-345-52253-5

Printed in the United States of America

www.delreybooks.com

19 18 17 16 15 14 13 12 11 10

Del Rey mass market edition: May 2011

Look, Mom, I made this!
Can we put it on the fridge?

Irish Pronunciation Guide

Let it be known from the beginning that readers are free to pronounce the names in this book however they see fit. It's supposed to be a good time, so I do not wish to steal anyone's marshmallows by telling them they're "saying it wrong." However, for those readers who place a premium on accuracy, I have provided an informal guide to some names and words that may be a bit confusing for English readers, since Irish phonetics aren't necessarily those of English. One thing to keep in mind is that diacritical marks above the vowels do not indicate a stressed syllable but rather a certain vowel sound.

Names

Aenghus Óg = Angus OHG (long *o*, as in *doe*, not short *o*, as in *log*)

Airmid = AIR mit

Bres = Bress

Brighid = BRI yit (or close to BREE yit) in Old Irish. Modern Irish has changed this to Bríd (pronounced like Breed), changing the vowel sound and eliminating the *g* entirely because English speakers kept pronouncing the *g* with a *j* sound. Names like Bridget are Anglicized versions of the original Irish name

Cairbre = CAR bre, where you kind of roll the *r* and the
     e is pronounced as in *egg*
Conaire = KON uh ra
Cúchulainn = Koo HOO lin (the Irish *ch* is pronounced
     like an *h* low in the throat, like a Spanish *j*, never
     with a hard *k* sound or as in the English *chew*)
Dian Cecht = DEE an KAY
Fianna = Fee AH na
Finn Mac Cumhaill = FIN mac COO will
Flidais = FLIH dish
Fragarach = FRAG ah rah
Granuaile = GRAWN ya WALE
Lugh Lámhfhada = Loo LAW wah duh
Manannan Mac Lir = MAH nah NON mac LEER
Miach = ME ah
Mogh Nuadhat = Moh NU ah dah
Moralltach = MOR ul TAH
Ó Suileabháin = Oh SULL uh ven (pronounced like
     O'Sullivan, it's just the Irish spelling)
Siodhachan = SHE ya han (remember the guttural *h* for
     the Irish *ch*; don't go near a hard *k* sound)
Tuatha Dé Danann = Too AH ha day DAN an

Places

Gabhra = GO rah
Mag Mell = Mah MEL
Magh Léna = Moy LAY na
Tír na nÓg = TEER na NOHG (long *o*)

Verbs

Coinnigh = con NEE (to hold, keep)
Dóigh = doy (to burn)
Dún = doon (to close or seal)
Oscail = OS kill (to open)

Trees

Fearn = fairn
Idho = EE yo
Ngetal = NYET ul
Tinne = CHIN neh
Ura = OO ra (make sure you're not turning this into a
military cheer. Both syllables are very clipped and you
roll the *r* a wee bit)

HOUNDED

Chapter 1

There are many perks to living for twenty-one centuries, and foremost among them is bearing witness to the rare birth of genius. It invariably goes like this: Someone shrugs off the weight of his cultural traditions, ignores the baleful stares of authority, and does something his countrymen think to be completely batshit insane. Of those, Galileo was my personal favorite. Van Gogh comes in second, but he really was batshit insane.

Thank the Goddess I don't look like a guy who met Galileo—or who saw Shakespeare's plays when they first debuted or rode with the hordes of Genghis Khan. When people ask how old I am, I just tell them twenty-one, and if they assume I mean years instead of decades or centuries, then that can't be my fault, can it? I still get carded, in fact, which any senior citizen will tell you is immensely flattering.

The young-Irish-lad façade does not stand me in good stead when I'm trying to appear scholarly at my place of business—I run an occult bookshop with an apothecary's counter squeezed in the corner—but it has one outstanding advantage. When I go to the grocery store, for example, and people see my curly red hair, fair skin, and long goatee, they suspect that I play soccer and drink lots of Guinness. If I'm going sleeveless and they see the tattoos all up and down my right arm, they assume I'm in a rock band and smoke lots of weed. It never enters their mind for a moment that I could be an ancient Druid—and that's the main reason why I like this look. If I grew a white beard and got myself a pointy hat, oozed dignity and sagacity and glowed with beatitude, people might start to get the wrong—or the right—idea.

Sometimes I forget what I look like and I do something out of character, such as sing shepherd tunes in Aramaic while I'm waiting in line at Starbucks, but the nice bit about living in urban America is that people tend to either ignore eccentrics or move to the suburbs to escape them.

That never would have happened in the old days. People who were different back then got burned at the stake or stoned to death. There is still a downside to being different today, of course, which is why I put so much effort into blending in, but the downside is usually just harassment and discrimination, and that is a vast improvement over dying for the common man's entertainment.

Living in the modern world contains quite a few vast improvements like that. Most old souls I know think the attraction of modernity rests on clever ideas like indoor plumbing and sunglasses. But for me, the true attraction of America is that it's practically godless. When I was younger and dodging the Romans, I could hardly walk a mile in Europe without stepping on a stone sacred to some god or other. But out here in Arizona, all I have to worry about is the occasional encounter with Coyote, and I actually rather like him. (He's nothing like Thor, for one thing, and that right there means we're going to get along fine. The local college kids would describe Thor as a "major asshat" if they ever had the misfortune to meet him.)

Even better than the low god density in Arizona is the near total absence of faeries. I don't mean those cute winged creatures that Disney calls "fairies"; I mean the Fae, the *Sidhe,* the actual descendants of the Tuatha Dé Danann, born in Tír na nÓg, the land of eternal youth, each one of them as likely to gut you as hug you. They don't dig me all that much, so I try to settle in places they can't reach very easily. They have all sorts of gateways to earth in the Old World, but in the New World they need oak, ash, and thorn to make the journey, and those trees don't grow together too often in Arizona. I have found a couple of likely places, like the White Mountains near the border with New Mexico and a riparian area near Tucson, but those are both over a hundred miles away from my well-paved neighborhood near the university in Tempe. I figured the chances of the Fae entering the world there and then crossing a treeless desert to look for a rogue Druid were extremely small, so when I found this place in the late nineties, I decided to stay until the locals grew suspicious.

It was a great decision for more than a decade. I set up a new identity, leased some shop space, hung out a sign that said THIRD EYE BOOKS AND HERBS (an allusion to Vedic and Buddhist beliefs, because I thought a Celtic name would bring up a red flag to those searching for me), and bought a small house within easy biking distance.

I sold crystals and Tarot cards to college kids who wanted to shock their Protestant parents, scores of ridiculous tomes with "spells" in them for lovey-dovey Wiccans, and some herbal remedies for people looking to make an end run around the doctor's office. I even stocked extensive works on Druid magic, all of them based on Victorian revivals, all of them utter rubbish, and all vastly entertaining to me whenever I sold any of them. Maybe once a month I had a serious magical customer looking for a genuine grimoire, stuff you don't mess with or even know about until you're fairly accomplished. I did much more of my rare book business via the Internet—another vast improvement of modern times.

But when I set up my identity and my place of business, I did not realize how easy it would be for someone else to find me by doing a public-records search on the Internet. The idea that any of the Old Ones would even try it never occurred to me—I thought they'd try to scry me or use other methods of divination, but never the Internet—so I was not as careful in choosing my name as I should have been. I should have called myself John Smith or something utterly sad and plain like that, but my pride would not let me wear a Christian name. So I used O'Sullivan, the Anglicized version of my real surname, and for everyday usage I employed the decidedly Greek name of Atticus. A supposedly twenty-one-year-old O'Sullivan who owned an occult bookstore and sold extremely rare books he had no business knowing about was enough information for the Fae to find me, though.

On a Friday three weeks before Samhain, they jumped me in front of my shop when I walked outside to take a lunch break. A sword swished below my knees without so much as a "Have at thee!" and the arm swinging it pulled its owner off balance when I jumped over it. I crunched a quick left elbow into his face as he tried to recover, and that was one faery down, four to go.

Thank the Gods Below for paranoia. I classified it as a survival skill rather than a neurotic condition; it was a keen knife's edge, sharpened for centuries against the grindstone of People Who Want to Kill Me. It was what made me wear an amulet of cold iron around my neck, and cloak my shop not only with iron bars, but also with magical wards designed to keep out the Fae and other undesirables. It was what made me train in unarmed combat and test my speed against vampires, and what had saved me countless times from thugs like these.

Perhaps *thug* is too heavy a word for them; it connotes an abundance of muscle tissue and a profound want of intellect. These lads didn't look as if they had ever hit the gym or heard of anabolic steroids. They were lean, ropy types who had chosen to disguise themselves as cross-country runners, bare-chested and wearing nothing but maroon shorts and expensive running shoes. To any passerby it would look as if they were trying to beat me up with brooms, but that was just a glamour they had cast on their weapons. The pointy parts were in the twigs, so if I was unable to see through their illusions, I would have been fatally surprised when the nice broom stabbed my vitals. Since I could see through faerie glamours, I noticed that two of my remaining four assailants carried spears, and one of them was circling around to my right. Underneath their human guises, they looked like the typical faery—that is, no wings, scantily clad, and kind of man-pretty like Orlando Bloom's Legolas, the sort of people you see in salon product advertisements. The ones with spears stabbed at me simultaneously from the sides, but I slapped the tips away with either wrist so that they thrust past me to the front and back. Then I lunged inside the guard of the one to the right and clotheslined him with a forearm to his throat. Tough to breathe through a crushed windpipe. Two down now; but they were quick and deft, and their dark eyes held no gleam of mercy.

I had left my back open to attack by lunging to the right, so I spun and raised my left forearm high to block the blow I knew was coming. Sure enough, there was a sword about to arc down into my skull, and I caught it on my arm at the top of the swing. It bit down to the bone, and that hurt a *lot*, but not nearly as much as it would have if I had let it fall. I grimaced at the pain and stepped forward to deliver a punishing open-hand blow to the faery's solar plexus, and he flew back into the wall of my shop—the wall ribbed with bars of iron. Three down, and I smiled at the remaining two, who were not so zealous as before to take a shot at me. Three of their buddies had not only been physically beaten but also magically poisoned by physical contact with me. My cold iron amulet was bound to my aura, and by now they could no doubt see it: I was some sort of Iron Druid, their worst nightmare made flesh. My first victim was already disintegrating into ash, and the other two were close to realizing that all we are is dust in the wind.

I was wearing sandals, and I kicked them off and stepped back a bit toward the street so that the faeries had a wall full of iron at their backs. Besides being a good idea strategically, it put me closer to a thin strip of landscaping between the street and the sidewalk, where I could draw power from the earth to close up my wound and kill the pain. Knitting the muscle tissue I could worry about later; my immediate concern was stopping the bleeding, because there were too many scary things an unfriendly magician could do with my blood.

As I sank my feet into the grass and drew power from it for healing, I also sent out a call—sort of an instant message through the earth—to an iron elemental I knew, informing him that I had two faeries standing in front of me if he wanted a snack. He would answer quickly, because the earth is bound to me as I am bound to it, but it might take him a few moments. To give him time, I asked my assailants a question.

"Out of curiosity, were you guys trying to capture me or kill me?"

The one to my left, hefting a short sword in his right hand, decided to snarl at me rather than answer. "Tell us where the sword is!"

"Which sword? The one in your hand? It's still in your hand, big guy."

"You know which sword! Fragarach, the Answerer!"

"Don't know what you're talking about." I shook my head. "Who sent you guys? Are you sure you have the right fella?"

"We're sure," Spear Guy sneered. "You have Druidic tattoos and you can see through our glamour."

"But lots of magical folk can do that. And you don't have to be a Druid to appreciate Celtic knotwork. Think about it, fellas. You've come to ask me about some sword, but clearly I don't have one or I would have whipped it out by now. All I'm asking you to consider is that maybe you've been sent here to get killed. Are you sure the motives of the person who sent you are entirely pure?"

"Us get killed?" Sword Guy spluttered at me for being so ridiculous. "When it's five against one?"

"It's two against one now, just in case you missed the part where I killed three of you. Maybe the person who sent you knew it would happen like that."

"Aenghus Óg would never do that to us!" Spear Guy exclaimed, and my suspicions were confirmed. I had a name now, and that name had been chasing me for two millennia. "We're his own blood!"

"Aenghus Óg tricked his own father out of his home. What does your kinship matter to the likes of him? Look, I've been here before, guys, and you haven't. The Celtic god of love loves nothing so much as himself. He'd never waste his time or risk his magnificent person on a scouting trip, so he sends a tiny little band of disposable offspring every time he thinks he's found me. If they ever come back, he knows it wasn't really me, see?"

Understanding began to dawn on their faces and they crouched into defensive stances, but it was much too late for them and they weren't looking in the right direction.

The bars along the wall of my shop had melted silently apart behind them and morphed into jaws of sharp iron teeth. The giant black maw reached out for them and snapped closed, scissoring through the faeries' flesh as if it were cottage cheese, and then they were inhaled like Jell-O, with time only for a startled, aborted scream. Their weapons clattered to the ground, all glamour gone, and then the iron mouth melted back into its wonted shape as a series of bars, after gracing me with a brief, satisfied grin.

I got a message from the iron elemental before it faded away, in the short bursts of emotions and imagery that they use for language: //Druid calls / Faeries await / Delicious / Gratitude//

Chapter 2

I looked around to see who might have witnessed the fight, but there wasn't anyone close by—it was lunchtime. My shop is just south of University on Ash Avenue, and all the food places are north of University, up and down both Ash and Mill Avenues.

I collected the weapons off the sidewalk and opened up the shop door, grinning to myself at the OUT TO LUNCH sign. I flipped it around to say OPEN; might as well do some business, since cleaning up would keep me tied down to the shop. Heading over to my tea station, I filled a pitcher with water and checked my arm. It was still red and puffy from the cut but doing well, and I had the pain firmly shut down. Still, I didn't think I should risk tearing the muscles further by asking them to carry water for me; I'd have to make two trips. I grabbed a jug of bleach from under the sink and went outside with it, leaving the pitcher on the counter. I poured bleach on every bloodstain and then returned for the pitcher to wash it all away.

After I'd satisfactorily washed away the blood, a giant crow flew into the shop behind me as I opened the door to return the pitcher. It perched itself on a bust of Ganesha, spreading its wings and ruffling its feathers in an aggressive display. It was the Morrigan, Celtic Chooser of the Slain and goddess of war, and she called me by my Irish name. "Siodhachan Ó Suileabháin," she croaked dramatically. "We must talk."

"Can't you take the form of a human?" I said, placing the pitcher on a rack to dry. The motion caused me to notice a spot of blood on my amulet, and I removed it from my neck to wash it off. "It's creepy when you talk to me like that. Bird beaks are incapable of forming fricatives, you know."

"I did not journey here for a linguistics lesson," the Morrigan said. "I have come with ill tidings. Aenghus Óg knows you are here."

"Well, yes, I already knew that. Didn't you just take care of five dead faeries?" I laid my necklace on the counter and reached for a towel to pat it dry.

"I sent them on to Manannan Mac Lir," she said, referring to the Celtic god who escorted the living to the land of the dead. "But there is more. Aenghus Óg is coming here himself and may even now be on his way."

I went still. "Are you quite certain?" I asked. "This is based on solid evidence?"

The crow flapped its wings in irritation and cawed. "If you wait for evidence, it will be too late," she said.

Relief washed through me, and the tension melted from between my shoulder blades. "Ah, so this is just some vague augury," I said.

"No, the augury was quite specific," the Morrigan replied. "A mortal doom gathers about you here, and you must fly if you wish to avoid it."

"See? There you go again. You get this way every year around Samhain," I said. "If it isn't Thor coming to get me, it's one of the Olympians. Remember that story last year? Apollo was offended by my association with the Arizona State Sun Devils—"

"This is different."

"—Never mind that I do not even attend the university, I just work nearby. So he was coming in his golden chariot to shoot me full of arrows."

The crow shuffled on the bust and looked uncomfortable. "It seemed a plausible interpretation at the time."

"The Greek deity of the sun being offended by an old Druid's tenuous relationship with a college mascot on the other side of the globe seemed plausible?"

"The basics were accurate, Siodhachan. Missiles were fired at you."

"Some kids punctured my bike tires with darts, Morrigan. I think you may have exaggerated the threat somewhat."

"Nevertheless. You cannot stay here any longer. The omens are dire."

"Very well," I sighed in resignation. "Tell me what you saw."

"I was speaking with Aenghus recently—"

"You spoke to him?" If I'd been eating anything, I would have choked. "I thought you hated each other."

"We do. That does not mean we are incapable of conversing together. I was relaxing in Tír na nÓg, thoroughly sated after a trip to Mesopotamia—have you been there recently? It is magnificent sport."

"Begging your pardon, but the mortals call it Iraq now, and no, I haven't been there in centuries." The Morrigan's ideas of sport and mine varied widely. As a Chooser of the Slain, she tends to enjoy nothing so much as a protracted war. She hangs out with Kali and the Valkyries and they have a death goddesses' night out on the battlefield. I, on the other hand, stopped thinking war was glorious after the Crusades. Baseball is more my kind of thing these days. "What did Aenghus say to you?" I prompted.

"He just smiled at me and told me to look to my friends."

My eyebrows shot up. "You have friends?"

"Of course not." The crow ruffled its feathers and managed to look aggrieved at the mere suggestion. "Well, Hecate is kind of funny and we have been spending a lot of time together lately. But I think he meant you."

The Morrigan and I have a certain understanding (though it's too uncertain for my taste): She will not come for me as long as my existence continues to drive Aenghus Óg into twitching spasms of fury. It's not exactly a friendship—she's not the sort of creature that allows it—but we have known each other a long time, and she drops by every so often to keep me out of trouble. "It would be embarrassing for me," she explained once as she was ushering me out of the Battle of Gabhra, "if you got yourself decapitated and yet you didn't die. I would have some explaining to do. Dereliction of duty is difficult to justify. So from now on, do not put me in a position where I must take your life to save face." The bloodlust was still on me at the time, and I could feel the power coursing through my tattoos; I was part of the Fianna during that episode, and there was nothing I wanted more than to have a go at that pompous snot King Cairbre. But the Morrigan had chosen sides, and when a goddess of death says to leave the battle, you leave the battle. Ever since I earned Aenghus Óg's enmity all those centuries ago, she has tried to warn me of mortal dangers coming my way, and while she occasionally exaggerates the danger, I suppose I should be grateful she never underestimates it or neglects to warn me at all.

"He could have been playing with your mind, Morrigan," I said. "Aenghus is like that."

"I am well aware. That is why I consulted the flight of crows and found them ominous regarding your position here." I made a face, and the Morrigan continued before I could say anything. "I knew that such augury would not be sufficient for you, so, seeking more specifics, I cast the wands."

"Oh," I said. She had actually gone to some trouble. There are all sorts of ways to cast lots or runes or otherwise practice divination by interpreting the random as the pattern of the future. I prefer them all to watching the flight of birds or watching clouds, because my involvement in the casting centers the randomness on me. Birds fly because they want to eat or mate or grab something for their nest, and applying that to my future or anyone else's seems a ludicrous stretch to me. Logically, throwing some sticks on the ground and making predictions is little better, except that I know that my agency and will in the ritual provide enough focus for Fortune to stop and say, "Here's what's coming soon to a theatre near you."

There used to be a class of Druids that practiced animal sacrifice and read the future from entrails, which I kind of thought was messy and a waste of a good chicken or bull or whatever. People today look at those practices and say, "That's so cruel! Why couldn't they simply be vegan like me?" But the Druidic faith allows for a pretty happy afterlife and maybe even a return trip or ten to earth. Since the soul never dies, taking a knife to some flesh here and there is never a big deal. Still, I never got into the whole sacrificing thing. There are far cleaner and more reliable ways to peek under Fortune's skirts. Druids like me use twenty wands in a bag, each marked with Ogham script representing the twenty trees native to Ireland, and each carrying with it a wealth of prophetic meaning. Much like Tarot, these wands are interpreted differently depending on which direction they fall in relation to the diviner; there is a positive set of meanings if they fall upright, a negative set if they fall downward. Without looking, the caster draws five wands from the bag and tosses them on the ground in front of him, then tries to interpret the message represented by their arrangement. "And how did they fall?" I asked the Morrigan.

"Four of them were fell," she said, and waited for that to sink in. It wasn't going to be a happy time.

"I see. And which of the trees spoke to you?"

The Morrigan regarded me as if her next words would cause me to swoon like a corseted Jane Austen character. "*Fearn. Tinne. Ngetal. Ura. Idho.*"

Alder, Holly, Reed, Heather, and Yew. The first represented a warrior and was simultaneously the most clearly interpreted and the most vague. The others all suggested that some pretty dire shit was going to befall said warrior, whoever he was. Holly signaled challenges and ordeals, Reed screamed of fear, Heather warned of surprises, and Yew prophesied death.

"Ah," I said as nonchalantly as I could. "And how, precisely, did the Alder and the Yew fall in relationship to each other?"

"The Yew crossed the Alder."

Well, that was fairly clear. The warrior was going to die. He'd be surprised by its arrival, scared witless, and he'd fight maniacally against it, but his death was inevitable. The Morrigan noted my acceptance of the casting and said, "So where will you go?"

"I have not decided yet."

"There are even more isolated places in the Mojave Desert," she suggested, with a slight emphasis on the name. I think she was trying to impress me with her knowledge of American geography since she had bungled the Iraq thing. I wondered if she knew about the dissolution of Yugoslavia, or if she even knew that Transylvania was now part of Romania. Immortals don't always pay much attention to current events.

"I mean, Morrigan, I have not decided to go yet."

The crow on the bust of Ganesha said nothing, but the eyes flashed red for a brief second, and that, I admit, made me a bit uncomfortable. She really wasn't my friend. One day—and it could be today—she would decide I'd lived far too long and grown far too cavalier, and that would be it for me.

"Just give me a few minutes to think about the casting," I said, and realized immediately afterward that I should have chosen my words more carefully.

The red eyes came back and the crow's voice was pitched lower than before, with minor harmonics in it that raised the hairs on the back of my neck. "You would pit your divination skills against mine?"

"No, no," I hastened to reassure her. "I'm trying to catch up with you, that's all. Now, I'm just thinking aloud here, okay? That Alder wand—the warrior—that does not necessarily have to mean me, does it?"

The red eyes faded back to a more natural black, and the Morrigan shifted her weight impatiently on the bust. "Of course not," she said in her normal tone. The minor harmonics were gone. "It could technically be anyone who fights you, should you prevail. But my focus was on you when I made the casting, and so you are most likely to be the warrior the Alder wand represents. This fight is coming, whether you will or no."

"But here is my question: You have let me live for centuries because it vexes Aenghus Óg. Aenghus and I are probably linked somewhat in your mind. So when you did the casting, is it not possible that Aenghus Óg was also in your thoughts?"

The Morrigan cawed and hopped onto Ganesha's trunk, then hopped back up to the top of the head, twitching her wings a bit. She knew the answer, but she didn't like it because she knew where I was going with this.

"Possible, yes," she hissed. "But it is unlikely."

"But you must admit, Morrigan, that it is also unlikely Aenghus Óg would leave Tír na nÓg to hunt me down himself. He is far more likely to employ surrogates, as he has done for centuries now." Aenghus's strengths ran to charm and networking—making people love him, in other words, so that they'd offer to do him any little favor, like killing wayward Druids. He'd sent practically every sort of thug and assassin imaginable against me over the years—my favorites were the camel-mounted Egyptian Mamelukes—but he seemed to realize that taking up the chase personally would diminish him, especially since I kept living to escape another day. A hint of smugness might have crept into my tone as I continued, "And I can handle any of the lesser Fae he should choose to send after me, as I proved just moments ago."

The crow leapt off the bust of Ganesha and flew straight at my face, but before I could get worried about a beak in the eye, the bird sort of melted in midair, reforming into a naked, statuesque woman with milk-white skin and raven hair. It was the Morrigan as seductress, and she caught me rather unprepared. Her scent had me responding before she ever touched me, and by the time she closed the remaining distance between us, I was ready to invite her back to my place. Or here would be fine, right here, right now, by the tea station. She draped an arm around my shoulder and trailed her nails down the back of my neck, causing me to shudder involuntarily. A smile tugged at the corners of her mouth at that, and she pressed her body against mine and leaned forward to whisper in my ear.

"And what if he sends a succubus to slay you, most wise and ancient Druid? You would be dead inside a minute if he knew this weakness of yours." I heard what she said, and a small corner of my mind realized that it could be of some importance, but the largest part of me could think of nothing except the way she was making me feel. The Morrigan stepped back abruptly and I tried to clutch at her, but she slapped me viciously across the face and told me to snap out of it as I crumpled to the floor.

I snapped out of it. The scent that had so intoxicated me was gone, and the pain spreading across my cheek banished the physical need I had felt.

"Ow," I said. "Thanks for that. I was about to go into full-on leg-humping mode."

"This is a serious vulnerability you have, Siodhachan. Aenghus could simply pay a mortal woman to do his work for him."

"He tried that when I was last in Italy," I said, as I grabbed the edge of the sink to help myself up. The Morrigan is not the sort to give a man a hand. "And I've faced succubi as well. I have an amulet to protect me against such things."

"Then why aren't you wearing it?"

"I took it off just a moment ago to wash it. Besides, I am safe inside my store and my home from the Fae."

"Clearly not, Druid, because here I stand." Yes, there she stood, naked. That could prove awkward if anyone walked through the door.

"Your pardon, Morrigan; I am safe from all save the Tuatha Dé Danann. If you look carefully, you will notice the bindings I have set about the place. They should hold against the lesser Fae and most anything he could send from hell."

The Morrigan tilted her head upward and her eyes lost focus for a moment, and it was then that a pair of unfortunate college lads wandered into my shop. I could tell that they were drunk, even though it was only mid-afternoon. Their hair was greasy and they wore concert T-shirts and jeans, and they had not shaved for several days. I knew the type: They were stoners who were wondering if I had anything smokable behind my apothecary counter. Conversations with them usually began with them asking if my herbs had medicinal benefits. After my affirmative response, they would ask me if I had anything with hallucinogenic properties. I usually sold these types a bag of sage and thyme under an exotic name and sent them on their merry way, because I have no scruples about separating idiots from their money. They would get headaches from the experience and never return. What I feared was that these particular lads would see the Morrigan and never leave alive.

Sure enough, one of them, wearing a Meat Loaf shirt, saw the Morrigan standing bare-assed in the middle of my shop, hands on hips, looking like a goddess, and he pointed her out to his friend in the Iron Maiden shirt.

"Dude, that chick is naked!" Meat Loaf exclaimed.

"Whoa," said Iron Maiden, who pushed his sunglasses down his nose to get a better look. "And she's hot too."

"Hey, baby," Meat Loaf said, taking a couple of steps toward her. "If you need some clothes, I'll be glad to take off my pants for you." He and his friend began to laugh as if this was incredibly funny, spitting out "hahaha" like automatic weapons fire. They sounded like goats, only less intelligent.

The Morrigan's eyes flashed red and I held up my hands. "Morrigan, no, please, not in my shop. Cleaning up afterward would cause me tremendous hardship."

"They must die for their impertinence," she said, and those hair-raising minor harmonics were back in her voice. Anyone with a cursory knowledge of mythology knows that it is suicidal to sexually harass a goddess. Look what Artemis did to that guy who stumbled across her bathing.

"I understand that this insult must be redressed," I

said, "but if you could do it elsewhere so that my life is not further complicated, I would appreciate the courtesy very much."

"Very well," she muttered to me. "I just ate, in any case." And then she turned to the stoners and gave them the full frontal view. They were overjoyed at first: They were looking down and so did not see that her eyes were glowing red. But when she spoke, her unearthly voice rattled the windows, and their eyes snapped up to her face and they realized they were not dealing with the average girl gone wild.

"Put your affairs in order, mortals," she boomed, as a gust of wind—yes, wind inside my shop—blew their hair back. "I will feast on your hearts tonight for the offense you gave me. So swears the Morrigan." I thought it was a bit melodramatic, but one does not critique a death goddess on her oratory delivery.

"Dude, what the hell?" Iron Maiden squealed in a voice a couple of octaves above his prior register.

"I don't know, man," Meat Loaf said, "but my chubby is gone. I'm bailin'." They tripped over each other in their haste to get out.

The Morrigan watched them go with predatory interest, and I kept silent as her head tracked their flight even through the walls. Finally she turned to me and said, "They are polluted creatures. They have defiled themselves."

I nodded. "Aye, but they are unlikely to provide you much sport." I was not about to defend them or beg for a stay of execution; the best I could do was imply that they were not worth the trouble.

"That is true," she said. "They are pathetic shadows of true men. But they will die tonight nevertheless. I have sworn it." Oh well, I sighed inwardly. I had tried.

The Morrigan calmed herself and returned her attention to me. "The defenses you have here are surprisingly subtle and unusually strong," she said, and I nodded my thanks. "But they will not serve you well against the Tuatha Dé Danann. I counsel you to leave immediately."

I pressed my lips together and took a moment to choose my words carefully. "I appreciate your counsel and I am eternally grateful for your interest in my survival," I replied, "but I cannot think of a better place to defend myself. I have been running for two millennia, Morrigan, and I am tired. If Aenghus truly means to come for me, then let him come. He will be as weak here as anywhere on earth. It is time we settled this."

The Morrigan tilted her head at me. "You would truly offer arms against him on this plane?"

"Aye, I am resolved." I wasn't. But the Morrigan is not renowned for her bullshit detection. She is more renowned for whimsical slaughter and recreational torture.

The Morrigan sighed. "I think it smacks of foolishness more than courage, but so be it. Let me see this amulet, then, your so-called defense."

"Gladly. Would you mind clothing yourself, however, so that we may avoid any further shocks to mortal eyes?"

The Morrigan smirked. She was not only built like a Victoria's Secret model, but the sun streaming through the windows lit up her smooth, flawless skin, which was white as confectioner's sugar. "It is only this prudish age that makes a vice of nudity. But perhaps it is wiser to bow to local custom for now." She made a gesture, and a black robe materialized to cloak her form. I smiled my gratitude and picked up my amulet from the counter.

It would perhaps be more accurate to describe it as a charm necklace—not charms like you will find on a Tiffany bracelet, but charms that will quickly execute spells for me that otherwise would take a long time to cast. It took me 750 years to complete the necklace, because it was built around a cold iron amulet in the center designed to protect me against the Fae and other magic users. Aenghus Óg's constant attempts to kill me had made it necessary. I had bound the amulet to my aura, an excruciating process of my own devising but worth every second in the end. To any of the lesser Fae, it made me an invincible badass, because as beings of pure magic, they cannot abide iron in any form: Iron is the antithesis of magic, which is why magic largely died on this world with the advent of the Iron Age. It had taken me 300 years to bind the amulet to my aura, providing me with tremendous protection and a literal Fist of Death whenever I touched one of the Fae; the remaining 450 were spent constructing the charms and finding a way to make my magic work in such close proximity to the iron and my newly tainted aura.

The problem with the Tuatha Dé Danann was that they were not beings of pure magic, like their descendants born in the land of Faerie: They were beings of this world, who merely used magic better than anyone else, and the Irish had long ago elevated them to gods. So the iron bars around my shop would not bother the Morrigan or any of her kin, and neither would my aura do them any damage. All the iron did was even the odds a bit so that their magic would not overwhelm me: They had to stoop to physical attack if they wished to do me any harm.

That, more than anything else, was the reason I was still breathing. The Morrigan aside, the Tuatha Dé Danann were loath to subject themselves to physical combat, because they were as vulnerable as I to a well-timed sword thrust. Through magic they had prolonged their lives for millennia (just as I had staved off the ravages of aging), but violence could bring an end to them, as it had to Lugh and Nuada and others of their kind.

It made them prone to use assassins and poisons and other forms of cowardly attack when their magic would not suffice, and Aenghus Óg had tried most of them already on me.

"Remarkable," the Morrigan said, fingering the amulet and shaking her head.

"It's not a universal defense," I pointed out, "but it's pretty good, if I do say so myself."

She looked up at me. "How did you do it?"

I shrugged. "Mostly patience. Iron can be bent to your will, if your will is stronger than the iron. But it is a slow, laborious process of centuries, and you need the help of an elemental."

"What happens to it when you change your shape?"

"It shrinks or grows to an appropriate size. It was the first thing I learned how to do with it."

"I have never seen its like." The Morrigan frowned. "Who taught you this magic?"

"No one. It is my own original craft."

"Then you will teach me this craft, Druid." It was not a request.

I did not respond right away but rather looked down at the necklace and grasped a single one of the charms. It was a silver square stamped in bas relief with the likeness of a sea otter, and I held it up for the Morrigan's inspection.

"This charm, when activated, allows me to breathe underwater and swim like I was native unto the element. It works in conjunction with the iron amulet here in the center, which protects me from the wiles of selkies, sirens, and the like. It makes me second only to Manannan Mac Lir in the sea, and it took me more than two hundred years to perfect it. And that is just one of the many valuable charms on this necklace. What do you offer me in exchange for this knowledge?"

"Your continued existence," the Morrigan spat.

I thought she would say something like that. The Morrigan has never been noted for her diplomacy.

"That is a good beginning for negotiations," I replied. "Shall we formalize it? I will teach you this new Druidry, painstakingly formulated over centuries of trial and error, in exchange for your eternal ignorance of my mortality—in other words, you will not take me, ever."

"You are asking for true immortality."

"And for this you receive magic that will make you supreme amongst the Tuatha Dé Danann."

"I am already supreme, Druid," she growled.

"Some of your cousins may beg to differ," I replied, thinking of the goddess Brighid, who currently ruled in Tír na nÓg as First among the Fae. "In any case, regardless of your decision, you have my word, freely given, that I will not teach this magic to any of them under any inducement."

"Fairly spoken," she said after a pause, and I began breathing again. "Very well. You will teach me how each charm on this necklace was achieved under the terms you described and how you bound the iron to your aura, and I will let you live forever."

Smiling, I told her to find a lump of cold iron to use as her amulet and then we could begin.

"You should still fly from here now," she told me when we had sealed the bargain. "Just because I will never take you does not mean you are safe from other gods of death. If Aenghus defeats you, one of them will come eventually."

"Let me worry about Aenghus," I said. Worrying about him was my specialty. If love and hate were two sides of the same coin, Aenghus spent an awful lot of time on the hate side for a god of love—especially where I was concerned. I also had to worry about the effects of aging, and if I lost a limb, it wasn't going to grow back. Being immortal did not make me invincible. Look at what the Bacchants did to that poor Orpheus fella.

"Done," the Morrigan replied. "But beware the agency of humans first. Working at the behest of Aenghus, one of them found you on some sort of new device called the Internet. Do you know of it?"

"I use it every day," I said, nodding. If it was less than a century old, then it qualified as new to the Morrigan.

"Based on the word of this human, Aenghus Óg is sending some Fir Bolgs here to confirm that Atticus O'Sullivan is the ancient Druid Siodhachan Ó Suileabháin. You should have used a different name."

"I'm a stupid git, and no doubt about it," I said, shaking my head, piecing together how they must have found me.

The Morrigan's expression softened and she grasped my chin in her fingers, pulling my mouth to hers. Her black robe melted away into nothingness, she stood before me like a Nagel poster come to life, and the heady scent of everything desirable to a man again filled my nostrils, though the effect was muted since I was now wearing my amulet. She kissed me deeply and then pulled away with that same maddening smirk on her face, knowing the effect she had on me, magically assisted or not. "Wear your amulet at all times from now on," she said. "And call on me, Druid, when you have need. I have some humans to hunt now."

And with that she turned back into the battle crow and flew out the door of my shop, which opened of its own accord to grant her passage.

Chapter 3

I have been around long enough to discount most superstitions for what they are: I was around when many of them began to take root, after all. But one superstition to which I happen to subscribe is that bad juju comes in threes. The saying in my time was, "Storm clouds are thrice cursed," but I can't talk like that and expect people to believe I'm a twenty-one-year-old American. I have to say things like, "Shit happens, man."

The Morrigan's exit did not put me at ease, therefore, because I fully expected the day to get worse from there. I closed up my shop a couple of hours early and headed home on my mountain bike with my necklace tucked inside my shirt, worrying a bit about what might be waiting for me there.

I headed west on University from my shop and took a left on Roosevelt, heading south into the Mitchell Park neighborhood. Before the dams got put up on the Salt River, the area was floodplain land, with very fertile soil. It was farmland originally, and the lots were gradually subdivided and built up from the 1930s through the '60s, complete with front porches and irrigated lawns. Usually I took my time and enjoyed the ride: I would say hello to the dogs who barked a greeting at me or stop to chat with the widow MacDonagh, who liked to sit on her front porch, sipping sweaty glasses of Tullamore Dew as the sun set. She spoke the Irish with me and told me I was a nice young lad with an old soul, and I enjoyed the conversation and the irony of being the young one. I usually did her yard work for her once a week and she liked to watch me do it, declaring loudly each time that "If I were fifty years younger, laddie, I'd jump yer wee bones and tell no one but the Lord, ye can be sure." But today I hurried, tossing a quick wave at the widow's porch and churning my legs as fast as they would go. I took a right onto 11th Street and slowed, stretching out my senses in search of trouble. When I pulled up to my house, I did not go in right away. Rather, I squatted near the street and sank the fingers of my tattooed right hand into the grass of my lawn to check on my defenses.

My house was built in the fifties, a north-facing cottage with a white-posted raised porch and a flower bed in front of it. The lawn in front is dominated by a single towering mesquite tree planted to the right of center, while a driveway on the right leads into a garage. A flagstone path goes from the driveway to my porch and front door. My front window told me nothing, being cast completely in late-afternoon shadow. But by examining my wards through the grass . . . yes. Someone was there. And since no mortal or lesser Fae could ever break through the wards on my house, that meant I had two choices: Get the hell out now, or go find out which member of the Tuatha Dé Danann had untied my knots and was waiting for me inside.

It could be Aenghus Óg, and the thought chilled me even though it was nearly a hundred degrees outside (Arizona does not cool down to sensible temperatures until the second half of October, and we were still a week or so away from that). But I could not imagine him leaving Tír na nÓg, despite the Morrigan's insistence that he was on his way. So I checked in with my pet—well, I should say in all honesty, my friend—Oberon, with whom I was specially bound.

How goes it, my friend?

<Atticus? Someone is here,> Oberon answered from the backyard. I did not pick up any tension in his thoughts. I rather got the impression that his tail was wagging. The fact that he had not been barking on my arrival was another clue that he thought everything was fine.

I know. Who is it?

<I do not know. I like her though. She said perhaps we would go hunting later.>

She spoke to you? In your mind, like me? It took some effort to make an animal understand human language; it was not a simple binding, and not all of the Tuatha Dé Danann would bother. Most often they confined themselves to communicating emotions and images, as one does when speaking to an elemental.

<Aye, she did. She told me I remind her of my sires of old.>

High praise. Oberon was indeed a magnificent specimen of Irish wolfhound, with a rich dark-gray coat and sturdy constitution. His sires of old were called warhounds, not wolfhounds, and they accompanied the Irish into battle, unhorsing cavalry and attacking chariots. The warhounds of my youth were rather less friendly creatures, not like the gentle wolfhounds of today. Indeed, most modern wolfhounds are so mild, bred for gentle dispositions for centuries, that they can scarcely conceive of attacking anything beyond a bowl of dry kibble. But Oberon personified a fine blend of characteristics, able to turn the savagery of his heritage on and off as occasion demanded. I found him online at a rescue ranch in Massachusetts, after becoming frustrated with breeders in Arizona. Everything they had was too tame. Oberon, once I flew out to visit, was practically wild by modern standards, but of course all you needed to do was talk to him. He simply wanted to hunt once in a while. Allow him that, and he was a perfect gentleman. *No wonder you like her. Did she ask you any questions?*

<She only wondered when to expect you.>

That was encouraging. She obviously wasn't looking for any of my treasures—and that meant she might not be in the employ of Aenghus Óg. *I see. How long has she been here?*

<She arrived here recently.>

Dogs are not all that great with time. They understand day and night, but beyond that they are nearly indifferent to its passage. So "recently" could mean anything from a minute ago to hours. *Have you taken a nap*, I asked, *since she got here?*

<No. We just finished speaking before you arrived.>

Thank you, Oberon.

<Will we go hunting soon?>

That depends entirely on the visitor. Whoever she is, she was not invited.

<Oh.> A hint of uncertainty crept into Oberon's thoughts. <Have I failed to protect you?>

Do not worry, Oberon, I said. *I am not displeased with you. But I am going to come back and get you, and we will enter the house together. I want you to guard me in case she proves not to be as friendly as you thought.*

<What if she attacks?>

Kill her. One does not give the Tuatha Dé Danann second chances.

<I thought you said never to attack humans.>

She hasn't been human for a very long time.

<All right. I do not think she will attack, though. She is a nice inhuman.>

You mean nonhuman. Inhuman is an adjective, I said,

as I rose from the lawn and padded softly around the left side of the house to the backyard.

<Hey, I'm not a native speaker. Give me a break.>

I left my bicycle resting in the street, hoping that it would not be stolen in a few minutes of neglect. Oberon was waiting for me as I opened the gate, his tongue lolling out and his tail wagging. I scratched him briefly behind the ears, and we walked together to my back door.

The patio furniture seemed undisturbed. My herb garden, planted in rows of boxes along the back fence and in much of the area normally reserved for a lawn, grew unmolested.

I found the visitor in my kitchen, trying to make a strawberry fruit smoothie.

"Manannan Mac Lir take this cursed thing to the land of shades!" she shouted as she smashed her fist onto the buttons of my blender. "The mortals always push these buttons and the bloody things work. Why won't yours work?" she demanded, flipping an irritated glance my way.

"You have to plug it in," I explained.

"What is this plug?"

"Insert the two-pronged device at the end of that cord into the slots on the wall there. That will give the blender its, um, animating force." I thought I could explain electricity later if necessary; there was no use burdening her with new vocabulary.

"Ah. Well met, then, Druid."

"Well met, Flidais, goddess of the hunt."

<Told you she was nice,> Oberon said.

I had to admit that of all the Tuatha Dé Danann it could have been, Flidais was one of the most agreeable to find in my kitchen. But you know that old saying about storm clouds being thrice cursed: Flidais brought the second one rolling behind her, and I never saw it coming.

Chapter 4

"You know you cannot get one of these drinks in Tír na nÓg?" Flidais said above the whine of my blender.

"I thought as much," I replied. "Blenders tend to be in short supply there. So how did you hear of them?"

"Only recently, as it turns out," Flidais said, puffing an errant wisp of curling red hair away from her eyes as she watched the strawberries puree. It was a somewhat windblown mane she had, a bit frizzy and so natural that I thought I spied a twig or two reclining lazily in her locks. "I was guesting in the forest of Herne the Hunter, and I caught a poacher driving through it in one of those monstrous truck things. He had taken a doe and covered it up in the back with a sheet of that black plastic material. Since Herne was not with me at the time, I took it upon myself to avenge the doe, and I followed him in my chariot to the city." She began to pour some of the smoothie into the glass, and it looked pretty good. I found myself hoping she was in a sharing mood. And then I remembered that Flidais has a chariot pulled by stags, and I thought that even the reserved British of today would behave badly when confronted with something like that on the highway.

"You were invisible to mortals during this chase, I presume?"

"Of course!" Her hands froze and her green eyes

flashed at me with a temper that matched the flame of her hair. "What kind of huntress do you take me for?"

Whoops! I lowered my eyes and spoke down to her boots, the soft brown leather sort with tough yet pliant soles like moccasins. They rose to her knees, where she had some tan leggings tucked into them—also leather and well worn. But the leather didn't stop there; she'd never met a piece of it she didn't like, as long as it wasn't black. Her belt and sleeveless vest were dyed forest green, and some supporting material underneath, the same chocolate brown of her boots, suggested that it loved its job. A strip of green rawhide was wrapped repeatedly around her left forearm to protect it from the lash of her bowstring, and it bore signs of recent abuse. "The very best, Flidais. My apologies." Flidais was one of the few who could pull off the invisibility trick. The best I could manage was a decent camouflage. She nodded curtly, acknowledging my apology as her due, and continued as if I had never bothered her with such sauciness.

"It quickly became a tracking operation, though. My chariot could not keep up with his truck. By the time I caught up with him, his truck was parked in one of those asphalt wastelands. What are they called again?" The Tuatha Dé Danann have no problem asking Druids for information. That's what we're for, after all. The secret to becoming an old Druid instead of a dead Druid is to betray nary a hint of condescension when answering even the simplest of questions.

"They are called parking lots," I replied.

"Ah, yes, thank you. He came out of a building called 'Crussh,' holding one of these potions. Are you familiar with the building, Druid?"

"I believe that is a smoothie bar in England."

"Quite right. So after I killed him and stowed his body next to the doe, I sampled his smoothie concoction in the parking lot and found it to be quite delicious."

See, sentences like that are why I nurture a healthy fear of the Tuatha Dé Danann. Now, I will be the first to admit that human life was not worth much to my generation in the Iron Age, but Flidais and her kind are forever rooted in Bronze Age morality, which goes something like this: If it pleases me, then it is good and I want more; If it displeases me, then it must be destroyed as soon as possible, but preferably in a way that enhances my reputation so that I can achieve immortality in the songs of bards. They simply do not think like modern people, and it is because of them that the Fae have such twisted senses of right and wrong.

Flidais took an experimental sip of her smoothie and her face lit up, very pleased with herself. "Ah, I think the mortals are on to something here," she said. "Anyway, Druid—what name are you using now?" A faint crinkle appeared between her eyes.

"Atticus," I said.

"Atticus?" The crinkle deepened. "Does anyone actually believe you are Greek?"

"Nobody pays attention to names here."

"Then what do they pay attention to?"

"Crude displays of personal wealth." I stared at the remaining liquid in the blender and hoped that Flidais would get the hint. "Shiny trucks, shiny rocks on their fingers, that sort of thing." Sure enough, she noticed that my attention was not totally centered on her.

"What are you—oh, would you like some of my smoothie? Help yourself, Atticus."

"That is most considerate of you." I smiled as I reached for another glass. I thought of the stoners who came into my shop earlier, probably already dead at the hands of the Morrigan, and how they would have been equally dead had they found Flidais in their kitchen.

They would have seen her and said something like,
"Yo, bitch, the fuck you doin' with my strawberries?"
and those would have been their last words. Bronze
Age manners are tough to fathom for modern men, by
and large, but it's fairly simple: The guest is to be treated
like a god, because he may, in fact, be a god in disguise.
I had no doubts on that score when it came to Flidais.

"Not at all," she replied. "You are a gracious host.
But to finally answer your question, I went into the
Crussh building and watched the mortals use these
machines to make smoothies, and that is how I learned
of them." She considered her drink for a moment, and
the crinkle appeared between her eyes again. "Do you
not find this age to be horribly strange, so much of the
sublime alongside the abominable?"

"I do indeed," I said as I poured some red slush into
my glass. "It is fortunate that we remain to preserve the
traditions of a better time."

"That's what I have come to see you about, Atticus,"
she said.

"Preserving traditions?"

"No. Remaining." Oh, bloody hell. That did not
sound good.

"I would love to hear about it. But may I first offer
you anything else by way of refreshment?"

"No, I am perfectly content with this," she said, wiggling her glass.

"Then perhaps we can retire to the front porch while
we talk?"

"That will serve nicely." I led the way, and Oberon
followed us out and sat between us on the porch. He
was thinking about hunting in Papago Park and hoping
we would take him there. My bicycle was still in the
street, to my relief, and I relaxed a little bit, until it
occurred to me that Flidais had probably not walked
here.

"Is your chariot safely stowed?" I asked her.

"Aye, there is a park hard by here, and I have bound the stags there until my return. Do not worry," she added when she saw my eyebrows rise, "they are invisible."

"Of course." I smiled. "So tell me, what brings you out to visit an old Druid long gone from the world?"

"Aenghus Óg knows you are here."

"So the Morrigan tells me," I replied equably.

"Ah, she's paid you a visit? Fir Bolgs are on their way too."

"I am well aware."

Flidais cocked her head and considered my air of unconcern. "And are you also aware that Bres follows them?"

I spewed strawberry smoothie into my flower bed at that, and Oberon looked at me in alarm.

"No, I suppose you had not heard that yet," Flidais said with a faint smile, and then she chuckled, pleased to have elicited such a reaction from me.

"Why is *he* coming?" I asked as I wiped my mouth. Bres was one of the meanest of the Tuatha Dé Danann alive, though he was not particularly bright. He had been their leader for a few decades, but eventually he was replaced for being more sympathetic to the monstrous race of the Fomorians than to his own people. He was a god of agriculture and had escaped death at Lugh's hands long ago by promising to share all he knew. The only reason he had not been killed since then was because he was husband to Brighid, and no one wished to risk her wrath. Her magical powers were unmatched, save perhaps by the Morrigan.

"Aenghus Óg has tempted him with something or other," Flidais said with a dismissive gesture. "Bres acts only when it is in his interest to do so."

"I understand that. But why send Bres? Is he to kill me?"

"I do not know. He certainly cannot be coming to outwit you. Truthfully, Druid, I hope the two of you do come to blows and you defeat him. He does not respect the forest as he should."

I offered no response, and Flidais seemed content to let me consider what she had said. She sipped her smoothie and reached down to give Oberon a friendly scratch behind the ears. His tail sprang to life and quickly thumped against the legs of our chairs. I could hear him begin to tell her of the sport to be had at Papago Park, and I smiled at the way he always kept his goals firmly in mind—the mark of a true hunter.

<There are desert bighorn sheep in the hills there. Have you ever hunted them?>

Flidais told him no, she had never hunted sheep at all. They were herd animals that offered no sport.

<These are not regular sheep. They are larger, they are brown, and they move very fast among the rocks. We have yet to corner one, though we have tried only a few times. I always enjoy the hunt anyway.>

"Does your hound jest with me, Atticus?" Flidais raised her eyes to mine, and a note of contempt crept into her voice. "You were unable to bring down a sheep?"

"Oberon never jests about hunting," I said. "Desert bighorns are nothing like the sheep you are used to. They are significant game, especially in the Papago Hills. Treacherous rocks there."

"Why have I never heard of these creatures?"

I shrugged. "They are native to this area. There are several desert creatures you would probably enjoy hunting here."

Flidais sat back in her chair, frowning, and took another sip of her smoothie as if it were an elixir to cure cognitive dissonance. She stared for a few moments at the low-hanging branches of my mesquite tree, which were swaying gently in a whisper of desert wind. Then, without warning, her face exploded in a smile and she laughed in delight—I would almost call it a giggle, but that would be beneath the dignity of a goddess.

"Something new!" she gushed. "Do you know how long it has been since I have hunted anything new? Why, it has been centuries, Druid, millennia even!"

I raised my glass. "To novelty," I said. It was a highly prized commodity amongst the long-lived. She clinked her glass against mine, and we drank contentedly and shared silence for a while, until she asked when we could begin the hunt.

"Not until a few hours after nightfall," I said. "We must wait for the park to close and the mortals to retire for the night."

Flidais arched an eyebrow at me. "And how shall we spend the intervening hours, Atticus?"

"You are my guest. We may spend it however you wish."

Her eyes appraised me and I pretended not to notice, keeping my gaze locked on my bicycle still lying in the street. "You appear to be in the summertime of youth," she said.

"My thanks. You look well as always."

"I am curious to discover if you still have the endurance of the Fianna or if you are hiding a decrepitude and softness most unbecoming a Celt."

I stood up and offered her my right hand. "My left arm was injured earlier this afternoon and is still not fully healed. However, if you will follow me and assist in mending it, I will do my best to satisfy your curiosity."

The corner of her mouth quirked up at the edge, and her eyes smoldered as she placed her hand in mine and rose. I locked my eyes on hers and didn't let go of her hand as we returned inside and went to the bedroom.

I figured, to hell with the bike. I'd probably feel like jogging to work in the morning anyway.

Chapter 5

Pillow talk in the modern era often involves the sharing of childhood stories or perhaps an exchange of dream vacations. One of my recent partners, a lovely lass named Jesse with a tattoo of a Tinker Bell on her right shoulder blade (about as far from a real faery as one can get), had wanted to discuss a science-fiction television program, *Battlestar Galactica,* as a political allegory for the Bush years. When I confessed I had no knowledge of the show nor any interest in getting to know it or anything about American politics, she called me a "frakkin' Cylon" and stormed out of the house, leaving me confused yet somewhat relieved. Flidais, on the other hand, wanted to talk about the ancient sword of Manannan Mac Lir, called Fragarach, the Answerer. It kind of killed the afterglow for me, and I felt myself growing irritated.

"Do you still have it?" she asked. And as soon as she did, I suspected that the entire visit—even the conjugal part—had been planned just so she could discover the answer. I had flat out lied to the lesser Fae who'd attacked me earlier, but I didn't feel safe doing the same to Flidais.

"Aenghus Óg certainly thinks so," I hedged.

"That is no answer."

"That is because I have reason to be cautious, or even

paranoid, where that subject is concerned. I mean you no disrespect."

She eyed me steadily for a full five minutes, trying to get me to talk by merely remaining silent. It works well on most humans, but the Druids taught that technique to the Tuatha Dé Danann before I was born, so I kept my smile on the inside and waited for her next move. I busied myself in the interim by trying to find patterns in the popcorn ceiling and idly stroking her right arm, which was tattooed like mine, ready to draw the earth's power with an effort of will. I found a woodpecker, a snow leopard, and what might have been the snarling face of Randy Johnson throwing a slider before she spoke again.

"Tell me the story of how you came to possess it in the first place, then," she finally said. "The legendary Fragarach, the sword that can pierce any armor. I have heard several versions of it in Tír na nÓg, and I would like to hear you tell it."

It was an appeal to my vanity. She wanted me to lapse into braggadocio and get so carried away with my tale that I'd wind up blurting out, "It's in my garage!" or "I sold it on eBay!" or something similar.

"All right. I stole it in the Battle of Magh Lena, when Conn of the Hundred Battles was so bent on slaying Mogh Nuadhat during the night that he hardly cared what weapon he was holding in his hand." I raised my fist as if it grasped a sword. "Conn was outnumbered and knew he'd have little chance of winning in a straight-up fight, so he decided to attack in the night to skew the odds in his favor. Goll Mac Morna and the rest of the Fianna refused to fight until the morning, citing something about honor, but I have never had much of that in the middle of a war. Being honorable is an excellent way to get yourself killed. Witness the British getting their hair lifted by this continent's natives in the eighteenth century because they refused to break their silly formations."

Flidais grunted, then said, "This was before Finn Mac Cumhaill led the Fianna?"

"Oh, aye, well before. So I slunk away from the Fianna's fires and went to join Conn in the slaughter. He was hacking his way amongst Mogh Nuadhat's army—which was about seventeen thousand Gaels and two thousand Spaniards, if you can believe it—when his hands, slick with the blood of his fallen enemies, slipped on the hilt of Fragarach as he raised it for another blow, letting this magnificent sword sail behind him, over his head, to literally fall at my feet in the chaos of a night battle."

Flidais snorted. "I don't believe you. He simply dropped it?"

"*Threw it* would be more accurate." I raised my right hand. "Every word is true or I am the son of a goat. I picked it up, felt the magic thrumming through my arm, wrapped myself in mist, and exited the field with my prize, never to return until the time of Cormac Mac Airt."

"Nay, they did not let you simply exit with Fragarach!"

"You're right," I chuckled. "There was a bit more to it than that. I thought you might enjoy the short version, though."

Flidais seemed to seriously consider whether or not she had enjoyed it. "I appreciated the denial of expectations; it is similar to when prey refuses to behave in standard fashion, making the hunt more interesting. But I know that you have skipped many details, and it already differs from what I have heard, so now I must know it all. Tell me the longer version."

"Wait. What did you hear in Tír na nÓg? The short version."

"I heard that you stole it from Conn through chicanery and guile. In some tales you put him to sleep through use of a potion; in others you switch swords with him using an illusion. You come across as little more than a scheming, cowardly footpad."

"How delightful. All right, then, I think perhaps it is crucial to know my state of mind leading up to the point where the sword dropped at my feet—for that is truly how it happened. Night battles are ridiculously crazy; I wasn't sure that I was always facing people from the opposing army, you know? The only illumination saving it from being black as tar was the pale glow of a crescent moon, the stars, and a few distant campfires. I may have accidentally killed a man or two on my own side, and I was paranoid about being cut down in a similar accident. So I was thinking, this is absurdly dangerous, why am I doing this, and why am I here, and the answer that I came up with was this: We were all killing one another in the middle of the night because Conn had a magic sword given to him by Lugh Lámhfhada of the Tuatha Dé Danann. Fragarach's power had allowed him to conquer most of Ireland. Great as he was, he could not have done it without that sword. Conn would have never had the stones to attack Mogh Nuadhat without it. Everyone who died in the battle to that point had done so because a single sword gave one man in power the lust for more. And as I maniacally hewed down whoever faced me, I realized that, even as we fought for Conn, Conn was fighting for the Tuatha Dé, manipulated by Lugh and his cronies as sure as a tree drinks water."

"I remember this now," Flidais said. "I stood apart because I have never had much interest in human affairs outside the forest. But Lugh was very interested, and Aenghus Óg even more so."

"Aye. I think they wanted to bring peace to Ireland at

the point of a sword. They encouraged Conn to do
what he did—and all the High Kings after him. And
perhaps it would have been the best thing for Ireland, I
don't know. What bothered me is that the Tuatha Dé
were manipulating human events, when they were supposed to have been removed from them centuries
before."

"Meddlesome, are we?" Flidais grinned sardonically.

"In that particular case you were. I was mentally cat-
aloging which of you were on Conn's side and who was
on Mogh Nuadhat's when the sword fell at my feet. I
knew immediately what it was; I could feel its power
pulsing through the ground, calling to me. And that's
when I heard a voice in my head, already half expected,
telling me to pick it up and exit the field. Pick it up, the
voice said, and I would be protected."

"Whose voice was it?" Flidais asked.

"Cannot you guess?"

"The Morrigan," she whispered.

"Yes indeed, the old battle crow herself. I would not
be surprised if she had something to do with it slipping
from Conn's grasp in the first place. So I picked it up.
When you're in the middle of a killing field and the
fucking Chooser of the Slain tells you to do something,
you do it. But of course there were many agents, human
and immortal, who objected to this."

"Conn came after you?"

"Not personally. He was too busy fighting for his life
with a normal sword he'd snatched from a corpse. He
was in the very thick of the mêlée, and thus he sent
some of his chiefs behind him to find Fragarach. What
they found was a Druid holding his sword and not particularly anxious to surrender it. In fact, they found me
trying to summon mist to cloak my escape."

"Only trying?" Flidais raised an eyebrow. I noticed
that she had a few freckles underneath her eyes, high on

her cheeks. She was comfortably pink all over and slightly bronzed from the sun, not the marble white of the Morrigan.

"It was rather difficult to concentrate. Aenghus Óg and Lugh were in my head, telling me to return the sword to Conn or die, and the Morrigan was telling me I would die if I gave it back. I said to the Morrigan that I wanted to keep Fragarach for my own, to which Aenghus Óg and Lugh both shouted no, so of course the Morrigan instantly agreed."

Flidais laughed. "You played them against one another. This is utterly delicious."

"But wait, it gets tastier. The Morrigan shielded my mind from Aenghus Óg and Lugh, and just in time. Conn's lieutenants tried to slay me and quickly discovered that, while Fragarach was a great sword in Conn's hand, it was a terrible sword in mine. They all shouted 'Traitor!' before they dropped in the mud, however, and I abruptly found myself surrounded by hostiles—hostiles egged on to kill me by Aenghus Óg and Lugh, no doubt. The Morrigan suggested to me that the best way out would be through Mogh Nuadhat's army. Charging in that direction, I whirled Fragarach around me with all the strength a Druid could muster from the earth, cleaving bodies in two and shearing anonymous torsos from their trunks. The flying halves of men bowled whole men over, and fountains of blood showered upon my erstwhile comrades. I eventually reached Mogh Nuadhat's Spaniards, who parted for me like the Red Sea for Moses—"

"For whom?"

"I beg your pardon. I was alluding to a figure from the Torah, who escaped an Egyptian army by appealing to the god Yahweh for aid. Yahweh parted the Red Sea for Moses and his Jewish friends to escape, and when the pharaoh's army tried to follow, the Red Sea fell upon them, drowning them all. And so it was when Conn's men tried to pursue me; the Spaniards closed ranks and thwarted them, and I ran freely to the other side of the field, thanking the Morrigan for her assistance. But that's when Aenghus Óg decided to take a very personal hand in the matter. He appeared before me, in the flesh, and demanded that I return the sword."

"You had better not be jesting with me now," Flidais said.

"I assure you I remember it very clearly. He was outfitted in some stunning bronze armor etched with lovely bindings and dark-blue pauldrons and bracers. Do you remember seeing it?"

"Mmm. Long ago, yes. But that proves nothing."

"Confirm it all with the Morrigan. For just as Aenghus and I were about to come to blows, she alighted on my shoulder as the battle crow and told Aenghus to back the fuck off."

"She actually said that?"

"No." I grinned. "I confess that was a bardic embellishment. She said I was under her personal protection and by threatening me he placed himself in mortal peril."

Flidais clapped her hands in delight. "Oh, I bet he nearly shat kine!"

That made me laugh—I hadn't heard that expression in a long, long time. I refrained from telling her that the modern expression would be "he had a cow," because I liked the original better.

"Yes, the kine he nearly shat would have fed several clans."

"What did Aenghus do then?"

"He protested that the Morrigan had gone too far and interfered beyond her compass. She replied that the battlefield was precisely her province and she could do as she wished. She tried to make him feel better by guaranteeing that Conn would survive the night and even win the battle. He accepted these concessions as his due but couldn't leave without threatening me personally. He glared at me with those flat black eyes and promised me a short, miserable life—and I'm grateful for that, because the Morrigan has tried to make it the opposite as much as possible.

"'You may enjoy this victory now, Druid,' he said, 'but you will never know peace. My agents, both human and Fae, will hound you until you die. Always you will have to look over your shoulder for the knife at your back. So swears Aenghus,' blah blah blah."

"Where did you go?" Flidais asked.

"At the Morrigan's suggestion, I left Ireland to make it tougher for Aenghus to kill me. But the bloody Romans were everywhere and they weren't friendly to Druids. It was the reign of Antoninus Pius, so I had to travel east of the Rhine to escape them and join the Germanic tribes holding the line there. I fathered a child, picked up a language or two, and waited a couple generations for people in Ireland to forget about me. By stealing Fragarach, I had ensured plenty more battles and horrible, bloody deaths. Conn wasn't able to fully unite all the tribes without Fragarach to enforce his will, and Aenghus Óg's dreams of some kind of Pax Ireland were ruined. Even though Conn won that battle and slew Mogh Nuadhat, he had to settle for a patchwork of truces and marriages to keep the illusion of peace, and it all fell apart after his death. The Morrigan has used my name to goad Aenghus Óg ever since, not that he needed it. After I bore witness to his cowering before her, there was nothing he wished more than to erase his humiliation by erasing me."

"How long since you have wielded Fragarach?"

"I will not say." The goddess's face fell a bit, clearly

disappointed that her gambit had failed, and I grinned. "But if you are wondering if I have kept up with my swordsmanship, the answer is yes."

"Oh? And with whom do you spar out here? I would imagine that there are few mortals alive who are truly skilled with a blade anymore."

"You imagine correctly. I spar with Leif Helgarson, an old Icelandic Viking."

"You mean he can trace his lineage back to the Vikings?"

"No, I mean he really is a Viking. Came to this continent with Eric the Red."

The brow of the goddess knitted in confusion. There were a few extremely long-lived mortals like me running around, but she thought she knew them all. I could tell she was reviewing them in her head, and when she failed to recall any Vikings, she said, "How is this possible? Has he made some sort of bargain with the Valkyries?"

"No, he's a vampire."

Flidais hissed and leapt out of bed, landing in a defensive fighting posture as if I was going to attack her. I very carefully did not move except to turn my head a little bit and admire her perfectly sculpted form. The last rays of the day's sun were filtering through the blinds, leaving soft striped shadows on her lightly tanned legs.

"You dare consort with the undead?" she spat.

I really hate that word, even though I occasionally catch myself using it. Ever since *Romeo and Juliet,* I am of Mercutio's mind when he takes issue with Tybalt's suggestion that he consorts with Romeo. To mask my irritation, I grinned and tried to affect an Elizabethan accent. "Zounds, consort? Wouldst thou make me a minstrel?"

"I speak not of minstrels," she scowled. "I speak of evil."

Oh well. Not a fan of the Bard, then. "Your pardon, Flidais. I was alluding to an old play by Master Shakespeare, but I can see you are in no mood for light banter. I would not say that I *consort* with the undead, for that would imply a relationship beyond what is minimally necessary for business. I merely employ Mr. Helgarson. He's my attorney."

"You are telling me that your lawyer is a bloodsucking vampire?"

"Yes. He is an associate at the firm of Magnusson and Hauk. Hauk is also my attorney; he's also Icelandic, but he is a werewolf and takes care of clients during the day, and Helgarson obviously does his business after sunset."

"Associating with a member of the Pack I can understand, and even approve. But frolicking with the undead, that is *tabu*."

"And a wiser *tabu* has never been enforced by any culture. But I have never frolicked with him and have no plans to do so. Leif is not the frolicking type. I merely use his legal services and occasionally spar with him because he is the finest swordsman available in the area—and the fastest as well."

"Why does the pack member work with the vampire? He should have killed the foul creature on sight."

I shrugged. "We are not in the Old World anymore. This is a new age and a new place, and they both happen to have a common enemy."

Flidais cocked her head sideways and waited for me to name said enemy.

"And that would be Thor, the Norse god of thunder."

"Oh." Flidais relaxed somewhat. "I can understand that, then. He could make a salamander team up with a siren. What did he do to them?"

"Helgarson won't tell me, but it must have been bad. His fangs pop out if you just say 'Thor' aloud, and he hunts carpenters simply because they use hammers. As far as Magnusson and Hauk go, Thor killed some of their pack members ten or so years ago."

"This Magnusson is a werewolf too?"

"Aye, he's the alpha. Hauk is his second."

"Did Thor have cause to attack them?"

"Hauk says they were on holiday in the old forests of Norway and it was nothing more than a capricious whim on Thor's part. Eight precisely aimed lightning strikes out of a sky that had been clear moments before. Couldn't possibly have been a freak occurrence." Silver isn't the only thing that can kill werewolves: Humans simply don't have access to weapons like bolts of lightning, which fry critters before they can heal.

Flidais was silent for a time and regarded me intensely.

"This desert seems to attract an unusual collection of beings."

I merely shrugged again and said, "It is a good place to hide. No easy access from the Fae planes, as you know. No gods stomping about, besides Coyote and the occasional visitor like yourself."

"Who is Coyote?"

"He's a trickster god of the natives. There are several versions of him running around all over the continent. He's a nice lad; just don't make any wagers with him."

"Isn't the Christian god prominent here?"

"The Christians have such muddled ideas of him that he usually can't take shape beyond the crucifix form, and that isn't much fun, so he rarely bothers. Mary will appear more often, though, and she can do some pretty awesome stuff if she feels like it. Mostly she sits around looking beatific and full of grace. Keeps calling me 'child,' even though I'm older than she is."

Flidais smiled and crawled back into bed with me, vampires forgotten. "When were you born, Druid? You were already old for a mortal when first I met you."

"I was born in the time of King Conaire Mor, who reigned for seventy years. I was nearly two hundred when I stole Fragarach."

She threw a leg across my body and then sat up so that she knelt astride me. "Aenghus Óg thinks Fragarach is rightfully his." Her fingers began to trace curling patterns on my chest, and I stopped her by covering her hand with mine, with seeming affection. It wouldn't do to have her put a binding on me. Not that I thought she would; it was merely my customary paranoia.

"The people here," I said, "have a saying: Possession is nine-tenths of the law. And I have possessed it for far longer than any other being, including Manannan Mac Lir."

"Aenghus Óg cares nothing for mortal sayings. He thinks you have stolen his birthright, and that is all that matters to him."

"His birthright? Manannan is his cousin, not his father. It's not like I stole his personal family heirloom. Besides, if it truly mattered to him, then he would have come to get it himself by now."

"You have not stayed long enough in one place to make it practicable."

I looked at her with raised eyebrows. "Is that all it takes to finally make this end? Just stay still?"

"I would think so. He will send surrogates after you first, but if you defeat them, he will eventually have no option but to come after you himself. He would be pronounced a coward otherwise and banished from Tír na nÓg."

"I will stay still, then," I said, and smiled up at her. "But you can move if you like. May I suggest a gentle rocking motion?"

Chapter 6

Located just north of the Phoenix Zoo, Papago Park is an odd formation of isolated hills surrounded by teddy bear cholla, creosote, and saguaro. The hills are steep red rock and riddled with holes, fifteen-million-year-old remnants of ancient mudflows that petrified and eroded over the ages. Now the hills are play-grounds for children in one part of the park, a chal-lenging day climb in some others, and, in a fenced-off area on zoo property, home to a score of bighorn sheep. These last can be viewed—occasionally, if they deign to show themselves—from a part of the zoo called the Arizona Trail. But even then the viewers may be forced to use binoculars to see them well, because it is not an exhibit so much as a tiny preserve, where the sheep are left largely to themselves and undisturbed—that is, until Oberon and I started terrorizing them.

When I hunted with Oberon, I took the form of a wolfhound with a red coat shot through with streaks of white, slightly taller in the shoulder than Oberon and with dark markings on the right side reminiscent of my tattoos. If I had gone out there with a bow and let Oberon flush them for me, it would have been far sim-pler but far less satisfying for both of us. Oberon wanted to bring them down in the "old way," never mind that wolfhounds were bred to chase down wolves in the forest and take out charioteers on the battle plain, not leap around rocky hills after nimble-footed rams.

The reason the sheep were so hard to bring down was that the terrain was steep, unkind to our paws, and a tumble from the rocks would probably land us in a cactus—and anyone who's ever tried to tangle with a teddy bear cholla knows there's a whole lot more bear than teddy to it. The conditions would simply not let us open up full bore and catch up to them.

When we got to the park, Oberon was ready to kill just about anything that moved. He'd been trying to intimidate Flidais's stags and found that they were not scared of him in the least, and it was practically making him rabid. I had overheard snatches of their conversation as we rode along in Flidais's chariot:

<If you were not under the goddess's protection, I would have you for supper,> he told them.

<Maybe if you had two score friends or so,> they taunted him. <A single puppy would never trouble us.> Oh ho!

<You would not be so bold if the goddess were not here.>

<Is that so? She leaves us alone for long periods of time, staked to a small area. Try to take us then and see what happens, runt.>

Oberon growled at them and bared his teeth, and I told him to hush, doing my best to hide my amusement. Oh, was he ever mad. Calling a giant like him a runt? They really knew how to push a dog's buttons.

Flidais asked me where she should park her chariot, and I suggested she leave it by Hunt's Tomb, a small white pyramid incongruously erected on one of the hills as the final resting place of Arizona's first governor. It was fenced off from the rest of the park, but the stags simply leapt over it, jerking the chariot abruptly behind but landing gracefully on the other side through some of Flidais's magic.

<Can you jump like that, little doggie?> one of the stags teased.

Oberon simply growled in response, far past the point of vocalizing. We got out of the chariot, and he barked at them once before I brought him to heel.

"We are after sheep tonight," I reminded him.

<Let's go, then,> he replied as the stags snorted their laughter.

"Get yourself ready, Druid," Flidais said as she slung her quiver over her head.

And so I cleared my head and summoned power through the tattoo that tied me to the earth, drawing strength up from the desert. I fell down on all fours as I bound myself to the shape of a hound.

A Druid's therianthrophy is nothing like the change of a werewolf, save in the sense that both are magical. One major difference is that I can change shape (or not) at will, regardless of the time of day or the phase of the moon; another is that it's fairly painless, unlike lycanthropy; yet another is that I can transform into different animals, albeit a limited few.

In practice, I do not stay for long periods in animal form, for psychological reasons. While I can eat anything the animal would eat and not suffer physically from it, mentally I have difficulty choking down whole mice when I'm an owl or eating raw venison as a hound. (We had taken down a doe in the Kaibab Forest a couple of weeks ago, and once she was down, I had walked off and waited until Oberon had had his fill.) So these hunts were for Oberon more than for me: I just enjoyed the chase and that warm fuzzy feeling you get when you know you're making someone happy.

But something was different this time when I changed to hound form. My mind felt befuddled, and I was more than a little bloodthirsty. I smelled the sheep scent on the night air, and the nearness of the stags, but instead of accepting this input coolly, I became ravenous and started drooling a bit. It was wrong, and I should have changed back right then.

Flidais strode to the fence and ripped a section of it from the ground with a single hand, whistling once and gesturing for us to run through. We scampered underneath the links and headed for the hills we had hunted before, keeping silent so as not to alert the sheep too early that we were coming for them. There was another fence to negotiate to get into the preserve portion of the park, and Flidais obliged us there as well.

"Now go, my hounds," she said as she ripped up another section of fence, and as she said it I felt as if I *was* her hound, not a Druid anymore, not even human anymore, but part of a pack. "Flush a ram out of the hills and bring him to my bow." And then we were off, running faster than we ever had before, dodging cacti in the weak starlight of a city sky, and I was only dimly aware that there was magic at work here that was not my own. The cold iron amulet necklace, now shrunk about my neck like a collar, should protect me from it if it was sinister, so I did not worry.

It didn't take us long to find the sheep. They were bedded down in a tangle of creosote, but they heard us scrabbling in the gravel of the desert floor and were already leaping up a nearly vertical hillside when we first laid eyes on them. Our legs spasmed as we tried to make that first leap up to the beginnings of a slope; I made it to a narrow precipice, though barely, but Oberon fell short and tumbled backward into the dirt with a whuff of breath.

<Go around the base and wait,> I said to him. <I will chase them over to you.>

<Very well,> he agreed. <Cunning is better than running.>

I kept my eyes on the retreating flanks of the sheep

ahead of me and kept pumping my legs up the hill. Incredibly, I seemed to be gaining ground on them, and I felt so triumphant about it that I let loose with a few barks to scare them stupid. But they were built to negotiate those hills with ease, and I was not, and eventually I lost some ground as I had to scramble for footholds and find better places to jump up. When they disappeared over the peak and were headed down the other side, I started barking again to make sure they knew I was close behind and there was no time to stop. I wanted them to head straight for Oberon.

I had no way of knowing precisely where he was waiting, of course, but hopefully my barking would give him an idea of where we were headed.

Going down was much more treacherous than going up. The way the shadows fell, it was difficult to tell if the next step was a foot down or a fathom. But the pale flanks bobbing up and down ahead of me in soft, night-blue streaks gave me a good idea of what to expect. They were headed almost due south, and I heard nothing beyond their hooves clattering amongst the rocks and my own panting and barking. If Oberon and Flidais were waiting ahead, they were being careful not to reveal their positions.

I kept barking, though it was more to drown out any small noises Oberon might make than any enthusiasm I had for closing the gap between us. I fetched up at a precipice and saw that I would have to travel around to the west a bit before I could find a way down, and with every second the sheep got farther away. So I remained where I was and watched, and sure enough, Oberon was hidden behind a creosote bush not far from where the sheep finally came down off the hill. There was a gap of fifty yards or so before the next hill reared up out of the earth, with nothing but sparse desert plants in the way. Oberon cut off their approach to the next hill, and I was barking behind them, so the sheep turned east up the pass between the hills. Once they silhouetted themselves against the sky, an arrow knocked one off its feet and sent it tumbling, bleating to its doom as its fellows fled.

Oberon closed on it to finish it off, but there was no need. Flidais's arrow had found its heart, and she would doubtless appear momentarily to claim her kill. I began to work my way down the hill, wondering if she would be satisfied. The hunt had not lasted long; we had flushed them too perfectly, owing perhaps to our recent visits and familiarity with the terrain.

But it seemed those recent visits had not gone unnoticed, unfortunately: As I reached the site of the kill, where Flidais was already gutting the animal and Oberon was standing nearby, a park ranger suddenly appeared, holding a flashlight and a gun. He demanded loudly that we freeze as he blinded us with a halogen glare.

We couldn't have been more startled. He should not have been able to sneak up on any of us, much less all three. But it is not wise to surprise one of the Tuatha Dé Danann. Flidais whipped her knife out of its sheath and threw it to the left of the flashlight before I had even finished turning my head toward the ranger. She had not aimed, or even looked, so the knife didn't kill him; it sank into his left shoulder and caused him to cry out and drop his flashlight, which would make it harder for him to aim that gun if he felt like shooting. It turned out he did; a few shots thundered in the night, and I felt one bullet whip over my spine and heard another smack into a barrel cactus to my left. Flidais grunted as she took a slug in the arm, then roared in outrage as she realized what had happened.

"Kill him!" she shrieked, and I unthinkingly leapt to obey, as did Oberon. But unlike Oberon, I managed an independent thought after the first couple of steps, and that stopped me. Killing a ranger would bring the law down upon us, perhaps forcing us to flee, and I did not want to leave Arizona. I changed back to my human form, and immediately the fog lifted from my mind. Flidais had been controlling me as a hound, just as she was controlling Oberon—just as she could control all animals. Unable to resist without the protection of cold iron, Oberon had not stopped, and now he had the man flat on his back, screaming. I tried to call him off, but it was no use with Flidais binding him to her will; I could not even feel his mental presence as I normally could.

"Flidais! Release my hound now!" I snapped, and the man's screams stopped. But it was already too late. Without ceremony, without any dramatic growls or shivering violins, my hound had torn out the poor man's throat.

Oberon's thoughts returned and a flood of questions filled my mind. <Atticus? What happened? I taste blood. Who is this man? Where am I? I thought we were supposed to be hunting sheep. I didn't do this, did I?>

Step away from him and I'll explain in a moment, I said. When one has seen as much death as Flidais and I have, there are no expressions of disbelief at a person's sudden end. There is no gibbering, no wailing, no tearing of hair. There is only a cool assessment of the consequences. But if the consequences are dire, then a display of emotion is allowed.

"That was *not* necessary!" I shouted, but carefully kept my eyes on the corpse. "We could have disarmed him. His death will cause me and my hound much trouble."

"I do not see how," Flidais replied. "We can simply dispose of the body."

"That is not so simple as it used to be. They will find it eventually, and when they do, they will find canine DNA in the wounds."

"You speak of the mortals?" the huntress asked.

What does one do when one needs to pray to the gods for patience but a god is causing the need for patience? "Yes, the mortals!" I spat.

"What is this DNA you speak of?"

I ground my teeth and heard the short yips of Coyote on the thin desert air. He was laughing at me.

"Never mind."

"I think it well he is dead, Druid. He shot me and tried to shoot you. And he also surprised me, which should not have been possible."

I had to admit that piqued my curiosity. I stepped closer to the body and warned Oberon off.

<Atticus?> he practically whined. <Are you angry with me?>

No, Oberon, I said. *You didn't do this. Flidais did. She used your teeth as a weapon, just as she would use a knife or her bow.*

He whined in earnest. <I feel terrible. Sick. Auggh!> He coughed and hacked, vomiting onto the dry, rocky soil.

I crouched down to take a closer look at the ranger. He was a young Latino with a wispy mustache and a pair of thick lips. His aura was already gone, his soul traveling elsewhere, but when I used one of my charms to check out the magical spectrum, I saw traces of Druidry in a diamond stud in his left ear. That set off alarms.

I rose and gestured at the man. "Flidais, his earring is magical. Can you determine its purpose, or perhaps its origin?" Its origin was clear to me, but the knots in these particular bindings were unfamiliar. My query was a sort of test: If Flidais confirmed their Druidic origin and even recognized their purpose, she was not playing double. If she tried to tell me it was Voudoun, however, or something else completely different, then she was on some other side than mine. Flidais's boots crunched toward me, her trophy ram and wounded arm forgotten. She squatted next to the ranger's head and examined the earring. "Ah, yes, I recognize these bindings. It's not the sort of thing the lesser Fae can do. This man was under the control of the Tuatha Dé."

"That is enough for me," I said, satisfied she was telling the truth. "I'm sure it was Aenghus Óg himself. He gave the man a cloaking spell and then broke it abruptly as he was about to speak, ensuring our surprise and the man's death. It is the sort of puppetry Aenghus enjoys." I did not mention that Flidais seemed to enjoy it too. I felt like joining Oberon in a nice, cathartic vomit, utterly repulsed by these beings who robbed creatures of their own free will.

I had looked up Aenghus Óg on the Internet once to see if the mortals had a clue about his true nature. They describe him as a god of love and beauty, with four birds following him about, representing his kisses or some such nonsense. Who would tolerate four birds flapping about his head, constantly letting loose their bowels and screeching? Not the Aenghus I know. But some accounts provide a better picture of his character by also telling of his deeds, such as taking his father's house from him by trickery and slaying both his stepfather and his foster mother. Or the time he left a girl who was hopelessly in love with him and who died of grief a few weeks later. That's more the kind of man we are talking about.

No, the Celtic god of love isn't a cherub with cute little wings, nor is he a siren born of the sea in a giant clamshell. He is not benevolent or merciful or even inclined to be nice on a regular basis. Though it pains me to think of it because of what it says about my people, our god of love is a ruthless seeker of conquest, wholly self-serving, and more than a little vindictive.

As if to punctuate that thought, emergency sirens began to wail in the night.

"That noise is used by mortal law enforcement, is it not?" Flidais asked.

"Aye, it is."

"Do you think it probable that they are headed here?"

"Of course. Aenghus sent this man to die," I said, waving at the ranger, "and he wants us to be inconvenienced as much as possible." The chance that the police would not know precisely where in the park to look for us was as close to zero as I could imagine.

"And I suppose," she said with asperity, "that you would not want me to kill the mortal authorities so that I can take time to harvest my trophy."

She was not joking. She really would have killed them without compunction. From her tone, it was clear that I should be grateful to her for recognizing that I might have a different set of priorities.

"You suppose correctly, Flidais. Living as I do amongst the mortals, I am subject to their laws and do not wish to draw undue attention to myself."

The huntress sighed in exasperation. "Then we must hurry. The best I can do is to have the earth swallow him," she said, yanking her knife out of the dead man's shoulder.

I shook my head. "The police will have him out of the ground again as soon as we leave. But go ahead, since it is the best we can do. It may contaminate the evidence somewhat."

Flidais spoke some of the old tongue, and the skin around her tattoos whitened briefly as she drew power from the land. She frowned a bit: There was not as much to be had out here as in the Old World, and it cost her more effort than it should have. But she waved her fingers, said, *"Oscail,"* and the dirt beneath the ranger obeyed. First the surface gravel began to skitter away from him, then the crust began to cave and ripple beneath him, and he sank. Once he was only a couple of feet below the surface, Flidais waved her fingers in the opposite direction, muttered, *"Dún,"* and the earth closed over him. It was magic I could have performed myself, albeit not so quickly. There was nothing subtle about it though. The earth looked churned up and disturbed, and the police would have little trouble deciding where to look for a freshly killed body. The sirens were close now.

"Back to the chariot," she said, and I nodded and set off at a ground-eating pace, calling Oberon to follow. Flidais paused only to collect her bow and pull her arrow out of the ram, then she caught up and ran with us.

The sirens stopped, and we heard the dull *whump* of car doors slamming to the south as we reached her chariot. If they had a guide, and I had no doubt they did, the police would reach the body in minutes.

<Why isn't your tail wagging, puppy?> one of the stags said.

<Were you a bad doggie?> the other chimed in.

Before I could, Flidais told them to shut up and thankfully Oberon bit back any response he would have given. Flidais cast invisibility on us—a wonderful trick, that—and we hoofed it out of there without delay.

The goddess of the hunt was seething. "My first new hunt in an age of man," she said through gritted teeth, "and it was ruined by Aenghus Óg. Well, I will be avenged. The huntress can be patient."

"You're better adjusted than I am," I said, though I thought her a dangerous sociopath. "I'm about out of patience."

Chapter 7

With much apologizing and simultaneous thanks for the gift of her company, I suggested to Flidais once I returned home that if I were to be attacked shortly by a party of Fir Bolgs, I had much to do in the way of preparation. She was only too happy to take the hint, and her leave.

"If you prevail, Druid, perhaps we can hunt at leisure in the near future. You have my blessing." She gave Oberon an affectionate pat on the head—from which he tried to recoil—bade us both farewell, then winked out of sight and returned to her chariot. We may have had her blessing, but we wouldn't have her bow at our back. She could not afford to be seen taking my side against the Tuatha Dé Danann.

I expelled a deep breath, releasing some of the tension her mere presence had caused, and sank into a chair by my kitchen table. Oberon approached me, head down, tail between his legs.

<Atticus, I'm sorry,> he said.

It was not your fault, I reminded him. *She used you like a weapon, and Aenghus Óg wanted that man to be killed. But now you and I must face the consequences.*

<Because I killed him,> Oberon said.

Flidais made you kill him. Nevertheless, that means

*that you will be killed in turn, if the police figure out
you're the one who did it.*

<I don't even remember doing it.>

*I know. And that is why we will never hunt with her
again. She had a strong influence on me as well, and I
did not like being under her control, even a little bit.*

<You never hunted with her before?>

*Never in animal form. I hunted with her for a good
while in the Ukraine once. She helped me out with my
archery on horseback. It's bloody tough, I'll tell you,
but Genghis Khan's hordes could do it, so of course I
had to learn.*

<I have no idea what you're talking about right now.>

*Never mind. Listen, we have to get you cleaned up.
Into the bath.*

<Can't I just roll around in the dirt?>

*No, we need to get you superclean. Any blood
found on you will automatically get you killed at this
point.*

<You won't let them find me, though, right?>

Not if I can help it, Oberon. Come on, let's go.

I rose from my chair, and Oberon began to trot in
front of me down the hall to the bathroom, his tail
wagging again. <Will you tell me about Genghis Khan's
whores while I'm in the bath?>

*Hordes, not whores. He had both, though, now that
you mention it.*

<Sounds like he was a busy guy.>

You have no idea.

We had a good time with the suds and the short version of Khan's empire, after which I had to see to my
preparations for the Fir Bolgs—the full extent of which
was nothing more than a good night's sleep. They
would not attack me in my home, figuring it would be
too well protected—and it was. They would wait for
me to set foot off my property, and then they would

gang up on me like a bunch of schoolyard bullies. So I relaxed and got my beauty rest.

In the morning, I calmly made myself an omelet with cheese and chives, poured some Tabasco on it, and nibbled on a piece of whole wheat toast. I cooked up some sausages too, but most of them went to Oberon. I made us a pot of coffee to wash it down, some freshly ground organic stuff from Central America (I usually take mine black, but Oberon likes it with Irish Crème Coffeemate and cooled down with a few ice cubes).

<Did Genghis Khan take his coffee black?> Oberon asked me. After my bathtime story, he wanted to be the Genghis Khan of dogs. He wanted a harem full of French poodles, all of whom were named either Fifi or Bambi. It was an amusing habit of his: Oberon had, in the past, wanted to be Vlad the Impaler, Joan of Arc, Bertrand Russell, and any other historical figure I had recently told him about while he was getting a thorough cleansing. His Liberace period had been particularly good for my soul: You haven't lived until you've seen an Irish wolfhound parading around in rhinestone-studded gold lamé.

He didn't drink coffee, I replied. *Genghis Khan was more of a tea man. Or yak milk. Coffee really wasn't around in his time.*

<May I have some tea, then?>

Of course. I will ice it for you after it brews so you won't burn your tongue.

After I cleared away the dishes and Oberon Khan had enjoyed his tea, it was time to make myself a target.

I strode out to my backyard, barefoot, and told Oberon to go into sentinel mode. I watered my herb garden from right to left, talking to the plants and encouraging them. The herbs grew in planter boxes around the circumference of my yard, all of which rested on shelves attached to my fence. Underneath these I grew some vegetables in the actual earth of my back-yard, leaving some real estate for Oberon to roll around on. The medicinal herbs took up most of the boxes, but I spared a few for culinary varieties.

While this mundane chore was going on, I was using my connection to the earth to review my domestic defenses. Sending my awareness down through my tat-toos, I looked for holes in my bindings, anything the least bit out of the ordinary, to make sure that I was alone and unwatched. There was a cactus wren check-ing me out from high up in my neighbor's palo verde tree, but he flew off when I made a throwing motion with my arm, thereby showing that he was a normal bird and not someone's familiar. When I came to the last planter box on the left, I put down the watering can and shook my head.

"There's never enough thyme," I said, and pulled the box of herbs off the shelf and upended it on the lawn. The smell of rich loam and compost wafted into my nostrils, and the sight of a long, narrow package wrapped tightly in oilskin greeted my eyes. "Oh, look!" I said in mock surprise. Oberon recognized my tone and didn't bother to turn his head. "Somebody has hid-den an ancient magical sword underneath my herbs. That's so silly."

This was my most vulnerable time, because while the sword's location was now revealed, there were three bindings and a cloak on the sword to prevent anyone—including me—from using it. The bindings were my own work, and it's pretty much all a Druid can do. We bind elements together or unbind them: When I shape-shift, I am binding my spirit to an animal's form. Summoning mist or wind—that's a form of binding too, as is camouflaging myself or allowing Oberon to hear my thoughts. It is all possible because we are already bound with the natural world by living in it. We could not bind anything if the strings connecting us to all of nature were not already there. And because we see these connections and know that seemingly disparate elements can in fact be closely related, Druids have a better grasp of divination than most other magical practitioners. Our knowledge of nature makes us superior brewers of medicines, poisons, and even potables. We're able to run tirelessly by drawing on the power of the earth, and we heal fairly quickly. We're useful to have around. But we don't shoot balls of fire out of our hands, or fly upon brooms, or make people's heads explode. That sort of magic is only possible through a radically different view of the world—and by binding one's spirit to extremely unsavory beings.

The bindings on Fragarach were simple but effective. One kept the oilskin sealed; one kept the sword in its scabbard; yet another prevented it from leaving the confines of my backyard. All of these could be undone with a bit of my blood and spit—fluids I don't give out for free.

But the best spell currently resting on Fragarach was a magical cloak around the whole thing, denying that there was anything magical about it in the slightest. Even though I knew my bindings were there, I could not detect them. And even though Fragarach is one of the most powerful magical items ever created, and it should be practically humming with Fae energies, it just lay there in front of me like a stage prop. I knew the cloak worked on the Tuatha Dé Danann too, because Flidais obviously had been unable to sense it during her visit.

The cloak was a spell far beyond my abilities: Those kinds of spells are not in the Druidic milieu. A friendly local witch named Radomila had cast it for me, and in return I had hopped a plane to San Francisco, driven up to Mendocino, and shape-shifted into a sea otter. This allowed me to retrieve an ornate golden necklace set with several large rubies, which were clutched in the hand of a buried skeleton she had stunningly accurate information on. She seemed mightily pleased to receive it, but even with two millennia of arcane knowledge in my head, I had no idea what it signified. That's witches for you.

What sealed the deal for me was that the cloak wouldn't come off without a generous donation of my tears. Those used to be almost impossible for me to summon, I admit, until I watched *Field of Dreams*. When Kevin Costner asks his dad at the end if he'd like to have a catch, I just completely lose my shit. Any guy who doesn't is either in mixed company when he sees it or was blessed with an unusually sensitive father. I blubber and sob like a jilted girl every time I watch that scene, or even when I think about it. My dad would never have played catch with me—never mind that he's been dead for more than two thousand years and baseball hadn't been invented then. My dad's idea of bonding was throwing me in the tar pits to teach me a lesson, though I'm not sure what the lesson was, except to stay the hell away from Da. So if I ever think of a reason why the cloak should come off, all I will have to do is think of Kevin Costner and his chance to have a moment of peace with his dad, and the tears will flow like mountain springs.

Bindings banished with a drop of blood pricked from my finger and a bit of spit, I unwrapped the oilskin carefully to reveal a finely tooled brown leather scabbard, above which rose a golden guard and a hilt wrapped in strips of ancient rawhide, the grain long worn away. The blade was not suffused with the watery swirls of cooled steel: It was merely straight and chiseled and deadly in its purpose.

A long leather strap attached to iron rings on the

scabbard allowed me to sling the sword across my back, and I did so to serve as both a lure and promise of punishment to those who would take it from me. I drew it thinking I needed to inspect the blade, but in truth it was more to admire it. I knew already that it was pristine: There had been no water damage to the scabbard. The blade sung and sparkled in the sunlight, and I marveled again at the strength of the cloak. Even though I knew it was Fragarach in my hand, its weight and balance and familiar knotwork etchings on the blade greeting me like old friends, the pulse of magic I usually felt was absent. The Fir Bolgs would not believe I had Fragarach in hand until it cut through their armor and bones as if they were rice paper.

"Come to heel, Oberon," I said aloud, as I sheathed Fragarach and rose. "Warn me of any approach, but do not attack unless I give you express permission."

<I'm coming to the shop with you?> he asked, his ears raised in query.

"Aye, you need to remain at my side until this business is finished. Do I need to remind you not to sniff my customers' asses?"

<You just did. And very subtly too, thank you very much.>

I chuckled. "I apologize if I have offended Oberon Khan. It is the stress of a death sentence that makes me speak without thinking."

<I will overlook it this time,> Oberon replied, his tail wagging in good humor.

"I am also going to cast camouflage on you," I said, "so that if you remain still—no tail wagging, no panting—no one will see you. Even when you move, you will be difficult to see, but you will be practically invisible when still."

<Why do I need to be invisible?>

"Because after last night, people may come hunting

you. And because if faeries come hunting me, I want you to take them by surprise."

<That's not very sporting.>

"It is fine to be sporting when we hunt. It is ridiculous to be sporting in war, and often fatal."

I cast the spell on him that binds one's skin and hair pigments to the hues of the surroundings, and he shook as if he were wet.

<Hey, that tickles,> he said.

"Good enough," I replied. He trotted next to me as I pedaled to work, his nails clicking on the asphalt of the street. Following the noise, all one could see was a sort of heat mirage, just a wavy fluidity to the air.

The widow MacDonagh was already out on her porch with her morning whiskey, and she waved to me as I rode by.

"Will y'be comin' by this afternoon, Atticus?" she called.

I quickly glanced at her lawn and saw that it was due to be mowed. Her grapefruit tree could use a trim as well.

"A bonny young lass like you need not ask a man twice," I shouted back, hoping her ancient ears understood me. I gave a thumbs-up to reinforce the message, just in case.

When I got to the store, my only employee was already there. Saturday mornings were always busy and I needed the help. I switched to silent communication with Oberon as I opened the door. *Go lie down behind my apothecary counter and keep your ears open.*

<Okay. What am I listening for, exactly?>

The approach of really heavy footsteps, the kind giants would make.

"Morning, Atticus," a bass voice rumbled in gnarly cheerfulness.

"Good morning, Perry," I replied. "You sound

abnormally happy. People will be on to you if you don't watch it."

A tall man of twenty-two years smiled back at me with recently bleached teeth. Perry Thomas had dark hair fastidiously groomed to look carelessly mussed, rectangular glasses with thick black rims, and a silver labret stud nestled like a pearl in the hair of his soul patch. He also had large silver gauges in both ears and a pale complexion that seemed to be the primary accessory for all Goths. He was dressed entirely in black, of course, with a concert T-shirt of the psychobilly group Mad Marge and the Stonecutters, a studded belt, and skinny-leg jeans that blossomed at the bottom into full-blown Doc Martens. Perry failed to notice Oberon padding right between us to take his appointed spot behind the counter.

"Yeah, I'm supposed to be jaded and mournful that the sun is shining, aren't I? Don't worry, I'll get into character once the store opens. Hey, cool sword."

"Thanks." I waited for him to ask me more about it, but Perry had apparently exhausted all he had to say on the subject. Young people can be so uncomplicated.

I glanced at the clock behind my counter. Five minutes to opening. "All right, give me a chance to get some tea brewing, then fire up the soundtrack and we'll get going. I want both registers working today." I had my apothecary counter and tea station on the east wall, immediately to the left, or south, of the store entrance. Wood shelves behind the counter held jars and little drawers of bagged herbs, many of which came from my backyard garden, and I had a couple of hot plates back there to heat kettles of water. There was a small fridge for milk, a sink, and some teacups always being washed and dried. I had a few packages of cookies and muffins for sale, but the lion's share of my apothecary business was in medicinal teas and bulk herb sales. I'd built up a regular clientele amongst the local senior citizens, who came in for a proprietary blended tea that eased their arthritis and gave them a boost of energy (I called it Mobili-Tea). They felt about ten years younger for about ten hours afterward, and they blessed me for it, bought newspapers, and had their morning arguments about politics and young people at the five tables I had placed in front of the counter. One register was there, and one was in the "back" of the store, on the west side, to handle customers who just wanted something from the bookstore.

My book inventory was basically an expanded collection of the Religion and New Age shelves in Barnes & Noble, but I also had some serious magical texts behind glass on the north wall. Buddhas and incense and various busts of Hindu gods were sprinkled amongst the shelves; I would have put some crucifixes around too if there had been any demand for that sort of thing, but devout Christians tended to avoid my store for some reason. Celtic crosses were popular, though, as were various representations of the Green Man.

Perry raised his eyebrows. "Open the second register? Think we're going to be that busy?"

I nodded. "I have a feeling it's going to be an unusual day." In truth, I simply didn't want him behind the apothecary counter where Oberon was hiding. "If you get some downtime, see if you can create an end display for the Tarot cards; maybe we can sell some more that way."

"Putting them out like that will make them easier to shoplift."

I shrugged. "I'm not worried about it." I wasn't. Everything in the store had the same binding spell on it that I had put on Fragarach in my backyard. Nothing could go out the door unless it had first been placed on

the counter next to one of the registers. More than one
would-be thief had been forcibly pulled back into the
store by the items in his pocket.

"Okay, I'll go turn on the music. Celtic pipes?"

"Nah, let's do some guitar this morning—that
Mexican duo, Rodrigo y Gabriela."

"Right." Perry headed toward the back of the store,
where the sound system was, and I filled a couple of kettles in the sink and put them on to boil. A couple of regulars would be coming in as soon as we unlocked the
door, so it was best to have the water ready. I glanced
over at the paper racks and saw that Perry had already
filled them.

Some Spanish guitar came on through the sound system, its World beat suggesting to customers that here
they could not only find refuge from corporate radio,
but also much else that was stale and prepackaged and
bereft of mystery. Perry strode back to the door, bran-
dishing his keys, and said, "Okay to open?" and I nodded at him.

The first person to walk through the door was my
daytime lawyer, Hallbjörn Hauk—he used the name
Hal for modern American usage. He was dressed in a
dark blue pinstripe suit with a white shirt and pale yellow tie. His hair, as ever, was immaculately styled in a
Joe Buck haircut, and the dimple in his chin smiled
sideways at me. If I didn't know he was a werewolf, I
would have voted for him.

"Have you seen the morning papers, Atticus?" he
said without preamble.

"Not yet," I admitted. "Good morning to you, Mr.
Hauk."

"Right. Well, then, perhaps you'd better take a look."
He grabbed a copy of *The Arizona Republic* and
slapped it down forcefully on the counter in front of
me, pointing to a headline on the right-hand column.

"Now, tell me, lad," he said in his best faux-Irish accent tinged with ancient Icelandic, "would y'be knowin' anything about this spot o' trouble here?"

The headline read, RANGER FOUND DEAD IN PAPAGO PARK.

Casting off my American accent, I replied in kind: "I'd be knowin' more than is comfortable, just between me and my attorney–client privilege."

"I thought as much. I heard Coyote laughin' last night, and he doesn't laugh at the harmless, does he now?"

"No, he doesn't, sir. I might be needin' your help sooner rather than later."

"Right. I'll be seein' you for lunch, then, at Rúla Búla?" He named the Irish pub at the north end of Mill Avenue that was my favorite hangout. "I'm thinkin' it's high time we had ourselves a heart-to-heart, and there's no reason it shouldn't be had over the best fish and chips in thirty states."

I nodded and said, "At high noon, sir," though I could not figure where he had pulled the number thirty from. Which twenty states had better fish and chips than Rúla Búla? He had evidently been paying more attention to fish and chip cuisine than I had, and I must admit that I felt a twang of guilt. The finest fish and chips in the land was more than a mere trivial pursuit for me, and I had sorely neglected it for an abominably long time. Most places excelled in either one or the other, but rare was the establishment that paid equal attention to both sides of the culinary complement. Rúla Búla was one of the few Irish pubs that savored the chip as well as the fish, and its presence had been a determining factor in my decision to grow roots in Tempe.

"Right," he said. "See you then," and he exited without another word.

My senior regulars came in: Sophie, Arnie, Joshua, and Penelope. Joshua grabbed a newspaper and pointed out the same article Hal had shown me. "God, would you look at this," he said, waving at it. "It's like we're back in New York." He said almost the same thing every day about one article or another, so I was oddly comforted by it.

A lone searcher arrived, seeking something that wasn't Judeo–Christian and buying a primer series in Buddhism, Hinduism, and Wicca. "May harmony find you," I said, and he dipped his head to me as he left. He had my respect: At least he wasn't content to be fed the diet on the television. And then something unusual walked through my door.

She was a witch. Her personal wards radiated warnings, and even though I was not adept enough to know what they did or what they protected her from, I knew by her aura what she was. I hastily muttered a binding under my breath to keep all my hairs on my body. Witches could do some pretty heinous stuff with hair, blood, or even nail clippings, and I didn't know yet if she was friendly or not. Her appearance marked her as nothing more than a trendy college student, however: no black robes or pointy hat, no hairy moles growing on the end of an oversize nose. She had her brown hair pulled back in a ponytail, as carefully considered a decision as the makeup applied to her face and the pink gloss on her lips.

She was wearing a white *bebe* tank top and a pair of oversize white-rimmed sunglasses. She carried a pink cell phone in one hand along with a jangling key ring. Her tanned, silky legs were bare beyond a pair of turquoise cotton shorts that strained at the boundaries of modesty. Her feet were slipped into a pair of pink flip-flops, her toenails painted pink with golden glitter sparkling in it.

She took a moment to look around, inspecting the unseen more than the seen, before she turned and strode to my apothecary's counter. She appeared to be my assumed age, twenty-one or so, but I knew how deceiving appearances could be. I could not tell her true age without more information, but the eyes behind those sunglasses were definitely older than twenty-one: She had seen things that separated her from the young and stupid. Still, she was less than a century old, judging by her aura, because it was still fluid and had none of the telltale markers of the truly old. If she could perceive the bindings around my shop and within them, she knew I was much older than I looked too.

"Are you the owner of this shop?" she said, approaching my counter.

"I am. What can I do for you?"

"You are Atticus O'Sullivan?"

"Uh-huh." I nodded once. Someone had told her whom to ask for. I did not put my name on the window.

"I have heard that you can brew some extraordinary teas."

"Well, yeah, I can make you some oolong with an antioxidant booster that's simply awesome. Would you like a cup of that?"

"That does sound fabulous, but that's not the sort of tea I'm talking about."

"Oh. Then whatcha lookin' for?"

"I need a tea that will . . . humble a man who is attracted to me. Make me unattractive to him."

"What? Wait. You wish to be unattractive?"

"To this one particular man, yes. Can you brew such a tea?"

"You want a sort of anti-Viagra, if I'm hearing you right."

"You have understood me perfectly."

I shrugged. "It oughtta be possible." She smiled. Her

teeth were very white and straight, a toothpaste commercial waiting to happen. "But how did you hear about me?"

"I am one of Radomila's coven," she said, extending her hand to shake. "The youngest, actually. My name is Emilia, but I go by Emily in America."

I relaxed a little bit: Radomila and I had a professional and cordial relationship. She was the leader of the Tempe Coven, thirteen witches who actually knew what the hell they were doing. They had a fancier name for themselves than that, but they didn't advertise it. Radomila was pretty powerful, and I would rather not get on her bad side. Oh, one-on-one I'd probably be able to dispatch her, but then her entire coven would come after me together, and they would chew me up and tell the Morrigan to go suck on it, because they most likely had their own goddess in their corner.

"Why do you need me, Emily?" I asked, shaking her hand once and knowing she was trying to gauge my power through the contact. That didn't work too well on Druids. We draw our power from the earth as needed, so she probably felt nothing more than the low-level power I was using to maintain Oberon's camouflage. It had caused more than one foe to underestimate me, so that was fine by me. I'm not into peacock displays of power. "Isn't Radomila capable of looking after her own coven anymore? For that matter, you could take care of this problem yourself. You don't need me."

"That is true," she said. "But Radomila wants no part in the crafting of this particular potion. Neither do I. We require . . . outside assistance."

"And so you came here? I'm just a friendly apothecary who knows that witches are for real."

"I pray you do not fence with me. I know full well what you are, Druid."

Well. That was putting the cards on the table. I took

another look at her aura, which was largely red and tossed about with the desire for power. She might be older than a century after all. College students these days didn't begin their sentences with "I pray you," and they thought fencing was selling stolen car stereos.

"And I know what you are too, Emily of the Sisters of the Three Auroras." Her mouth formed a tiny O of surprise at my use of her coven's true name. "If you don't want to humble this guy yourself, then I don't want to either."

"If you would agree to this thing, then Radomila and her coven would be in your debt," Emily said.

I arched an eyebrow. "Are you authorized to commit Radomila to such a pledge?"

"I am," she said, and pushed a note across the counter to me. It was in Radomila's hand. And the splatter beneath it was Radomila's blood—even dried, I could see the power in it. Oh, yes, she had authorization.

I snatched the note off the counter and pushed it down into my pocket. "Very well," I said. "I will agree to make this tea against your coven's pledge of future favor, provided that you personally agree to follow my instructions to the letter and pay my customary fees."

She bristled a little bit, obviously expecting the note to take care of everything, but eventually she nodded curtly. "Agreed," she said.

"Very well." I smiled. "How long do you wish to remain unattractive to this man?"

"A week should suffice."

"Then you will appear here tomorrow at this hour to drink a tea I will prepare for you and every day thereafter for a week. Failure to appear will void our contract with no monies refunded."

"I understand and agree."

"Tomorrow you will bring me a cashier's check for ten thousand dollars."

Her eyes widened. "Outrageous!" she spat, and she had a point. I never charged more than two hundred dollars for my apothecary services. "That cannot be your customary fee!"

"If the Tempe Coven is unwilling to take care of your paramour's libido on its own, which they could do far more simply than I, then I am owed danger pay," I said.

"But not that much!" she fumed, all but admitting the danger was real.

I produced the note and offered it to her. "Then I bid you good day."

Emily's shoulders sagged. "You bargain well," she said, her eyes downcast to my countertop. Her hands made no move to take back the note, but I kept it raised within her reach.

"You will bring me the cashier's check tomorrow, then?" I asked.

"Aye," she said, and with that I put the note back in my pocket.

"Then we will begin tomorrow."

"Not now?"

"Until I have the check, no."

"Then if I bring the check today, you will begin?"

"Aye, Emily, that is the contract I propose."

"And once begun, you will not renege?"

It was an unusual request to put so bluntly, but not an unreasonable one. All contracts should allow the customer a reasonable expectation of completion. But it seemed an awful lot of trouble to go through to make one guy go limp for a week.

"You have my word, Emily, that once payment is received, I shall execute the contract as stated, so long as you appear daily at the same hour to drink my tea."

She spat in her hand and extended it to me. "Contract offered?"

I stared at her hand and made no move to take it. If

I spat in mine and shook her hand, then she would have some of my spittle to work with. Giving a witch your body fluids is akin to slicing off a choice cut of your buttocks and offering it to a werewolf. "Received," I said, keeping my hands on the counter. "You may consider my word my bond."

She smiled triumphantly, not in the least offended, and exited my shop without feigning interest in any of my wares, though she pointedly waved at Oberon behind the counter and said, "Bye, puppy," just to show me she had seen through the camouflage. And I wondered, far too late, whether I had behaved wisely in agreeing to this business. Probably not. Witches had better ways of controlling their bodies than drinking a Druid's brews, and if they were willing to put their entire coven in magical hock to me and pay me ten thousand ducats to boot to get rid of one horny guy, then I was probably dealing with an incubus or something similarly nasty.

The magic of attraction is little more than science these days. I would brew her a blend of herbs that would suppress her natural pheromones, which were currently exciting the fella, and then, with a bit of clever binding, cause her to emit the chemical signature of a skunk instead. Unless this guy was a closet skunkophile, she'd be looking at a wet noodle all night. On top of that, I was going to make sure she didn't get excited either, throwing in some natural monoamine suppressants. I had made this sort of brew before: I sold it to sorority girls as Humili-Tea. They used it on their exes or their stalkers or sometimes to end a relationship when they had no good reason to do so.

Back when I first learned how to make a tea like this, I didn't have names for all the chemical reactions caused by the herbs—the herblore was just as magical to me as my bindings were to a layperson. Science had taken away some of the mystery of the process but none of the utter coolness I felt knowing that I could whip up compounds the pharmaceutical industry could only dream of.

But I will not pretend I was helping Emily to feel cool. I figured to come out far ahead in the deal, because having a coven in your debt was serious mojo, and I could use plenty of that if the Morrigan's casting were to come true.

Chapter 8

It actually turned out to be quite a busy morning, making my opening of the second register seem like genius. Perry never found time to mess with the Tarot display until much later, and I never got time to read the full article about the park ranger. But I figured Hal would fill me in once I got to Rúla Búla.

Come on, Oberon. Lunchtime.

<Burgers?> He lifted his head up hopefully.

Fish. And we're going to be in a restaurant, so you need to behave and stay out of the way.

<Same rules wherever we go. Behave and stay out of the way.>

I waved at Perry and told him I'd be back in an hour or so. "Mind the fortress, will you?"

He waved back. "No problem."

I slipped out the door and opened it wide so Oberon could follow me, then unlocked my bike from the stand and hopped on.

No stopping to smell the trees and fire hydrants, I said. *I can't be calling back to an invisible dog every few minutes to hurry it up.*

<When do I get to have some fun?> he whined.

After I close up shop. You can play around at the widow's house. You can chase her cats in camouflage and totally freak them out. Heh!

Oberon made chuffing noises, which was the canine equivalent of laughter. <Oh, now that sounds like a good time! I can sneak up on that calico one and bark right behind it. It'll hit the ceiling.>

We chuckled about it together as we made our way up Mill Avenue, passing the bars and boutiques and the occasional gallery. Oberon told me about his plans to just put his paw down on the Persian's tail and watch what happened.

Hal Hauk had already secured a table inside Rúla Búla near the window, and he had ordered a pint of Smithwick's for each of us. I was both pleased and disappointed by the gesture, for it meant I wouldn't get to go to the bar myself and take a whiff of the barmaid.

That's not as creepy as it sounds.

Granuaile, the redheaded siren behind Rúla Búla's bar, was not entirely human, but I still didn't know what she was, and her scent was my only clue. She was a mystery to me, and a beautiful one at that. Long locks of curly red hair cascaded over her shoulders, which were always covered in a tight but otherwise chaste T-shirt. She did not earn tips from her cleavage, like many barmaids do, but rather depended on her green eyes, her pouty lips, and the light dusting of freckles on her cheeks. She had pale, creamy skin and a few fine golden hairs on her arms, which led eventually to fingernails she had painted green to match her eyes.

She was not one of the Fae: I could see through all their glamours, and in any case she never blanched at my iron amulet. Neither was she undead, or she would hardly be working the day shift. She wasn't a were of any kind, which Hal had mentioned but I had already determined using my own methods. I had thought she might be a witch, but she didn't have the telltale signs in her aura. If she had been anything sent from hell, I would have smelled the brimstone, but instead she gave off an ineffable scent that was not quite floral, more like a pinot grigio and mixed in with something that reminded me of India, like saffron and poppies. I was left to conclude that she was a goddess of some sort, masking her true nature and slumming here incognito like so many other members of the supernatural community, displaced from points all over the world. The bonny Irish lass façade was even more shameless than mine, for I doubted that she was truly Irish underneath it all: She must be from some foreign pantheon, and I was determined to figure it out without asking her a thing.

She flashed a smile at me as I walked in, and my heart sped up a bit. Did she have a clue as to my true nature, or did she only see the dim college kid disguise?

Her face fell as I walked past the bar toward Hal's table. "You're not sitting with me today, Atticus?" she said with a pout, and I almost changed course right there.

<Down, boy,> Oberon said at my heels with ironic relish. I ignored him.

"Sorry, Granuaile"—that simply could not be her true name; she had to have picked it out on purpose to fit in at an Irish bar—"I have to talk a little treason with my friend," I said, gesturing toward Hal.

She smiled. "If it's a conspiracy, I want in on it. I can keep a secret."

"I'll bet you can," I said, and she arched an eyebrow at me. I felt a foolish grin spread across my face.

"Ahem. Time is money, Mr. O'Sullivan," Hal called, and I snapped my head around, suddenly realizing I had stopped in the middle of the bar and forgotten what I was doing there. Hal's time was worth $350 an hour.

<Next time you take me to the dog park and you yell at me to stay away from the French poodles, I'm going to remind you of this,> Oberon said.

Embarrassed, I stalked over to Hal's table and sat myself across from him. Oberon squeezed underneath the table next to the window and waited for food to rain down from the sky.

Hal frowned. "I smell your dog."

"He's under the table, camouflaged," I said.

Hal's eyes widened as he processed the sling across my chest and the hilt peeking out over my shoulder.

"Is that the sword I think it is?" he asked.

"Yes," I replied, and took a long pull from the Smithwick's.

"Was it employed in last night's mischief?"

"No, but I believe in being prepared. There's more trouble on the way. A whole lot more."

"Do I need to tell the Pack?" Hal asked.

Werewolves. Their pack always came first. "Hey, it's my ass in the meat grinder here, not the Pack's," I said. "You don't need to tell anyone but Leif about this business. In fact, I want to see him as soon as he wakes up tonight. Send him to my house."

Hal looked as if I had just asked him to lick up vomit. "Will you be paying the firm for his time, or will he?" He was referring to the business arrangement I had with the vampire. Leif and I had a unique understanding: Sometimes I paid cash for his services, and sometimes I paid him in fine liqueur—that is to say, my blood. (I had carefully neglected to mention that to Flidais.) The blood of a 2,100-year-old human, and a Druid no less, was a powerful, intoxicating, and extremely rare vintage for a vampire. I slashed my arm, drained a wineglass full for him, and then healed myself, and that was worth twelve hours' billing to him. Then I washed out the glass and made sure he hadn't spilled any, because I was paranoid about my blood getting into the hands of witches. He paid the firm out of his own pocket for such a drink, and he had grown powerful over the years by it. I never saw him use the power, because nothing locally wanted to mess with him, but I think Leif was trying to become strong enough to mess with Thor someday.

"Does it matter?" I said. "The firm gets paid either way."

Our waitress arrived, and we paused to order three plates of fish and chips—the third was for Oberon, who was doing a good job of remaining invisible. When she left, Hal spread his hands and said, "Okay, tell me everything." I told him about Flidais but left out the Morrigan; it wasn't everything, but close enough.

"So a goddess from your pantheon has come and gone," he said when I had finished, "and you could get a visit from two more Irish gods before this business is through?"

"Right. Aenghus Óg and Bres. Plus Fir Bolgs."

"Plus those. I've never seen one. What are they like?"

"To you they'll look like a biker gang or something similar, but they will smell like shit."

"Biker gangs can smell like shit sometimes."

"Well, that just makes the disguise better," I said. "The point is, you won't see what they're really like, because they wear glamour when they walk in the mortal world. In truth, they're giants with bad oral hygiene and a predilection for wielding spears. They used to be an independent people in the old days, but the Tuatha Dé Danann use them as thugs now."

"How much of a threat are they?"

"To my life? I am not particularly worried. I'm more worried about collateral damage than anything else."

"That will bring the police into it."

"Which I'm sure is the point of sending them. Fir Bolgs are not renowned for their discretion."

Our fish and chips arrived and I sighed happily. It is life's small, simple pleasures that make it worth living longer than a century or two. I dropped a piece of cod down to Oberon and covered up his noisy chomping sounds with some noises of my own.

"So how can I keep Oberon from going to Animal Control?" I asked around a mouthful of chips and beer.

Hal shrugged. "The simplest way is to do what you're doing and lie," he replied. "Keep him hidden, and tell anyone who asks that he escaped and ran away. In a month or even less, they'll be so swamped with other cases that they won't be able to keep tabs on whether he's with you or not. Then you tell all your neighbors you've given up, you're going to get a new dog, and voilà, Oberon reappears. Oh, and I wouldn't go hunting in the Papago Hills for a year or so."

Oberon whined at that, and I hushed him by dropping another piece of cod on the floor.

"This is all supposing the police actually track him to your place," Hal said. "They haven't shown up yet, have they?"

I shook my head. "Not yet. But since I think someone is leading them around, I have no doubt they will show up soon. Now tell me what to do if I don't want to lie."

Hal stopped chewing and regarded me steadily for a few seconds. "You don't want to lie?" he said, completely off his guard.

"Of course I do! I just want to know what else I can do that I haven't thought of already. That's why I pay you, Hal. I mean, shit, come on."

Hal smiled. "You really sound like one of these modern kids. I have no idea how you do it."

"Blending in is the best survival skill I have. It's just listening carefully and parroting, really. So tell me what to do if I'm forced to play it honest."

"Honest as in the police can see through your camouflage spell and know that Oberon is right in front of them?"

"Sure. Pretend I'm an ordinary guy with no magic at my disposal. Then how do I protect Oberon?"

The werewolf took a long drink of Smithwick's and belched discreetly as he thought about it. Then he placed his hands flat on the table and said, "Well, the only way they would be able to build a case without witnesses is to use DNA matching. Oberon has no rights, but as his owner you can demand they get a warrant before they do the whole unreasonable-search-and-seizure thing. If they come with a warrant, though, you pretty much have to let them do what they want. And judging from what you've told me, if they get a DNA sample from him, the case will be pretty solid."

"That's right," I said, nodding.

"Well, another way we can delay things is to lodge some protest on religious grounds."

"How's that?"

"You protest against the DNA testing of your dog on the grounds that's it's against your religion."

I looked at him as if he were trying to sell me the ShamWow and the Slap Chop for only $19.99 plus shipping and handling. "My religion has no objection to DNA testing. We didn't know what the hell DNA was in the Iron Age."

Hal shrugged. "They don't know that." Neither of us would ever get an award for ethics. "The Iron Age, eh?" Hal had been trying to guess my age for a good while, and I had carelessly given him another clue.

I ignored his query and frowned skeptically. "Will that argument work?"

"No, the judge will throw it out on the grounds that your dog cannot possibly share your religious views or something like that, but it will delay things for a good long while, long enough for you to figure out where to hide Oberon if, as you say in this entirely hypothetical situation, you can't do it magically."

"Good show, old sod," I said in a cheerful accent straight out of Piccadilly Circus. "I knew there was a jolly good solicitor in you somewhere."

"Oh, bugger off," Hal replied in kind. "Just hide and lie and keep it simple for everyone, all right?"

I grinned at him. "Will do. Where is the Pack going to run next full moon?"

"In the White Mountains near Greer. Did you want to come along?" Occasionally the Pack would let Oberon and me run with them, and it was always a good time. The only touchy part was my status within the group, because werewolves are obsessed with status. Magnusson didn't like to have me along, because technically he'd have to be submissive to me—if I gave a damn about such things—and alphas aren't comfortable showing any kind of submission in front of their packs. I couldn't blame him, of course, so we worked out a compromise where I was a "friend" of the Pack, a guest on equal footing with every member, essentially outside their hierarchy, and that kept everyone's hackles from rising. But it also meant that Hauk, not Magnusson, had to be my lawyer. As a second, he was already submissive and did not have to worry about debasing himself by serving my legal needs.

"I would love to, but it falls around Samhain, and I have some of my own rituals to attend to," I said. "I thank you for the offer, though."

"My pleasure." He extended a hand across the table to me. I shook it and he said, "I'll take care of this bill and let Leif know you want to see him when he wakes for the night. You call me if you need anything else. And stay away from that redheaded bartender. I don't know what she is besides trouble."

"That's like asking a bee to stay away from flowers." I grinned back at him. "Thanks, Hal. Give my regards to the Pack. Come on, Oberon." We both rose and headed for the door. Granuaile waved at me and smiled.

"Come back soon and see me, Atticus," she called.

"I will," I promised.

<You don't even know if she really likes you,> Oberon said as we exited and I unlocked my bike. <She could be doing her customer-service routine and stringing you along in hopes of a big tip the next time you come in. With dogs you just go up and smell their asses and you know where you stand. It's so much easier. Why can't humans do that?>

Perhaps if we had a better sense of smell, we would, I said. *Nature clearly favored your kind in that regard.*

When I returned to the store and told Perry he could take off for lunch, Emily the witch was already there waiting for me, drinking a cup of chamomile tea Perry had made for her. He wasn't skilled behind the tea station, but he could boil some water and pour it on top of pre-made sachets as long as I labeled them carefully.

"Back so soon?" I said. "You must be eager to begin."

"True enough," she said. She stood from the table and minced over to me in her affected Barbie-doll stride. She waved a check at me before placing it in my hand and saying snarkily, "Here's your danger pay, though there's nothing dangerous about making some tea. I never figured Druids would be so avaricious."

I took it from her hand and made a show of examining it carefully, because I knew it would annoy her. She'd deliberately tried to provoke me, and one cannot sass me with impunity. I saw her face flush and knew she wanted to say something about my dilatory manner, but she wisely kept her mouth shut and contained herself to huffing.

Eventually I said, "This appears to be in order. I will begin your treatment because your coven has done right by me in the past, but if this fails to clear the bank, then of course that will be a breach of contract." Now, that was just unnecessary—even insulting—for me to say, but she was such a snot I felt she deserved it.

"Fine," she ground out, and I smiled and went behind my counter to begin brewing her tea. I worked in silence for a while. We were the only people in the store, and neither of us was in the mood to make small talk. Oberon picked up on it.

<Genghis Khan would never put up with so much attitude,> he said.

You speak the truth, my friend. But I'm as guilty as she is. We are not being very nice to each other.

<So I gathered. But why not? Isn't she the sort of female you normally find attractive?>

If that was really what she looked like, sure, I said. *But in reality she's probably pushing ninety or so, and besides, I don't trust witches.*

<You think she's going to try something? Should I move behind her?>

No, she knows you're here. She can see through the camouflage. But I think she's hiding something from me, and I'm waiting for the other shoe to drop.

<When did she drop the first shoe? I missed it.>

Never mind. Just listen. Once she drinks the tea, she will try to surprise me with something. She is waiting for the contract to be fully in effect before she says anything.

<Well, then, give her back the check and send her packing! We don't need to play her witch's games. They always want to get you and your little dog, too.>

I knew I never should have let you watch The Wizard of Oz.

<Toto didn't deserve that kind of trauma. He was so tiny.>

When Emily's tea was finished steeping, I set it on the

counter for her. "Drink it as is," I said. "No sweet-
eners, and nothing sugary for at least three hours
afterward. Be careful from this day forward not to
eat anything for three hours before drinking this tea
either. Insulin will interfere with metabolizing the
medicinal compounds in the tea." That was complete
bunk. I just made that up to mess with her. "And it
will take a couple of hours for the results to show up,
so don't go hopping into his bed right away."

"Fine," she said, and she began chugging the tea as if
it were an Irish Car Bomb, completely disregarding the
damage the hot liquid might do to her tongue and
throat. She really wanted to get this over with. She
slammed it down forcefully, as if it were a shot glass
instead of a teacup, and she smiled malevolently at me.

"And now, Druid, now that you have entered into a
contract from which you cannot withdraw without
severe consequences, I have the pleasure of informing
you that the man you're rendering impotent with this
brew is none other than Aenghus Óg."

Chapter 9

Now, that was a pretty good bomb to drop on me. It raised all sorts of questions, foremost among them, "Where is Aenghus Óg right now?" If he was already in town and diddling the local witches to pass the time, then my paranoia was well justified. It meant he was far more directly involved in last night's mischief than I had thought. And it meant something else, which Emily was obviously waiting for me to realize: Providing her with the agent for his humiliation would make Aenghus Óg duty-bound to kill me as soon as possible. He would no longer feel comfortable in taking the occasional pot shot at me from a distance; he'd have to actively hunt me down and make me pay.

Yep, storm clouds are thrice cursed. First the Fae found out where I was hiding, then my dog killed a human, and now I'd earned the very personal enmity of a god who had been content for centuries to simply let his minions slap me around.

Emily wasn't going to get an expression of even mild concern from me, though. She wanted to see terror in my eyes, but I walled that all off and pretended she was talking about someone harmless, like Snuffleupagus or Captain Kangaroo.

"So you've come to me to make him wilt like lettuce?" I said. "You could have done the job yourself by shedding that skin and showing him what you really look like."

Wow. I couldn't believe I'd just said that. Her eyes bulged with the offense, and she whipped her right hand toward my face for a slap. Now, a slap from a normal woman I could handle. Heck, I'd suggest I needed one after saying something like that to a regular college kid. But a slap from a witch is simply not permissible, because sure as the moon rises full once a month, she'd use her nails to scrape some skin off my cheek, perhaps even draw some blood, and then she'd have me. A friend of mine fell prey to precisely this sort of trick centuries ago, and it had poisoned me against witches ever since. She had goaded him into saying something rude, slapped him and left marks on his face, and then that very night his heart exploded inside his chest. I don't mean he had a heart attack: His heart had literally blown apart as if someone had planted explosives in it, long before gunpowder was invented. Some other Druids and I had taken him to the grove and done a rudimentary autopsy to see if we could puzzle out why he'd dropped dead so abruptly, and we found this crater inside his rib cage. That's when I realized he'd been killed the moment she slapped him.

I'd never avenged him—the witch got away—and it still stung centuries later. That's why Emily's attempt to slap me got a very violent reaction: I knocked her arm down by crossing my right hand over my face, then I backhanded her really hard, much harder than I should have. I shouldn't have hit her at all; I should have just backed up out of her reach, but I tend to flare up when people try to kill me—which was what she was trying to do, make no mistake. She squealed and staggered back a few steps, holding her nose.

I had broken it, and I sort of felt like an asshole even though she had planned to do much worse to me.

While she was still in shock and processing what had happened, I took the opportunity to try to talk her down from escalating it. "You offered me violence and I defended myself. I know that a slap from you would have meant the end of my life, or at least the threat of it, and I could not permit that. And if you are thinking about using magic against me in my own shop, I would remind you that discretion is sometimes the better part of valor."

"And I would remind you that I am not powerless. Radomila will hear of this!"

"That's fine. I'll show her my security tape," I said, gesturing to the video camera mounted on the wall above the register, "which clearly shows you swinging first. On top of that, you have now given me cause to believe you are a close associate of an old enemy of mine. I'd be within my rights to treat you as hostile."

"Go ahead and try something!" she challenged, eyes blazing.

"I don't need to try anything," I chuckled. "I'm in control here."

"You go on thinking you're in control, Druid," she spat, heading for the door in a fury, her flip-flops flapping noisily. "You'll soon find out you are very mistaken."

"See you tomorrow for tea," I waved cheerily as she slammed through my door.

<Oh, she's going to want some revenge,> Oberon said after the door closed and we were alone.

"Don't worry about her," I said, grabbing a spoon and moving quickly around the counter. "She's not the sharpest tool in the shed."

<What are you doing?> Oberon asked. He followed me out to the floor, curious. I had squatted down on my haunches, examining the carpet.

"Ah, there we go." I found a droplet of blood on the

carpet that hadn't soaked thoroughly into the weave; it was not much, but it would be enough. I scraped it off the surface and walked toward the door, peering through the glass window to see if Emily was visible. She was getting into her car, parked across the street a short distance north, a bright yellow Volkswagen Beetle. She would have to turn over her left shoulder to see me, so I darted outside, telling Oberon I'd return in a moment, and kicked off my sandals. I sank my toes into the same narrow strip of grass that had helped me heal my arm the day before, and I chanted a binding as I drew power from the earth. Emily felt the draw somehow, whipped her head around, and saw me standing there. I showed the spoon to her and smiled; her mouth dropped open in horror as she realized how careless she had been. I saw her lips move and her brow furrow in concentration, so I had no time to waste. I licked her blood off the spoon and completed the binding just in time. She flicked her fingers at me and I knew she had just hurled something my way, but all I felt was a gentle breeze.

A couple of seconds later her upper body was thrown painfully forward into her steering wheel, which caused the car's horn to beep. Ha! She had tried to blow the spoon out of my hand—and knock me down in the process, off the grass strip and my source of power. Clever. But not fast enough. The binding I had performed was actually a ward, which meant that any spell she sent against me would rebound against her. The only way she could get out of it would be to get herself some new blood.

She leaned back slowly and clutched her chest. Probably bruised a rib or two. On top of a broken nose and wounded pride, she'd had a rough day visiting the local Druid. It made me wonder what she'd been told about me. Did she know how old I was? Did she think

I was some sort of lame-assed neo-Druid, mucking about with holly branches and mistletoe? She turned around to stare daggers at me, and I gave her a jovial wave, then blew her a kiss. She flipped me off—a gesture that had zero cultural relevance to me—and then started up her Beetle and screeched away toward University Drive.

Chuckling to myself, I reentered the store, and Oberon came over and nuzzled against my legs, which was somewhat startling when he was in camouflage.

<Nobody's here now. I want a scratch behind the ears.>

I searched and found his head and gave him a good head rub for a minute or so. "Yes, you've been very patient, haven't you?" I said. "Tell you what. Next time we go hunting, we'll head down to the Chiricahua Mountains. That's south of here and I think you'll like it."

<What's down there?>

"Mule deer. Maybe some of those bighorn sheep, if we get lucky."

<When can we go?>

"Probably not until this business is over," I admitted. "I know it will be a long wait for you, but I promise we'll do nothing but hunt once we go. The trip will be for you. But that's not to say you're going to be totally bored in the meantime. We'll probably get attacked at any moment."

<Really?>

"Well, it's more likely going to be after we leave the store."

Oberon's ears perked up and he turned to the door. <Someone's coming.>

A customer walked in, looking for a copy of *The Upanishads,* and after that a fairly steady stream of people were either browsing or buying something. The lunchtime lull was over, and soon enough Perry came back to help out. After giving a regular his customary cup of Daddy's Little Helper (my code for a tea designed to promote prostate health), the phone rang. It was a call from one of Radomila's coven.

"Mr. O'Sullivan, my name is Malina Sokolowski. May I speak to you about what occurred between you and Emily this afternoon?"

"Well, sure. But I cannot speak frankly right now. I have customers in the store."

"I understand," she replied. She had a warm voice and a faint accent that had to be Polish, judging by her name. "Let me ask you this: Do you consider the contract between you and Emily to still be in effect?"

"Oh, absolutely." I nodded as if she could see it. "Nothing happened to nullify that."

"That is reassuring. Would you mind terribly if I accompanied her for tomorrow's tea?"

"I suppose that would depend on your intentions."

"I will not fence with you," Malina said. What was this coven's obsession with fencing? "My intention is to defend Emily in case you attack her again."

"I see. And, according to Emily, how many times have I attacked her so far?"

"Once physically and once magically."

"Well, at least she got that part right. But in both cases, Malina, it was she who initiated the attack. I was able to redirect both attacks against her; hence the injuries you have no doubt seen."

"So it's her word against yours," she sighed.

"Yes. And I understand that you must take her word against mine. But you must understand that she told me her lover is a sworn enemy of mine. By doing so, she has allied your entire coven with him."

"No, that's unthinkable!" Malina objected. "If we were allied with this individual, then we would not be trying to humiliate him."

"Why *are* you trying to humiliate him?"

"That is a question better answered by Radomila."

"So put her on. Is she there?"

"Radomila is indisposed." For normal people, that would mean she was taking a shower or something. In Radomila's case, it probably meant she was in the middle of a complicated spell involving tongue of frog, eye of newt, and maybe a packet of Splenda.

"I see." A customer with greasy black hair hanging over his face came up to the counter with a bulk bag of incense sticks. "Look, I have to go. You're welcome to come with Emily tomorrow, but it would be best to counsel her to keep silent around me. I can make her tea in silence, and she can drink it in silence; that way no one will get offended or injured. If you'd like to stay behind afterward, perhaps we can talk without coming to blows."

Malina agreed, said she looked forward to it, and we rang off. The greasy man asked me if I had access to medical marijuana as an apothecary, and I pasted a sorrowful expression on my face and told him no as I rang up the incense he needed to mask the stink of his habit.

Drug addicts perplex me. They're a relatively recent development, historically speaking. Everyone has their theories—monotheists like to blame it on Godlessness— but I think it was a plague that developed in the sooty petticoats of the Industrial Revolution and its concomitant division of labor. Once people specialized their labors and separated themselves from food production and the daily needs of basic survival, there was a hollow place in their lives that they did not know how to fill. Most people found healthy ways to fill it, with hobbies or social clubs or pseudo-sports like shuffleboard and tiddlywinks. Others didn't.

Perry finally found some time to mess around with the Tarot decks and had a serviceable display up by closing time. I rode quickly to the widow's house after locking up the store and retrieved the push mower from her shed in the backyard.

"Ah, yer a fine boy, Atticus, and that's no lie," she said, saluting me with her whiskey glass as she came out to the front porch to watch me work. She liked to sit in her rocking chair and sing old Irish songs to me—old for her, anyway—over the whirl of the lawnmower blades. Sometimes she would forget the words and simply hum the tune, and I enjoyed that just as much. When I was finished, I always spent a pleasant time with her, hearing stories of her younger days in the old country. That day, as the sun was setting and the shadows were lengthening, she was telling me something about running around the streets of Dublin with a bunch of ne'er-do-wells. "This was all before I met me husband, o'course," she made sure to add.

I had Oberon stationed as sentinel on the edge of the lawn, close to the street. As the widow regaled me with tales of her Golden Age debauchery, I was depending on him to tell me of approaching danger.

<Atticus,> he said, as the widow was winding up her tale with a sigh over better days in a better land, <someone comes on foot from the north.>

Is he a stranger? I had put Fragarach aside while I talked with the widow, but now I stood and slung the scabbard back over my head, causing the widow to frown.

<Yes. He is very strange. I can smell the ocean on him from here.>

Uh-oh. That's not good. Stay still and try not to make any noise.

"Excuse me, Mrs. MacDonagh," I said, "someone's coming and he might not be friendly."

"What? Who is it? Atticus?"

I couldn't answer yet, so I didn't. I kicked off my sandals and drew power from the widow's lawn even as I walked toward the street and peered northward. One of the charms on my necklace has the shape of a bear on it, and its function is to store a bit of magical power for me that I can tap when I'm walking on concrete or asphalt. I topped off the magical tank as a possible antagonist approached.

A tall, armored figure clanked noisily on the asphalt a couple of houses away, and it raised a hand to hail me when I came into view. I activated a different charm that I call "faerie specs," a sort of filter for my eyes that lets me see through Fae glamours and detect all sorts of magic juju. It showed me the normal spectrum, but then there was also a green overlay that revealed what was going on magically, and right now the two layers showed me the same thing. So whoever he was, I was looking at his true form. If he had something similar to my faerie specs, he might be able to see through Oberon's camouflage, but then again, he might not.

He was wearing rather gaudy bronze armor that no one would have worn in the old days. The cuirass, faced in hardened leather dyed with woad, covered too much and restricted movement. He had leaf-shaped tassets hanging down over a bronze mail skirt. He also had five-piece pauldrons and matching vambraces and greaves. It would have been hot enough to wear such armor in Ireland, but here the temperature was still in the low nineties, and he must have been broiling in it. His helmet was beyond ridiculous: It was one of those medieval barbutes that didn't become popular until a thousand years after his halcyon days of slaughter, and he must have been wearing it as a joke, though I did not find it especially funny. A sword hung in a scabbard at his side, but thankfully he did not carry a shield.

"I greet you, Siodhachan Ó Suileabháin," he said. "Well met." He flashed a smug grin at me through his helmet, and I wanted to slay him on the spot. I kept my faerie specs on, because I simply didn't trust him. Without some way to pierce his glamour, he could make my eyes think he was standing three feet away with his hands on his head while he was really plunging a dagger into my belly.

"Call me Atticus. I greet you, Bres."

"Not well met?" He tilted his head a bit to the right, as much as the barbute would let him.

"Let's see how the meeting goes. It's been a long time since we have seen each other, and I wouldn't have minded if it were longer. And by the way, the Renaissance Festival doesn't arrive here until next February."

"That's not very hospitable," Bres said, frowning. Oberon was right: He smelled of salt and fish. As a god of agriculture, he should smell of earth and flowers, but instead he retained the stink of the dockside, owing perhaps to his Fomorian ancestors, who lived by the sea. "I could take offense if I wished."

"So take it already and be done. I can't imagine why else you would be here now."

"I am here at the request of an old friend," he said.

"Did he request that you dress like that? Because if he did, he's not your friend."

"Atticus, who is that?" the widow MacDonagh called from her porch. I didn't take my eyes off Bres as I called back to her.

"Someone I know. He won't be staying long." Time to set up my flanking maneuver. Speaking mind to mind, I said to Oberon, *Remain still. But when I say, get behind him, grab a leg, and just yank him off his feet. Once he's down, jump clear.*

<Got it,> Oberon said.

Bres continued as if the widow had never spoken. "Aenghus Óg wants the sword. Give it to me and you'll be left alone. It's that simple."

"Why isn't he here himself?"

"He's nearby," Bres said. That was calculated to ratchet my paranoia up a few levels. It worked, but I was determined it would not work in his favor.

"What's your stake in this, Bres? And what's with the armor?"

"That does not concern you, Druid. Your only concern is whether you will agree to give us the sword and live, or refuse and die." The last fingers of the sun were waving good-bye over the horizon, and twilight was upon us. Faerie time.

"Tell me why he wants it," I said. "It's not like Ireland has a High King who needs the Tuatha Dé Danann to help him out uniting all the various tribes."

"It is not for you to question."

"Sure it is," I said, "but I guess it's not for you to answer. Fragarach is right here." I gestured to the hilt peeking over my shoulder. "So if I give it to you now, you walk away, and I never hear from you or Aenghus again?"

Bres peered intently at the hilt for a few moments, then chuckled. "That is not Fragarach. I have seen it, Druid, and I have felt its magic. You have nothing in that scabbard but an ordinary sword."

Wow. Radomila's magical cloak just rocked.

And then the green overlay in my vision started to differ from the normal spectrum. Bres was pulling his sword out of his scabbard in a leisurely fashion and watching my face to see if I reacted, so I tried to stay relaxed and let him think I was clueless. Either he knew that I really had Fragarach on my back and he wanted to double-cross me, or he simply wanted to kill me to burnish his reputation. He'd make a fine tale of the battle, no doubt, in spite of the fact that he was planning the equivalent of a stab in the back.

"I assure you it's the real thing," I said to him, and to

Oberon I said, *Change in plan. Just lie down behind him when I say. I'll push him over your back so he falls down.*

<Okay.>

Bres's glamour form shrugged and said, "You can give your cheap sword to me if you'd like. It will only delay things, and I'll have to come back again with another offer. But I can guarantee that offer won't be as generous as the one I'm giving you now."

And that was when the true Bres on the green overlay grinned wickedly and raised his sword over his head in a two-handed grasp, ready to split me in two.

Now, Oberon, I said, keeping my face pensive as if I were thinking over Bres's words. I started talking out loud to hopefully mask any sounds Oberon made as he moved.

"Bres, I think you're missing something important," I said, even as he brought his sword down with all his strength and I stepped out of the way to the right at the last instant. His glamour persona was still standing there, smirking, but I didn't pay attention to that one anymore. The green one—the real Bres—had just tried to slay me. While he was hunched over awkwardly on his follow-through, I kicked at the nerve cluster in his wrist to make him drop the sword, then put another one in his face to make him stand back up. It didn't get through his helmet, but any blow to the head is going to make you pull away. Then I pivoted on my left foot and spun clockwise, delivering a roundhouse into his solar plexus before he could set himself. He staggered backward and fell over Oberon in a tremendous clatter of bronze and hardened leather, still not hurt but pretty humiliated by this point. He gave up on the glamour, and the smirking Bres merged with the one on the ground, so that my faerie specs and my normal vision showed the same thing again.

I could have left it there. He was disarmed and no danger to me now, and if any of the Fae had been around to see him fall flat on his ass, he would be shamed in a legendary fashion. Except that he had tried to kill me with a glamour. He would never fight me fairly, because he could not win that way—he'd never been much of a terror on the battlefield. If I let him live, then he would send a series of assassins my way, just as Aenghus Óg had been doing for centuries. I didn't need twice the headache I already had.

Plus, in the parlance of our times, he was a douche bag.

So I didn't leave it there. While he was still on the ground, I whipped Fragarach out of its scabbard and plunged it straight through the center of his bronze cuirass, which offered no resistance to the magical blade. Bres's eyes bulged and he stared at me in disbelief: After surviving the epic battles of ancient Ireland (in respectable armor), during which he could have died heroically, he was going to meet his end in a fight that lasted less than ten seconds because of his own overconfidence.

I didn't gloat over him, because that's how people get cursed. I yanked Fragarach out of him quickly, causing him to gasp in pain, and then I brought the sword down on his neck, severing his head before he could utter a death curse against me.

<When he said to give him the sword, I don't think he meant for you to stick it in his guts,> Oberon said.

He took a swipe at me with his sword, I replied.

<He did? I didn't see that.>

He didn't see you either. Well done.

"Ye killed him," I heard a tiny voice say. I turned to see the widow standing up, whiskey glass trembling in her hand before it slipped out and shattered on her porch. "Ye killed him." Her voice quavered. "Are y'goin' to kill me too now? Send me home to the Lord so I can be with me Sean?"

"No, Mrs. MacDonagh, no, of course not." I re-sheathed Fragarach to remove the threat it represented, even though the blade wasn't clean. "I have no reason to kill you."

"I'm a witness to yer crime."

"It wasn't a crime. I had to kill him. It was self-defense."

"Didn't look like self-defense to me," she said. "Ye kicked him and pushed him and then ye stabbed him and cut off his head."

"I don't think you saw the whole thing," I replied, shaking my head, "because I was partially blocking your view. He tried to stab me with his sword. See it lying there on the ground? I didn't pull that out of its scabbard. He did." I stayed where I was and let her process it. When someone thinks you might kill them, the last thing you want to do is edge closer to them in an attempt to comfort them, but people always seem to do it in the movies.

The widow squinted at the dim outline of the sword, and I watched the doubt seep into her expression. "I thought I heard him threaten ye," she said, "but I didn't see him move until y'kicked him. Who was he? What did he want?"

"He's an old enemy of mine—" I began, and the widow interrupted.

"Old enemy? Aren't ye only twenty-one? How old could yer enemies be?"

Gods Below, she really had no idea. "He was old in the way I see things," I said, and then I thought of a story to tell her. "He was really an old enemy of my father's, so he's been my enemy from the day I was born, if you see what I mean. And after my father passed away years ago, I became the target instead.

That's why I moved here, you know, to get away from him. But I heard a couple days ago that he had found me and was coming, so I started wearing this sword to protect myself."

"Why didn't ye get yerself a gun like all these American boys do?"

I grinned at her. "Because I'm Irish, Mrs. MacDonagh. And I'm your friend." I modulated my expression to earnest pleading and clasped my hands together. "Please, you have to believe me, I had to kill him or be killed myself. And I hope you know that I would never, ever hurt you."

She was still unconvinced but was wavering. "What was the nature of the argument he had with yer da?" she asked.

I couldn't fabricate a plausible lie on the spot, so I told her a part of the truth. "It was about this sword, actually," I said, jerking my thumb back to the hilt. "Da stole it from him long ago, but in a way it's more like he brought it home. It's an Irish sword, you know, but this bloke had it in his private collection, and it didn't seem right, him being British and all."

"He's British?"

"Aye." I felt ashamed for pushing the widow's buttons like this, but I couldn't afford to keep talking all night with a decapitated body in the street. Her husband had been in the Provos during the Troubles and was killed by the UVF, whom the widow had always assumed, rightly or not, to be puppets of the British.

"Ah, well then ye can bury the bastard in me backyard, and God damn the queen and all her hellish minions."

"Amen," I said, "and thank you."

"Not at all, me boy," the widow said, and then she laughed. "Ye know what me Sean used to say, God rest his soul? He said, 'A friend will help ye move, Katie, but a *really good* friend will help ye move a body.'" She cackled hoarsely and clapped her hands together. "Not that I can help ye move a big bugger like that. D'ye know where the shovel is?"

"Aye, that I do. I wonder, Mrs. MacDonagh, if you would have some lemonade or something in the house? I have a feeling I'll need it."

"Oh, sure, me boy, I can whip something up. Ye just get busy and I'll come out with a glass."

"Thank you so much." As she disappeared inside, I turned back to Oberon, who was still in camouflage. *Think you can carry the head back to the backyard? We need to get this out of sight.* Night had fallen, but the streetlamps were coming on, and anyone driving down the street would see a slight problem in their headlights.

<Not much to grab on to with that helmet on. I guess I could nudge it along with my nose.>

Good enough, I said. As I bent down to pick up the body and Oberon began playing a macabre game of snout soccer, the battle crow showed up. It took one look at the carnage and squawked angrily at me.

"I know," I said in an urgent whisper. "I'm in deep trouble. If you will follow me to the backyard, we should be able to speak privately there." The crow squawked once more before launching itself into the air and flapping over the roof.

I hauled Bres off the street and slung him over my shoulder in a fireman's carry. I felt his blood oozing through the back of my shirt—I'd have to burn it.

When I got to the backyard, the Morrigan was already in human form, standing pale and silent with her hands on her hips. Her eyes were glowing. This wasn't going to be a nice chat.

"When I agreed to your immortality, that did not give you permission to kill the Tuatha Dé Danann," she spat.

"Surely I don't need permission to defend myself?" I asked. "He tried to use his glamour to cut me down, Morrigan. If I hadn't been wearing my necklace, I never would have seen the sword he pulled on me."

"You would have survived," the Morrigan pointed out.

"Aye, but in what condition? Forgive me if I do not wish to experiment with various levels of pain and disembowelment," I said, as I lowered my shoulder and let Bres fall unceremoniously onto the widow's Bermuda grass.

"Tell me precisely what happened, every word that passed between you."

I told her, and she regarded me with stony silence, except for those red eyes. They finally dimmed when I told of how I had used a camouflaged dog to trip him and finish him off.

"Well, that was unforgivably arrogant of him. He deserved to die a fool's death," she said. "And look at that horrendous armor." But then she looked at his head resting a yard to the right, and her eyes blazed red again. "When Brighid hears of this, she will want me to bring her *your* head! And I will have to tell her no! Do you know what position that puts me in, Druid?"

"I am sorry, Morrigan. But perhaps if you tell Brighid precisely how he died, she will be less inclined to demand blood for blood. Think of your own reaction to it: His death was the most dishonorable of any of the Tuatha Dé Danann. And why was he doing Aenghus's bidding, anyway? Demanding restitution for one such as he would be almost ridiculous."

Her eyes cooled down as she considered my words. "Hmm. You reason well. Perhaps we can avoid conflict if we present it to her properly." She looked again at Bres's headless body and his head sitting at Oberon's feet. "Leave the body with me," she said. "I will take care of it."

I was only too glad to let her. "My thanks. If you have no objection, I will go wash the blood out of the street."

"No, go ahead." The Morrigan flicked her hand dismissively, her eyes still on the body, and I took off before she changed her mind. Besides, I honestly didn't want to see what she was going to do.

I grabbed the garden hose attached to the front of the house and turned it on full blast. The widow came out with a glass of lemonade for me and a fresh whiskey for herself, surprised to see me back so soon.

"Have y'buried the fecking tea bag already?" she said.

"No," I admitted, and tried to cover my shock at the widow's language. "I just came back to wash the blood out of the street."

"Ah, well, then, I'll leave ye to it," she said, handing me the glass and patting me gently on the arm. "I think it's time for *Wheel of Fortune,* y'know."

"Good night, Mrs. MacDonagh."

She swayed a bit as she searched for the door handle. "Yer a good lad, Atticus, mowin' me lawn and killin' what Brits come around."

"Think nothing of it, please," I said. "And it's probably best if we kept this between us."

"O'course," she said, finally finding the door and yanking it open. "G'night."

As the door closed behind her, Oberon said, <You know, I think the television might have desensitized her to violence.>

That or living in Northern Ireland during the Troubles, I said.

<What were the Troubles about?>

Freedom. Religion. Power. The usual. Would you mind standing sentinel again on the edge of the lawn while I do this?

<No problem.>

I took out Fragarach first to hose it down, then pointed the spray at the street to wash the worst of the gore away. I was just about finished when I heard Oberon's voice in my head, sounding very tense. <Hey, you said to listen for heavy footsteps. Well, I hear a whole bunch of them, and I think they're coming this way.>

Chapter 10

"Time to go home!" I said, throwing down the hose and scrambling back to turn off the water. I hopped onto my bike and told Oberon we were going full tilt. I had to get away from the widow's house or she could become a casualty.

<What's making that noise?> he asked, his long stride keeping pace with my bike as I pumped furiously to get some speed.

Those are the Fir Bolgs, I told him in my mind, saving my breath for bike riding.

<I think they sped up. They're running now.>

They've spotted us. Don't look back, keep going. Now, listen: These guys carry spears, but you won't see them. Just trust me, they will have them. They're not going to see you either. What I want you to do is go for their left legs, that soft spot above the ankles.

<The Achilles tendon? I remember that.>

Good. But you need to go for their calves. These guys are actually a lot bigger than they look, and their Achilles tendons are going to be about where a human's calf would be. I want you to bite them once and then get the hell out of the way before they fall on you or take a swipe at you.

<But what if they're wearing armor?>

They won't be. Anything you see is an illusion.

They're going to be barefoot, most likely. They have pretty tough hides. I risked a look back up Roosevelt as I turned the corner onto 11th. My normal vision showed me nine assholes in Harley-Davidson riding gear running after me under the streetlights as if I'd just toppled their bikes outside the pool hall. My faerie specs showed me nine nearly naked Fir Bolgs wearing nothing but breechclouts and woad. They carried spears in their right hands and large wooden shields in their left, and they were grinning in anticipation, because they were gaining on me.

When I got to my house, I rode up on the lawn and leapt off my bike, letting it roll, riderless, up to the porch. I heard a curse coming from the porch and I drew Fragarach from its scabbard, wondering who was lying in wait for me there.

"Damn you, Atticus, what are you playing at?" a familiar voice said as my bike came to an abrupt halt and then got tossed half the distance back to me.

I felt my face relax into a brief grin. "Leif!" I called, and he could not help but hear the relief in my voice. "I'm glad you're here." I had forgotten I'd asked Hal to send him as soon as the sun set. "I hope you're dressed for a fight."

"A fight? Is that what I hear coming down the road?" My vampire attorney stepped from the shadow of the porch into the dim glow of the streetlights. A white mane of hair floated around his pale face, which was scowling at me above an impeccably tailored suit. Not dressed in his fighting togs, then.

The Fir Bolgs rounded the corner, and the noise of their approach became intimidating, even without the senses of a vampire.

"I didn't intend this, Leif," I said. "But if you don't help me now, you might not have your favorite client around anymore. There's two glasses in it for you."

"In addition to my fees?" he raised his eyebrows.

"No, one glass is your fee, the other is off the books for your help in this fight."

There was no time to negotiate. He nodded once and said, "They do not look very tough."

"They're giants using glamour, so don't trust your eyes. Use your other senses. What does their blood smell like?"

They were almost upon us, but it was a worthwhile question. Leif's eyes widened as he caught the scent of their blood. "They are strong," he said. "Thanks, Atticus." He grinned, his fangs lengthening as he smiled. "I have not had my breakfast yet."

"Look at it like an all-you-can-eat buffet," I said, and then there was no more time for talking. Not one to be shy, Leif launched himself in a superhuman leap against the leading Fir Bolg, far above where his head was according to mortal eyes. That's because the giant's neck was actually about three feet higher, and the Fir Bolgs slowed down when they saw their leader taken down by a guy in an English business suit. But slowing down wasn't the same thing as stopping.

Go, Oberon! Good hunting! He loped away and I drew power from my front lawn, exulting in the feeling as it coursed through my cells after channeling through my ancient tattoos. The intricate knotwork traveled from the sole of my right foot, up the outside of my ankle and right side, until it snaked over my right pectoral muscles and around to the top of my shoulder, where it fell like an indigo waterfall to the middle of my biceps; there it looped around five times until it threaded down my forearm, ending (if Celtic knots can be said to end at all) in a loop on the back of my hand. The tattoos were bound to me in the most intimate way possible, and through them I had access to all the power of the earth, all the power I would ever need, so long as my bare foot touched the ground. In practice, that meant I would never, ever tire in battle. I suffered no fatigue at all. And if I needed it, I could whip up a binding or two against my enemies or summon up a temporary burst of strength that would allow me to wrestle a bear.

It had been a long, long time since I had felt the need to summon so much power. But then again, I hadn't been in a scrap like this since I'd waded into the mosh pit at a Pantera concert. Nine Fir Bolgs—well, eight now—were a few more than I had been expecting.

I moved to put my mesquite tree behind my back as an obstacle in case any of them were thinking about surrounding me. Then I pointed my finger at the first Fir Bolg to set foot on my lawn and said, *"Coinnigh"* —literally, *hold* or *detain*—and the earth moved to do my will. It gave way and then re-formed around the Fir Bolg's feet, rooting him abruptly and very firmly to the spot. To say he was surprised would be putting it mildly. With so much forward momentum, his bones had no choice but to break above the ankle when his feet were suddenly and inflexibly held in place. The bones ripped out through the back of his calf, and he flopped facedown in front of me, sans feet and screaming. That was not the way I had envisioned things working out. I had hoped he would brace himself, keep his feet, and serve as a wall between me and the fellows behind him. No such luck. His buddies kept coming, enraged rather than cautioned by their comrade's fall, and I now had to deal with three spears thrusting at my vitals.

Real fights don't look as pretty as the ones you see in movies. Those are choreographed, especially the martial arts ones, to seem so beautiful that they are practically dances. In true combat, you don't pause, pose, and preen. You just try to kill the other guy before he kills you, and "winning ugly" is still winning. That's what Bres failed to understand, and that's why I got rid of him so easily. Fir Bolgs have none of that pretentiousness—and even if they did, they would have lost it quickly after seeing Leif take down their leader in the street and then another one lose his feet in my lawn. No, these lads were betting that I wouldn't be able to dodge three spears thrust at me from a height from three different angles. I might be able to deflect one and dodge another, but the third one would get me. If I jumped straight up or back, I'd get tangled up with my own mesquite tree. If I rolled forward, beneath their thrusts, they'd just stomp on my dumb ass. I was guessing these guys were pushing six hundred pounds, so I didn't want to be in the middle of their clog dance. That meant I had less than a second to do some impossible shit. The ones on the left and the center had solid footing for their thrusts, but the one on the right had to plant his foot squarely on the back of his fallen, screaming, footless friend, so that was the one I was willing to take my chances with. I leapt to the left, leaving the ground, which they obviously did not expect. Since the lad on the right was out of reach, I slashed at the spearheads of the other two and was gratified to see Fragarach cleave through them easily. But it was too easy: The cut was so clean that, while the heads careened off at an angle, the shafts continued on course, and so both of them caught me full force—one in the shoulder, one in the gut. They threw me backward to crack my back painfully against the trunk of my mesquite tree. And I had been planning such a graceful tuck and roll too.

The Fir Bolg on the right had missed completely, his thrust stabbing the air where I had been, but he was stepping off his screaming friend's back and preparing for another thrust. "*Coinnigh*," I said, pointing at him, and he unexpectedly found himself immobile. While he tried to figure out what to do about his captured feet, I returned my attention to the first two giants, who were now holding long wooden staves. I assumed that the other four Fir Bolgs were anxious to get at me too, but perhaps Leif and Oberon were keeping them busy. I saw nothing beyond my own personal battle. The one who had been the center attacker decided to steal the spear of his footless friend, since he wasn't doing anything except bleeding to death. As he bent down to retrieve it, the one on the left decided he would try playing golf with my head. Well, that was easy enough to deal with. I held out Fragarach in the path of his swing, and then I was able to spend a couple of seconds concentrating on the pain my tumble had caused. The blow to my shoulder had deeply bruised the muscle, and it wouldn't be much use until I healed it. The shot to my abdomen was much more serious: It had penetrated, though not through to the intestines, and I was bleeding freely. As for my back, I was damn lucky I had not broken it. It was probably a chiropractor's wet dream as it was.

I wished I could do one of those ridiculous fairy-godmother routines, where you just wave a wand, some sparkly lights fill your vision, and then everything is all better, but my magic doesn't work like that. I can start the healing process and accelerate it, and I can force my body to ignore pain, but I cannot simply make damage disappear. So I did what I could in two seconds: I activated the healing charm on my necklace, which blocked pain and put me firmly on the mend, and then I had to move. Golf Boy was getting ready to take another swing, his first one shortened a foot or so by Fragarach. The lad from the center now had his footless mate's spear and was ready to skewer me with it; the immobilized one had decided to throw his spear at me, off balance though he might be. It was time to take the offensive.

I gathered myself into a crouch and then leapt, but this one was more like Leif's: I put some earth power behind it, so I was fairly launching myself at the Fir Bolg's would-be Phil Mickelson. He saw my intent and raised his shield, but that was what I was counting on: I slashed down from right to left and followed through as I arrived, cutting cleanly through both his shield and his skull before crashing my right shoulder into the remainder of his shield and sliding back down to the earth with his crumpling body.

The Fir Bolgs get my highest marks for battle savagery: The slain giant's fellows spared him not a single thought but only looked for vulnerabilities my attack might have exposed. I had to whip Fragarach back up across my body to deflect a thrown spear from the immobilized one, then back down to neutralize the thrust of the other.

"*Coinnigh,*" I said once more, and now the latter was frozen in place too. I could safely move away to confront other threats and come back to finish them off later. Another of the Fir Bolgs had tried to flank me, but in doing so he had strayed too close to my house and activated the wards. He was busy fighting off some tangling bougainvillea vines that were trying to bring him to ground, and he wasn't enjoying the thorns.

I spun around to the street, trying to get some perspective on the remaining foes, and saw that two more were down in the street. One was dismembered, and another had Leif attached to his neck and drinking deeply.

There was one more, and this one was spinning around clumsily, counterclockwise, and stabbing at the ground at something unseen. It was Oberon, harrying the Fir Bolg's legs.

I could not bear it if my friend was lost, so I sprang to help. I lopped off the giant's spear arm at the elbow the next time he spun around, and then I thrust Fragarach underneath his ribs to end it.

<Thanks,> Oberon said as the giant fell heavily into the street. <They have tougher skin than I thought. All I was able to do was tick him off.>

That was enough, my friend. Stay here while I take care of the stragglers. I cast camouflage on myself and my sword, and then I crept up behind the two immobilized Fir Bolgs and stabbed Fragarach up into their kidneys. Cowardly? Bleh. Tell you what: Let's debate the meaning of honor and see who lives longer.

The last Fir Bolg died in a mess of vines and blood, and only then did I relax the bindings of my lawn, allowing the earth to spit the giants' feet back up. I dropped my camouflage and swept the area with my eyes and my other senses, looking for additional threats, but all I saw were nine massive corpses and a whole lot of blood. The Fir Bolgs' glamours had died with them, leaving me with a colossal cleanup problem.

I didn't want to ask the earth to swallow these guys; I had asked so much of it already, and besides that, I doubted there would be time. I wasn't as fast as Flidais when it came to moving large amounts of earth, and I imagined someone had called the police by now.

As if on cue, I heard sirens in the night air, and that drew my gaze to the parted living-room blinds of my neighbor across the street, whose large round eyes were staring fearfully at me as if I somehow was the bad guy. Great.

"Leif?" I said. "Hey, Leif, aren't you full yet?"

"Ahhh," my lawyer said, tearing himself away from his breakfast and belching softly. "Very full, thank you."

"Well, if it wouldn't be too much trouble, perhaps you could help me here? The police are on their way and we have a lot of evidence to hide."

"Oh," the vampire said, seeming to remember suddenly that his job was to keep me out of jail. He looked down at his tailored English business suit, now stained with copious amounts of blood, and then back up at my shirt, which was rather bloody as well. "Yes, it would appear that there is a lot of evidence to hide."

"Go inside and change real fast. There's a suit in my closet, and you can grab me a fresh shirt," I said, pulling mine off and handing it to him. "Then come back and do your freaky memory thing with my neighbor across the street. He's the source of our police problem."

Leif moved with all the speed at his disposal. He knew we had a couple of minutes at most, probably less, before the police would arrive. In that time we had to make it look as if no one had died here tonight. I went back to my lawn and summoned some more power. It allowed me to drag six-hundred-pound giant bodies quickly to the east side of my lawn, farthest from my driveway, and stack them on top of one another. The ones in the street would have to be Leif's problem: The power stored in my bear charm would drain quickly if I tried to handle them alone. But what I could do was cast camouflage on all the bodies and the spreading pools of blood. Oh, and maybe I should conceal my sword too. Nothing to see here, coppers. Move along.

Leif returned in a minute, wearing a suit I had bought at the Men's Wearhouse. "So did you like the way you looked wearing this?" he said, mocking the commercials as he tossed me a fresh T-shirt. It didn't fit him perfectly: It was tight across the chest, and he was a little longer of limb than I—he was a bloody Viking, after all.

The sirens were awfully close. "You need to get those bodies out of the street and put them over there," I said, pointing to the pile I had made. "And then take care of my neighbor's delusions."

"No problem," he said, and then he zipped out into the street and started tossing giants, being careful not to get blood on his hands. I pulled on the clean shirt and kept my eyes on the blinds across the street. My neighbor, Mr. Semerdjian, had always been the snoopy sort. He had held me in deep suspicion from the day I moved in, because I did not own a car.

I started casting camouflage on every spot of blood I could find and then on the pile of bodies as well. Leif ran across the street to lay some vampire hoodoo on Mr. Semerdjian: "Look into my eyes. You didn't see anything." It was like an old Jedi mind trick.

I was fairly confident I had taken care of all visible evidence before the first patrol car rounded the corner. If they went snooping around the east side of my lawn, they would run into some major invisible evidence, but hopefully they would never have reason to do that. As they wailed down the street, I muttered a little something to magnify the scent of local plant life, which would hopefully mask the scent of so much spilled blood.

I sent Oberon to sit quietly on our front porch while Leif and I dealt with the authorities. He probably needed another bath anyway.

Three black-and-whites pulled up to my house, alerting all my other neighbors that the noise they had been ignoring was something to worry about after all. Six officers jumped out of the cars and pointed guns at us over their car doors.

"Freeze!" one of them shouted, even though we were standing perfectly still. Another one snarled, "Hands above your head!" and yet another said, "Drop the sword!"

Chapter 11

How can one freeze and put their hands above their head at the same time? Do they teach cops to shout contradictory instructions at suspects at the academy for some sinister purpose? If I obeyed one cop, did the other cop get to shoot me for resisting arrest? The only one who worried me was the guy who told me to drop my sword. It was camouflaged but still hanging in its scabbard across my back. Could he see through the camouflage?

"Good evening, gentlemen," Leif said smoothly. Neither of us raised our hands. "I am an attorney for Mr. O'Sullivan here." All the cops looked at him standing there serenely in his suit and got real quiet.

I am an attorney is a trigger phrase for cops. It tells them they have to go slow and follow procedures or their case will get tossed out of court. It meant that they wouldn't be able to wave their guns around and bully me into anything. Unfortunately, it also told them that I needed an attorney at my house after normal business hours. If I were a mind reader, I would be hearing the same thing from each one of their heads: "This bastard is so guilty he already has his lawyer here."

"What can we do for you tonight?" Leif asked pleasantly.

"We received a call that there was someone cutting down people with a sword here," one of them said.

Leif snorted in amusement. "A sword? Well, I suppose that's refreshing, perhaps even charmingly retro. But would there not be some signs of struggle if that were the case? People missing their arms, lots of blood, and maybe an actual sword in somebody's hand? You can see for yourselves that nothing like that is going on here. All is well. I think you received a crank call, officers."

"Then why are you here?" the cop asked.

"I'm sorry, Officer . . . um?"

"It's Benton."

"Officer Benton, I am Leif Helgarson. I am here because Mr. O'Sullivan is not only my client, he is my friend. We were simply standing here, enjoying the autumn evening and discussing baseball, when you drove up and pointed your weapons at us. Speaking of which, isn't it about time you put those away? Neither of us is about to threaten you."

"Let me see your hands first," Officer Benton said.

Leif slowly took his hands out of his pockets and I did the same, raising them to shoulder height. "Look," Leif said, wiggling his fingers like they were jazz hands. "No swords."

Officer Benton scowled at him, but then he reluctantly put away his sidearm and the other officers followed his example. "I think we should take a look around, just to be thorough," he said, stepping around his car door and walking toward us.

"You do not have probable cause to look around," Leif told him as he lowered his hands and crossed his arms. I put mine in my pockets.

"The 911 call gave us probable cause," Benton countered.

"A crank call that clearly has no basis in fact. The only disruption to the peace in this neighborhood tonight has been your sirens, and if you want to search my client's property, you should go get a warrant."

"What is your client trying to hide?" Benton asked.

"It is not a matter of hiding anything, Officer Benton," Leif said. "It is a matter of protecting my client against unreasonable search and seizure. You have absolutely no reason to search these premises. Your call described a sword fight in progress, but nothing like that has gone on here, so I think your time would be better spent protecting the city from real threats instead of imaginary ones. In addition, if the caller was the elderly Lebanese gentleman across the street, he has a long history of harassing my client over imagined trespasses. We are considering a restraining order against him."

Officer Benton looked supremely frustrated. He knew, he just *knew*, I was hiding something, and of course he was right. But he wasn't used to dealing with lawyers—detectives usually handled them—and he wasn't confident enough to proceed when he couldn't see anything wrong. Apparently the officer who had told me to drop the sword couldn't see it strapped to my back either, because he hadn't said a word since he got out of the car. He must have been shouting at me based on the 911 call. All hearsay. But Benton couldn't resist trying to bully me anyway.

"Haven't you got anything to say, mister?" he sneered at me. "Why did we get called out here?"

"Well," I said, "I cannot say for certain, of course, but it might be because Mr. Semerdjian across the street there really doesn't like me. You see, about three years ago my dog escaped and pooped on his lawn. I apologized and cleaned it up, but he's never forgiven me."

<Hey, I heard that!> Oberon called from the porch. <You *told* me to poop on his lawn!>

Yeah, so what's your point? I asked.

<You're making it sound like I'm some ordinary dog who just poops anywhere.>

I know, but it's going to get that Semerdjian guy in trouble.

<Oh. Well, that's okay, then. I don't like him.>

Officer Benton glowered at me for a moment, and then at Leif, but if he was expecting us to confess, he was going to be disappointed.

"Sorry for disturbing you," he finally growled, and then thought to amend his tone. "Have a nice night." He turned his back on us and stalked across the street to Mr. Semerdjian's house, muttering to two of the officers that they could go, he'd write it up. They made good-bye noises at him and climbed back into their cars, turning off their lights and motoring away as Officer Benton pounded on Semerdjian's door.

"Should we worry about him remembering anything?" I whispered to Leif.

"No, he is still completely in my thrall," he replied in the same low tone. "How were you planning to get rid of the Fir Bolgs?"

"I actually hadn't planned that far yet."

"You know, for another glass of that fine vintage you have, I can take care of it. Just help me haul them over to Mitchell Park."

I took time to consider. Burying the bodies of nine giants would not be easy, even if they were already in pieces. Calling on Radomila's coven to take care of it was a possibility, but I really didn't want to use up their favor on something like this.

"How would you take care of it?" I asked.

He shrugged. "I know some ghouls. I make a couple calls, the guys come over for dinner, problem solved."

"They can put away nine whole giants? There's that many ghouls in town?"

"Probably not," Leif admitted. "But whatever they do not eat tonight, they'll take the rest to go."

I stared at him in disbelief. "You mean like a doggie bag?"

The vampire nodded with a thin trace of a smile. "They have a refrigerated truck, Atticus. These are practical guys. I employ them often, and so does Magnusson on occasion. It is a satisfactory arrangement for everyone."

"So I would owe you three glasses," I said.

"That is correct. And I want them sooner rather than later, since you are apparently marked for death."

"Hmm," I said, to buy myself some time. Officer Benton was writing out a citation for a bewildered Mr. Semerdjian across the street. False calls to 911 are a no-no.

"Can I pay you one tonight for your firm, and the other two tomorrow night?" I asked.

"Why not simply give them all to me tonight?" Leif replied. "You heal rapidly."

"Well, that's what I'm doing right now," I said. "I have some torn abdominal muscles, a deeply bruised left shoulder, and a couple of vertebrae are out of place."

"Should you not be screaming in pain, then?" Leif regarded me skeptically.

"Yes, but I've blocked my pain receptors. And I'm going to need my strength if I want to be good as new by morning."

"What are the odds of you surviving until morning?"

"I think they're excellent. I was warned about the arrival of Bres and the Fir Bolgs, and both have now been dispatched."

"Bres is dead? The former king of the Tuatha Dé Danann?" Manannan Mac Lir take me for a fool, I shouldn't have told him that! It was too late to backpedal, though. If I lied he'd know it.

"Aye, he lost his head up the street moments before I arrived."

"And you did it?"

"Guilty."

"Then I want all three glasses tonight, Atticus, and to hell with your healing. Brighid is going to kill you, and this will be my last drink."

I sighed heavily in defeat. I was not about to explain the details of my arrangement with the Morrigan to him. "We wait for Officer Benton to leave," I said, "then you make your calls and we haul the bodies over to the park. Only after I'm in the clear and my front yard can pass inspection without camouflage will you get your rare vintage."

"Agreed," the vampire said. "I am full right now anyway. I need to work some of this off." He dug a cell phone out of his—or, I should say, my—breast pocket and used a speed-dial number to call someone named Antoine. "I have dinner for the whole crew at Mitchell Park in Tempe right now. Bring the truck. . . . Yes, there is enough for everybody, trust me. See you there."

Whoa. He had ghouls on speed dial. My lawyer kicks so much ass.

Chapter 12

Ugggh. Yuck. Gack.

I woke in my backyard, stiff from a night spent on the ground and itchy from the grass. Oberon was nestled around my legs, his head resting on my shin. I tried to gently extricate myself so he could continue sleeping if he wished.

The night outside had been necessary to speed my healing, especially after surrendering three wineglasses of blood for Leif. I had needed the contact with the ground and the power of the earth. Worth a bit of itching? Definitely.

I sat up and checked my abdomen: Some stiffness there, no real pain, and the skin had already scabbed over and fallen off, showing me a shiny new pink epidermis. The shoulder was good as new, and my back, while still a bit sore, at least felt like it was straight again. I grinned. After 2,100 years, I still thought magic was pretty damn cool.

Oberon picked up his head as I got to my feet, and he took that as his cue to stand and stretch.

<Morning, Atticus.>

"Morning. You want a belly rub? Better take it while I'm offering."

<Okay!> He promptly flopped down next to me, lifting his front paws to give me better access. I squatted

down and rubbed him vigorously for a few minutes while his tail thumped happily against my leg.

"So what would you like for breakfast today?"

<Sausage.>

"You always say that."

<That's because it's always tasty.>

"I'm out of sausage. How about some pork chops?"

<I don't know. Did Genghis Khan eat pork chops?>

"Well, I doubt he ate chops, because that's a fairly modern way to cut it. He probably ate slices off a whole ham or something that they had roasted in the ground all day."

<Can I have some of that, then?>

"I don't have a whole pig to roast, nor do I have the time to do it properly. Can't you settle for some chops and just pretend?"

<All right. But after that can we conquer Siberia or something?>

"Not today, Oberon," I chuckled. "I have a contract to fulfill with the witches. And someone is bound to come by and threaten me today, or try to kill me. And we have to make sure the widow is okay. We left her house rather abruptly last night." I rose from my haunches and brushed the grass off my shorts. "Come on, let's go inside and make breakfast."

<All right, but I think we should start recruiting a horde now and have them muster on the Mongolian steppes. We can join them in the spring and then ride to glory.>

"Where are we going to recruit a horde?" I asked him as we stepped inside. Fragarach was lying where I left it on the kitchen table.

<I don't know. You're the bloody Druid here, not me. But I think you should start with getting me a sufficient number of French poodles, and you can find those in the classified section of the newspaper. Hold on, I'll go get it.>

"No, no, don't go out there," I said. "You're still in hiding, remember? I'll go get it." I wanted to see what could be seen in the daylight, anyway. I dissolved the camouflage bindings on my lawn to evaluate the signature of last night's carnage. There were some messy patches of gore we had missed last night, especially on the eastern side, and I pulled out the garden hose to see how much of it I could spray away. Most of it obligingly melted into the soil under a jet stream, but some of the grass remained tinted an unhealthy shade of pink. That was a problem I couldn't simply camouflage away, because the only thing around the pink grass was more pink grass. I'd have to come up with an excuse if anyone asked. Maybe that giant animated jar of Kool-Aid met his untimely end here?

Other than pinkness, there was no evidence of the violent demise of nine very large creatures. I scooped my newspaper off the driveway and returned to the house, where Oberon was waiting with his tail wagging. <Any French poodles for sale?> he asked hopefully.

"I haven't had a chance to look yet," I laughed.

We discussed the logistics and supply we'd need for our invasion of Siberia as I made a pot of coffee for us and two separate entrées: a skillet full of chops in melted butter for Oberon, and a cheese and chive omelet for myself. I also toasted a slice of whole wheat bread and slathered it with butter and blackberry preserves.

It was domestic bliss there for a while, with the sound of our breakfast cooking, mourning doves cooing in the backyard, and a conversation that was little more than an exercise in silliness. Oberon's ability to distract me from life's worries was one of the reasons I adored him. But then I sat down at the kitchen table with my food and looked at the newspaper, and the worries came back.

There was a follow-up story on the death of the

ranger. The headline said, RANGER DEATH CAUSED BY CANINE, and a subhead said, *Police following several leads*. The food I had been intent on savoring got shoveled into my mouth mechanically as I read.

PHOENIX—Lab reports revealed that the death of Phoenix park ranger Alberto Flores was caused by a canine, and not by a knife wound as originally believed.

Dr. Erick Mellon, Maricopa County Coroner, discovered that Flores's throat wounds bore signs of tearing associated with teeth. DNA tests on samples collected from the wound detected the presence of canine saliva.

That evidence, along with several dog hairs found underneath Flores's fingernails "and other clues," according to Phoenix Detective Carlos Jimenez, have led police to believe that he was attacked and killed by a large dog, possibly an Irish wolfhound.

"They got that lab report back awfully fast," I said aloud, and Oberon asked me what I was talking about. "They're on your trail, buddy." I gestured at the newspaper. "They know a dog killed the ranger. How they know an Irish wolfhound did it, I have no idea. As far as I know there isn't a test to isolate breeds. I bet you the police are getting help from someone."

Oberon's ears pricked up and he swiveled his head toward the front room. <Someone is coming to knock on the door,> he said.

Don't bark, I told him silently. *Don't make a sound or do anything to indicate you're here. I'm going to camouflage you again.* And then four sharp knocks echoed through the house. I quickly cast camouflage on Oberon before walking noisily to the front door. Pausing to look through the keyhole, I saw two men standing there in shirts and ties. I turned on my faerie specs, but there was nothing to see. They were humans, then, either cops or missionaries. Since it was Sunday morning and all the missionaries would be on their way to church, I was betting on cops.

I opened the door and stepped out quickly, taking them by surprise and forcing them to step back a little bit. I closed the door behind me and smiled winningly at them. "Good morning, gentlemen," I said. "How may I help you?" I kept my hands in plain sight at my sides, doing my best to appear friendly and harmless. I also stepped a bit to the left, so that they would be facing away from the pink grass.

The cop to my right wore a blue shirt with a striped tie in navy and white. He wore a jacket to conceal his firearm, certainly not to keep warm, and I got the feeling he would rather walk around with his gun in plain view. He was Latino, looked to be in his mid-thirties, and carried a bit of extra gravity in his jowls.

On the left was the lad assigned to look dumber and meaner. He was going for a Michael Madsen attitude, wearing polarized sunglasses and leaning against my porch railing with his arms crossed. I guessed he wouldn't be talking much. He was even younger than the other guy and wore a white shirt and skinny black tie, no jacket, like a refugee from a Tarantino film. He was scowling at me because I had stepped out onto the porch before they could ask to come in, which took away one of their primary methods for putting me on the defensive. If they can force you to run around playing the host, then they get a chance to snoop while you serve them.

The Latino guy answered me, as expected. "Mr. Atticus O'Sullivan?"

"The same."

"I'm Detective Carlos Jimenez from the Phoenix police, and this is Detective Darren Fagles from the Tempe police. May we speak to you inside?"

Ha! He asked to come inside anyway. Not gonna happen, buddy. "Oh, it's such a nice morning, let's just talk out here," I said. "What brings you to my door today?"

Jimenez frowned. "Mr. O'Sullivan, this is really best discussed in private."

"We're plenty private right here." I grinned at him. "Unless you're planning to shout. You aren't going to shout at me, are you?"

"Well, no," the detective admitted.

"Great! So why are you here?"

Resigned, Detective Jimenez finally got to the point. "Do you own an Irish wolfhound, Mr. O'Sullivan?"

"Nope."

"Animal Control says you have one licensed under the name of Oberon."

"That's true, I do; well done, sir."

"So then you do own one."

"Nope. He ran away last week. I have no idea where he is."

"So where is he?"

"Didn't I just say I have no idea?"

Detective Jimenez sighed and pulled out a notebook and a ballpoint pen. "When, precisely, did he run away?"

"Last Sunday. That would be a week ago, as I said. I came home from work and he was gone."

"What time was that?"

"Five-fifteen p.m." Time to play the bewildered citizen. "Why are you asking about my dog?"

Jimenez ignored my question and asked me another one. "When did you leave for work that day?"

"At half past nine."

"And where do you work?"

"At Third Eye Books on Ash Avenue, just south of University."

"Where were you on Friday night?"

"I was here at home."

"Was anyone with you?"

"Well, that can hardly be any of your business."

"It's precisely my business, Mr. O'Sullivan."

"Oh. Are you going to tell me what this is about now?"

"We are investigating a murder committed Friday night in Papago Park."

I frowned and squinted at him. "Am I a suspect? I didn't do it."

"Do you have an alibi?"

"I wasn't in Papago Park Friday night. Isn't it supposed to be closed at night?"

"Who saw you Friday night?"

"No one. I was home alone, reading."

"With your dog?"

"No, not with my dog. He ran away last Sunday, remember? You wrote it down in your little book."

"Would you mind if we verify that your dog is not at home?"

"How do you mean?"

"We'd like to take a look in your backyard and your house to make sure he's not at home."

"Sorry, I'm not entertaining houseguests today. Especially ones who assume I'm lying."

"We can come back with a warrant, Mr. O'Sullivan," Detective Fagles said, speaking up for the first time. I turned my head to glare at him.

"I'm well aware, Detective. If you'd like to waste your time, go right ahead. My dog is not here, nor will he be here if you come back. Why are you looking for my dog, anyway? What led you to my door?"

"We're not at liberty to discuss details of the investigation," Jimenez said.

"It sounds like a pretty good one. Colonel Mustard

did it in the park with the wolfhound, eh? I can hardly believe you'd be checking every single wolfhound owner in the valley. If you heard I still had a wolfhound from my neighbor across the street, he's not exactly a reliable witness. Last night he was cited by Officer Benton of the Tempe PD for making a false 911 call."

The two detectives exchanged a glance, and I knew that was it. Mr. Semerdjian was at it again. I'd have to ask Oberon to leave him a present on his front doorstep. He'd do it camouflaged too, so that even if Mr. Semerdjian was watching—and he probably would be—it would appear to be undeniable, physical evidence that, sometimes, shit just happens.

"Have you checked the animal shelter for your lost dog, Mr. O'Sullivan?" Jimenez asked. Fagles went back to glaring at me from behind his sunglasses.

"Not yet," I said.

"Aren't you concerned about his welfare?"

"Of course I am. He's properly licensed and has my phone number on a tag around his neck. I'm expecting a call any minute."

They stared at me stone-faced for a few moments to let me know that the sarcasm wasn't appreciated. I stared back to let them know I wasn't intimidated. Your move, youngsters.

I could tell they didn't quite know what to make of me. Seeing the world through a perp filter as they did, I must look to them like a sullen stoner punk pretending to attend college, but I wasn't behaving like one. I was too alert, too sharp. Maybe that made me a dealer. Perhaps they assumed I wasn't letting them in because they'd find my hydroponic weed operation and psychedelic mushrooms in the closet, or maybe a three-foot-tall bong made of blown glass in Day-Glo hippie colors sitting on the coffee table.

Finally Jimenez broke the silence. He gave me a business card and said, "We'd like you to call us if you find your dog."

I took the card and slipped it into my pocket without looking at it. "Good day, gentlemen," I said, giving them a broad hint to get the hell off my porch. Jimenez took the hint, but Fagles remained. Apparently he wanted to have a staring contest or mutter a threat to me. What an idiot. I knew how to be patient. I put my hands in my pockets and flashed him a fake smile. That got a reaction.

He uncrossed his arms, pointed a finger at me, and said, "We'll be watching."

Please. Whatever. I kept on smiling and said nothing.

Jimenez paused in the street and turned around, that being the point where he was supposed to realize Fagles hadn't followed him off the porch.

"Detective Fagles, we have other people to talk to," he called.

What a lovely straight line. Keeping his voice pitched for my ears only, Fagles said, "Yeah, like the judge." Gods Below, did this routine work on anyone? With one last aggressive clenching of his jaw, Fagles turned and stepped off the porch. As he did, he turned his head toward the east side of the lawn, where all the pink grass was. Just looking around. No reaction. The grass probably didn't look pink through those tinted sunglasses of his. Good job, Detective! Jimenez was oblivious as well. He was watching me to see if my body language screamed "GUILTY!" Then he strolled unhurriedly to their unmarked Crown Victoria once Fagles had caught up.

I returned inside once they had driven off, and Oberon nuzzled my hand at once.

<I was quiet,> he said, very pleased with himself.

I chuckled and scratched him behind the ears. "Yes, you were. Genghis Khan would have admired your craftiness."

I lifted the camouflage off him so that he would feel comfortable, and then I sat back down to a half-eaten lukewarm omelet and a cup of coffee I had to warm up to make palatable. After cleaning up, I set about looking for anything the cops would find incriminating should they come in here with a warrant. They would be supposedly searching for a dog, but that wouldn't stop them from snooping around either, unless I had a lawyer here. Even then, they might stumble across something or damage something in the process of their search that I didn't want them to—mostly my books. I had some pretty arcane titles behind glass in my study, with paper so old it was ready to crumble. Cops wouldn't be gentle with those if they wanted to rifle through them; I'd need to pay Hal $350 an hour to camp here and make sure they didn't look for Oberon inside my books. What a pain in the ass. Well, they should owe me some time after all that blood I gave Leif last night. That battle had taken much less than an hour, and the cleanup lasted maybe another, so I should be paid up for ten hours already. Speaking of blood, I put the scrap of paper with Radomila's blood on it inside an old collection of stories about the Fianna and locked it away in the glass bookcase in my study.

To be safe, I camouflaged my herbs in the backyard so it looked like I had nothing along my fence but empty shelves. No telling what the cops would think about all the plant life back there; they'd probably assume some of it must be illegal and confiscate the lot of it to have it analyzed, and I'm sure it would come back to me half dead or worse. Fagles would do it just to get back at me for staring him down.

While it was a load of inconvenience, I couldn't get myself too angry with them. They were only doing their jobs, and, after all, I really was the bad guy in this case—or, at least, Oberon was.

Satisfied that I had hidden what needed hiding, I put in a call to Hal on his cell phone and explained my extraordinary needs for a Sunday. If Jimenez could get a warrant on Sunday, then I could get a lawyer. Hal said he'd send over a junior associate to guard the castle.

"Is he a pack member?" I asked.

"Yes. Does that matter?"

"Just tell him to keep a sharp ear and nose out. If one of my pantheon is behind this, then there might be some magical skulduggery going on. The police might bring someone along who isn't entirely human, for example."

"They probably won't show up at all. I've never heard of a search warrant for a dog. You may be the most paranoid man I've ever met."

"I'm certainly the longest lived you've ever met."

"Point taken. I'll tell him."

I showered and dressed, cast camouflage back on Oberon, and slung Fragarach across my back. I was anxious to visit the widow's house and make sure she was okay.

Nothing looked amiss from the street. The blood had washed away or soaked into the asphalt sufficiently. Going around to the back, I saw nothing, not so much as a disturbed patch of ground. With a shudder, I considered the likelihood that the Morrigan had eaten him. Shaking my head to clear the grisly image, I walked back to the front, Oberon panting softly behind me. I knocked on the widow's front door and she answered after a minute, looking spry and chipper.

"Ah, me dear boy Atticus, 'tis a pleasure to see ye again and that's no lie. Have ye killed any more Brits for me?"

"Good morning, Mrs. MacDonagh. No, I haven't killed any more Brits. I hope you won't be talking about that with anyone."

"Tish, d'ye think I'm daft? I'm not there yet, thank the Lord. It's all due to clean livin' and good Irish whiskey. Would y'be havin' some with me? Come on in." She opened the screen door and beckoned.

"No, thank you, Mrs. MacDonagh, it's not yet ten in the morning, and it's Sunday."

"An' don't I know it? I have to be goin' to Mass soon enough at the Newman Center. But the father can drone on at times, and he keeps preaching to the youngsters what go there, all those ASU kids, y'know, who have those merry sins of the flesh to worry about, so I find a finger or two o' the Irish helps me bear it with patience."

"Wait. You go to church drunk?"

"*Mellow* is the word I'd be usin', if y'please."

"You don't drive there, uh, mellow, do you?"

"Of course not!" She looked affronted. "I get a ride from that nice Murphy family what lives down the street."

"Oh. Well, that's fine, then. I just wanted to make sure you were all right, Mrs. MacDonagh. I have to go to work now, so you can go, uh, get mellow, and enjoy your day. Peace be with you."

"And also with you, m'boy. Are y'sure I can't convince ye to get baptized?"

"Quite sure," I said. "But thank you again for the offer. Bye now."

<Um, Atticus?> Oberon said as he trotted behind my bike, once we were safely on the way to the store, <What's baptized mean?>

It means a priest dunks you in some water and when you come out you're reborn.

<Really? So if I got baptized I'd be a puppy again?>

No, you're not literally reborn in the physical sense. It's a symbolic thing. Your spirit is supposed to be reborn because you're washed clean of sins.

Oberon took twenty yards or so to consider this, his

nails clicking on the sidewalk as we turned right on University Drive. <But the water just gets your skin and fur wet, right? How can it wash your spirit clean? Especially without soap?>

Like I said, it's symbolic. And it's a different belief system.

<Oh. Like going to church drunk is really going to church mellow?>

I laughed. *Yeah. Kinda like that.*

I put Fragarach on a shelf underneath my apothecary counter, let Oberon circle around a few times and get himself settled, and then opened the door for Perry, who looked appropriately gloomy for a Goth guy this morning.

Sundays at the shop were usually decent business, as if all the non-Christians wanted to make a point of buying something pagan while everyone else was in church. You could always tell the ones who had been raised in a strict Christian environment: They'd put their books on Wicca or Aleister Crowley down on the counter and grin nervously, amazed at themselves for having the stones to buy something their elders told them not to buy. And their auras almost always churned with arousal, which I did not understand when I first opened the shop, but eventually it made sense: For the first time in their lives, they were going to read about a belief system where it was okay to have sex, and they could hardly wait for the validation.

By the same token, you could always spot the ones who were a part of the serious magical community. They had auras that shouted their mojo, for one thing, but they also wore one of three expressions on their faces when looking at the magical wannabes buying their first pack of Tarot cards: They either sneered contemptuously, grinned faintly in amusement, or looked nostalgic for a time when they themselves were clueless.

Emily the snotty witch was the contemptuous, sneering sort. She stormed into the shop dressed like a pampered horror from Scottsdale and promptly stuck her tongue out at me.

"Emily!" a voice snapped from the open door before I could say anything. A frowning woman stepped in after the classic parenting reprimand—just shout the kid's name in public and let the tone do the work—and Emily's eyes widened a bit. She knew she was in trouble.

Chapter 13

I assumed that the frowning woman must be Malina Sokolowski. She looked to be in her early thirties, but if Emily was the youngest of Radomila's coven, then Malina's real age had to be pushing a century or more. She was a true blonde, with pale yellow hair cascading past her shoulders in soft waves that shampoo companies like to put in commercials. It looked glossy, fragrant, and utterly mesmerizing. It fell onto a squarely cut red wool coat, which would be too warm to wear for another month or so but which provided a magnificent contrast in both color and texture.

At that point, my amulet shut the noise down and I snapped out of it. Whoa. She had some kind of beguilement charm on her hair. It was something the wards on my shop weren't designed to take care of, but the cold iron of my amulet caused it to fizzle. That meant it was not the everyday sort of witches' magic. Cool. Scary, but cool.

Her hair really did look good, but now I was able to look away from it and assess the rest of her. Pale eyebrows, just a shade or two darker than her hair and now drawn together in disapproval, provided a roof for a pair of startlingly blue eyes. She had a patrician nose and what looked like a generous mouth, but now it was drawn tightly down, lips painted to match the color of her coat. Pale skin—not the unhealthy pallor of Goths, but the white porcelain sheen of European nobility stretched over a faint blush—made a pillar of her neck, which betrayed a hint of a gold necklace before it disappeared underneath her coat.

Nonverbal signals are so powerful at times that I wonder at our need to speak. Without looking at her aura, I already knew that Malina was classy where Emily was not; far more mature, intelligent, and powerful; and was reluctant to give offense where Emily could not wait to give it. And I also knew she was more dangerous by several orders of magnitude.

"I thought I had made it clear you were to offer no offense to Mr. O'Sullivan," she said. Her Polish accent was more pronounced than it had been on the phone, perhaps owing to her irritation. Emily lowered her eyes and muttered an apology.

"I'm not the one who needs an apology. It's Mr. O'Sullivan you have insulted. Apologize to him this instant." Wow. She was scoring points with me already. But then I remembered that she was a witch, and they might have planned this whole scene ahead of time. Still, Emily looked as if she would rather mate with a goat than apologize to me, so I was enjoying it, even if it was a performance. Other customers were looking around at Malina's raised voice, their gazes lingering on the two women. They were difficult to look away from, albeit for very different reasons.

When Emily took too long, Malina's voice lowered to a threatening growl so that only Emily and I could hear. "If you do not apologize to him right now, then I swear by the three Zoryas that I will measure your length on this floor and put you in breach of contract. You are in so much trouble already, you will be cast out from the coven."

Apparently that was worse than mating with a goat,

because Emily suddenly could not be more sorry for her behavior and hoped I would forgive her discourtesy.

"I accept your apology," I said at once, and the tension in their shoulders eased.

Malina finally turned her attention to me. "Mr. O'Sullivan. I am so embarrassed by our entrance. I hope you will forgive me as well. I am Malina Sokolowski." She smiled brightly and extended a hand to me—gloved, I noticed, in brown leather—and I shook it once.

"Forgiven," I said, "though there is really nothing to forgive. You're welcome to look around if you'd like, or if you'd simply rather wait for the tea, you can sit at one of the tables over there while I make it."

"That's very kind, thank you," Malina replied.

"It will just be a couple of minutes."

"Great." She gestured toward the tables and gently pushed Emily in that direction. "After you, miss," she said.

<I like the blond one. She knows how to show respect,> Oberon said from behind the counter.

I busied myself making Emily's tea and spoke to him through our link. *Yes, well, she's decided to take the high road, so I'll be happy to walk it with her as long as she likes.*

<You don't trust her?>

Nope. She's a witch. A polite witch, but still a witch. She's got a charm on her hair that would have had me giving her anything she wanted if I hadn't been wearing protection. Don't take anything from her, by the way.

<You think she's going to pull a sausage out of her coat or something? She doesn't even know I'm here.>

Oh yes she does. Emily has probably already told her.

<Okay, fine. But seriously. You think she has a magic sausage for me?>

How would you know the difference if she did? You think all sausages are magic.

Serving Emily her tea was quite nearly magical for me. I set it down in front of her and she drank it straight down, despite its heat, without making eye contact. When she was finished, she rose from her chair, said, "Excuse me," and left the shop without another word.

"That was great," I said to Malina. "Can you come with her every day?"

Malina chuckled throatily, then clapped a hand over her mouth. "Oh, I shouldn't laugh. It's just that I empathize with you. She is not well behaved."

"So what's she doing hanging out with you?"

Malina sighed. "That is a very long story."

"Haven't you heard? I'm a Druid. I like long stories."

The witch looked around. There were still quite a few customers in the store, and someone scruffy had walked up to my apothecary counter and was squinting at the labels on my jars. "While you have a lovely place here," Malina said, "I do not think it is the right time for such a story."

"What? You mean the customers? Perry will take care of them." I walked to the counter and put a CLOSED tent sign significantly in front of the scruffy man.

"Whoa, man. You're closed?" He frowned at me but was not to be deterred. He had something on his mind. "Hey, dude, you got any medical marijuana back there?"

"No, sorry." These guys just wouldn't leave me alone.

"It's not for me, I swear. It's for my grandma."

"Sorry. Try back next week."

"Hey, really?"

"No."

I turned my back on him, pulled up a chair next to Malina, and plastered an attentive look on my face.

"You were telling me why you tolerate Emily in your coven."

Scruffy Weed Man interrupted before she could answer. "You have really beautiful hair," he said to Malina. She looked annoyed and told him curtly to go away, and he promptly turned and exited the store. Pretending to be self-conscious, she pulled at a lock of her hair near her shoulder and muttered something under her breath, no doubt dispelling the charm. She'd forgotten she had it on. I pretended not to notice.

She arched an eyebrow at me. "So. I was telling you all that? What if one of your customers hears us talking about covens and such things?"

"We're in the perfect place to talk of them. They'll assume you're Wiccan. And if you're going to go way back in history and anyone is rude enough to interrupt and ask you about it, like that guy who just left, we'll say we're part of the SCA."

Her brow crinkled in confusion. "The Society for Cruelty to Animals?"

"No, I think you mean the SPCA, where the *P* stands for Prevention."

"Ah. Of course."

I shot a quick thought to Oberon. *See? Witches.*

<I see what you mean now. She'd probably give me a sausage and it would have broccoli in it.>

Trying not to laugh at Oberon's one-track mind, I said, "Yes, well, the SCA is the Society for Creative Anachronism. People get together and dress in medieval garb and actually have battles in armor and everything. Lots of these modern folk romanticize the old days and enjoy role-playing. It's the perfect cover for talking about magic in front of average people."

She scrutinized me closely for a moment, trying to decide whether I was lying or not. Apparently satisfied, she took a breath and said, "Very well. The short version of the long story is that she came with me to America. We were living in the city of Krzepice in Poland when the Blitzkrieg arrived in September 1939. I saved her from being raped, and she sort of became my responsibility after that. I couldn't just leave her. Her parents were dead."

"Ah. Your parents as well?"

"Yes, but the Nazis had nothing to do with that." She smiled grimly. "I was already seventy-two in 1939."

You hear that? The nice blonde in her thirties is actually more than 140 years old.

<She must use that Oil of Olay stuff. I wonder if it would get rid of the wrinkles on a shar-pei?>

"Impressive. And Emily was how old?"

"She was only sixteen."

"She still acts like she's sixteen. Is everyone in your coven from Krzepice?"

"No, only Emily and me. We all came to America together, however, once we found one another in Poland."

"And you came straight to Tempe?"

"No, we have lived in several cities. But we have stayed here the longest."

"Why, may I ask?"

"No doubt for the same reason you have stayed here. Few old gods, few old ghosts, and, until recently, no Fae at all. Now, I have answered five questions truthfully. Will you answer five of mine in the same fashion?"

"Truthfully, yes. Not necessarily completely."

She accepted my qualification without comment. "How old are you?" she asked.

That's one of the most probing questions you can ask someone who isn't a standard human anymore. It was one way to gauge power and intelligence, and if she didn't already know my age, then I would rather keep it that way. I prefer to be underestimated; fights go better for me when my enemies do not know what they're truly dealing with. There is an opposing school of thought that says if you display your power, you avoid getting into fights in the first place—but that is true only in the short term. Enemies may not confront you openly or as often if they know you're powerful, but they will still plot against you and be more likely to try something sneaky. Now, Malina had been very forthcoming with me about her age, but I didn't feel comfortable responding with the same level of candor, because telling her would be telling the whole coven. So I settled for a dodge.

"At least as old as Radomila."

That set her back a bit. She was wondering if she should ask how I knew Radomila's age or let it slide. I didn't know Radomila's age, but I knew damn well I was older than she was. Malina was smart, though, and decided to ask other things instead of following up on a line of query that wouldn't get her anything more specific.

"Aenghus Óg told Emily you have a sword that belongs to him. Is this true?"

I chose to answer only part of the question. Sloppy of her. "No. It does not belong to him."

She hissed in frustration, seeing her mistake. "Do you still have this sword he believes is his?"

"Yes, I do." It occurred to me that it was odd of her to be asking me about it, because Radomila had been the one to slap a magical cloak on it. Did Malina not talk to her coven leader?

"Is it here on the premises?" Oh, now *that* was a good one. Much better than asking where it was, which would allow me to be vague. This was a yes or no, and unfortunately, since the answer was yes and I had promised to answer truthfully . . . Well, I could lie.

Except that I thought she would know it, and it would be the same as saying yes while giving her just cause to swerve off the high road.

"Yes," I admitted. She beamed at me.

"Thank you for not lying. Last question: Which member of the Tuatha Dé Danann have you most recently seen in corporeal form?"

Whoa. Why did she want to know that? "The Morrigan," I replied.

Her eyes widened. "The Morrigan?" she squeaked. Oh, now I got it. She had expected me to say Bres, and then she could surmise that I had killed him with the sword that I still had on the premises. But now she couldn't surmise that at all. She could surmise, instead, that since I'd seen the Morrigan and lived, I had a death goddess in my Five or My Circle or whatever. And maybe the reason Bres didn't "come home" last night was because of the Morrigan, and not because of me. But this line of reasoning implied that she knew about Bres coming to see me yesterday.

"How many people in your coven are helping Aenghus Óg to take the sword from me?"

A veil fell across her features. "I am sorry, but I cannot answer that."

Bingo, as they say in church halls on Wednesday nights. "That's a shame. And we were being so candid with each other."

"We can still be candid about other subjects."

"I doubt that. It sounds to me like you are allied with Aenghus Óg."

"Please." The witch rolled her eyes. "As I said on the phone yesterday, if that were true, then why would we want to humiliate him?"

"You tell me, Malina Sokolowski."

"Fine. We do not want anything to do with the Tuatha Dé Danann. Mortals who have dealings with them rarely end happily, and while we are not your average mortals, we still are not in their weight class, if you will allow me to use a boxing metaphor."

"I will allow it this once. I would find it more amusing if you would use gamer jargon from now on, like, 'If we fought the Tuatha Dé Danann, we'd get so *pwned.*'"

She smiled at me, understanding that I had made a joke even if she had no clue what being *pwned* meant. "We would actually like to help you, Mr. O'Sullivan. We think Aenghus Óg will be displeased if he discovers why he is unable to perform, and he may turn his wrath against us as well as you. So if you two are to fight, we would like to ensure that you are the winner. To that end, is there anything we can do to help?"

There was no way I was going to let them "help." I was sure it would backfire on me. But this was a golden opportunity to fish for information.

"I'm not sure," I said. "Tell me about the Zoryas you mentioned. Are they the source of your power?"

"When did I mention the Zoryas?"

"You swore by them when you threatened Emily."

"Ah. Well, yes, the Zoryas are star goddesses known throughout the Slavic world. The midnight star, Zorya Polunochnaya, is a goddess of death and rebirth, and, as you might expect, she has quite a bit to do with magic and wisdom. It is she who gives us much of our knowledge and power, though the other two Zoryas are helpful as well."

"Fascinating," I said, and I was being serious. I hadn't heard much about the Zoryas before—old Slavic deities had rarely come up as a topic of conversation in my travels. I'd need to do some research. "You don't do any mucking about with the moon, then?"

"No." She shook her head. "That's another kind of craft."

"Then I'm at a loss as to how you can help me. What sort of thing did you have in mind?"

"Well, since you seem to be fairly accomplished at wards"—she gestured around at the store to the spells she could sense—"perhaps we could help you with some offensive capabilities. How were you planning to attack Aenghus Óg?"

Did she really think I would answer that? "I think I'll just improvise."

"Well, we could increase your speed."

"Unnecessary, but thank you."

Malina frowned. "I get the feeling that you do not really want our help."

"You are correct. I am very grateful for the offer, however. It is kind of you."

"Why would you refuse our aid?"

"Look, I understand you would like to expiate the debt your coven owes me for Emily's treatment, but this is not the sort of service I am interested in."

"You think you are a match for Aenghus Óg?"

I shrugged. "That remains to be seen. He has not exerted himself overmuch to fight me. Perhaps he thinks I am."

Malina looked incredulous. "Are you anything more than a Druid?"

"Of course I am. I own this shop and I play a mean game of chess, and I've been told that I'm a frakkin' Cylon."

"What's a frakkin' Cylon?"

"I don't know, but it sounds really scary when you say it with a Polish accent."

Her brows drew together and her accent thickened. "You are being flippant with me now, and I do not appreciate it. You have implied that a member of the Tuatha Dé Danann is afraid of you, and yet you offer no credible reason why this may be true."

"It doesn't matter to me whether you believe it or not."

Malina's eyes turned icy as she glared at me. "It seems we have some trust issues to work out between us."

"Ya think? Tell me your coven isn't plotting with Aenghus Óg against me."

"My coven isn't plotting against you with Aenghus Óg."

"Now make me believe it."

"That appears impossible. But you have a document with Radomila's blood on it. I think that indicates that she trusts you, at least. I was under the impression that you and Radomila had exchanged favors in the past and were very cordial to each other."

"Yes, that's true. That was before members of her coven began sleeping with my mortal enemy."

"Well, I do not know how to allay your suspicions," she said, and pushed her chair back from the table. "So I will take my leave for now."

"Thank you for controlling Emily. I really did appreciate that," I said. "And I was pleased to have met you."

"Good day," she said, apparently not as pleased to have met me, and tossed her mane of luxurious hair over her red shoulder as she exited, prim and stately and Polish and oh so witchy.

<She's kind of like a Mary Poppins just before she turns to the dark side of the Force,> Oberon said. He was still behind the counter, but he had had a good look at her as she exited. <Let go of your anger, Malina! There's still good in you! The Emperor hasn't driven it from you fully!>

I clearly need to get you some new videos to watch while I'm at work.

<I'd rather come to work with you from now on. It's fun to watch you pretend to be normal.>

At that moment, the door opened on its own and

the Morrigan sailed through it, squawking loudly in her battle-crow form and scaring the bejesus out of my customers—again. Sigh.

When all had exited except for Perry, I told him to take a lunch break.

"You're just, uh, gonna take care of that giant freakin' bird all by yourself, then?" he asked, never taking his eyes from it. "The one with the razor-sharp beak and the spooky eyes that look like they're lit with the fires of hell?"

"Yeah, don't worry about it," I said casually. "Enjoy yourself. Take your time."

"Well, okay, if you're sure. I'll see you later, then." He circled around to the door cautiously, never taking his eyes off the bird, and then slipped out. I went to the door and locked it behind him, flipping the reversible sign around to say CLOSED.

"Okay, Morrigan, what's on your mind?"

She shifted into her human form and remembered this time to clothe herself in black. She was upset, though; her eyes were still glowing red.

"Brighid is on her way to see you. She will be here in moments."

I jumped up and down and swore violently in seventeen languages.

"I feel the same," the Morrigan said. "I do not know what she intends. I told her I had taken Bres and the manner of his death, as you suggested, and she merely listened. When I finished speaking, she thanked me and said she would be coming to see you. Then she asked me for privacy, so I know nothing of her true feelings. She has been traveling across the desert this morning on this plane. She is alone."

"Great. What if she decides to kill me?"

"That will test our bargain quite severely," the Morrigan replied with a smirk.

"Morrigan?"

"Relax. We have a bargain. But have the good grace to pretend to be dead if she decides to kill you."

"What if she decides to set me on fire and watch me burn?"

"Then that's going to hurt. Scream all you want, but turn it off at some point and she'll figure you for dead. I'll help you once she's gone."

"That makes me feel so much better. Hey," I said, suddenly remembering, "were you aware that Flidais came to see me and warn me about Aenghus Óg as well?"

"No." The Morrigan frowned. "When was this?"

"The same day you came to warn me here. When I went home, she was waiting for me there."

"I do not know why she would suddenly be interested in your welfare."

"I was thinking the same thing. Especially since she got me and my hound into some trouble with the local authorities."

"What sort of trouble?"

"My wolfhound is wanted for murder. He killed a park ranger who surprised us during a hunt. And this ranger was wearing an earring enchanted with Fae stealth spells."

The Morrigan's eyes flashed even redder. "There are clearly machinations going on in Tír na nÓg of which I am unaware. I dislike being left out; it gives me the feeling that I may be a target." She huffed and shook her head. "I must investigate. I will linger on this plane awhile to see what Brighid does—but after that, I am going back to Tír na nÓg to get some answers."

Her eyes cooled down abruptly and she turned toward the door. "She comes," the Morrigan said. "It would not do for her to see me here. Farewell for now, Siodhachan Ó Suileabháin."

She melted back into a crow and flapped her wings toward the door, which unlocked and opened for her as she flew through, leaving me alone with Oberon, who was enjoying all the comings and goings from his position behind the counter.

<You know, Atticus, that turning-into-a-crow business is pretty slick, but that's not her best godlike power by a long shot. She can sense when specific people are approaching in time to avoid them! Wouldn't it be cool if you could automatically avoid assholes for the rest of your life?>

"Hush, Oberon," I said. "Brighid is coming. You need to be polite. Keep yourself still back there and don't come out unless I give you express permission. She can fry us to bacon as easily as breathing."

I'd no sooner finished speaking than a ball of flame blew through my door, breaking the glass and melting my door chimes. It extinguished itself in front of me, leaving a tall, majestic, fully armored goddess in its place. It was Brighid, goddess of poetry, fire, and the forge.

"Old Druid," she said in a voice of music and dread, "I must speak with you about the death of my husband."

Chapter 14

Brighid was a vision. I don't think there's ever been a hotter widow in history. Even though she was in full armor and all I could see of her actual person were her eyes and her lips, well, I felt like a horny teenager again. I really, really wanted to flirt, but seeing as I was the guy who widowed her, I thought perhaps there was a line somewhere I shouldn't cross.

I cleared my throat and licked my lips nervously. "You'd just like to speak about his death?" I asked. "No summary incinerations or anything like that?"

"We will speak first," she said severely. "What comes afterward depends on what you say. Tell me of his death."

I told her everything. One doesn't even attempt to lie to Brighid. I sort of left out precisely how I had seen Bres pull his sword on me—I was rather hoping she wouldn't notice my necklace or how much power it held—but I told no untruths.

"The Morrigan told me the same story," she said.

"It was purely self-defense, Brighid," I said.

"I realize that." Her manner softened. "And in truth, Druid, I owe you my thanks. You have relieved me of an odious task."

Gadzooks! Brighid just said she owed me. That was a huge admission, and not what I had expected at all. "I beg your pardon? I do not understand."

Brighid removed her helmet, and her red hair spilled out across her pauldrons like one of those self-inflating life rafts. It wasn't sweaty or tangled from being confined in a helmet across miles of desert. It was glorious, shining, Age of Aquarius hair that would make Malina Sokolowski envious, a full-blown movie star 'do that a team of stylists would spend three hours teasing before the cameras rolled. It smelled of lavender and holly. I remembered to breathe only with some effort.

"I will explain," Brighid said. "But might you have any tea? It has been a long journey from Tír na nÓg."

I leapt to my feet and hurried behind the counter where Oberon waited patiently. "Oh, certainly," I gushed. Making tea for the goddess of fire was so much better than being summarily incinerated by the goddess of fire.

<Can I say hello to her?> Oberon asked meekly.

Let me check, I told him. "My wolfhound would like to greet you, Brighid. Would that be acceptable to you as I brew your tea?"

"You have a hound here? Where is he?"

I dispelled Oberon's camouflage and told him to mind his manners. He trotted into view and padded up to Brighid with his tail wagging like a metronome set to something allegro. She had seated herself at one of my tables, and she smiled at his enthusiasm.

"My, you are impressive. Can you speak?" She was binding her consciousness to his so that she'd be able to hear his answer.

<Yes, Atticus taught me. My name is Oberon. Nice to meet you, Brighid.>

"And it's nice to meet you, Oberon, Shakespeare's King of the Fae." She smiled, scratching him behind the ears with a gauntleted hand. "Who is Atticus?"

"That would be me," I admitted.

"Oh? Nobody told me you were using a new name.

They always use your proper name when they speak of you in Tír na nÓg. I suppose you must make interesting choices, living amongst the mortals as you do. But you," she said to Oberon, cupping her hand underneath his jaw, "I hear you killed a man. Is that true?"

I had been measuring loose-leaf tea into sachets as the water boiled, but at this I looked up sharply. Oberon's tail stopped wagging and dropped between his legs. He sat down and whined. <Yes. I didn't mean to. Flidais commanded me and I had to obey.>

"Yes, I know. I don't blame you, Oberon. In a way, it was my fault. I sent Flidais to see your master."

Gods Below! If she kept dropping bombs like that, I'd have to be very careful when handling the boiling water.

"Things didn't go the way I planned at all," she added. She began removing her steel gauntlets to pet him better. They clanked noisily on the table, and the magic in them was palpable. The armor of a forge goddess would be *sans pareil*—I wondered what it would take to even scratch it. Like, Fragarach, maybe? "And now things have gotten to the point where I need to get directly involved."

<Can you make the cops forget about me?> Oberon asked hopefully.

"I might be able to in normal circumstances. Unfortunately, someone is trying very hard to make sure that they don't forget about you."

"Wait, please, don't say anything else," I said. "Let me just pour this water and sit down, then we can talk."

"Very well. Would you like a belly rub while we wait, Oberon?"

<Oh, I like you a lot,> Oberon said, and he flopped down happily at her feet, his tail swishing across the floor.

Trivia: Brighid takes milk and honey in her tea. Just like me.

"Thank you," she said, before taking a sip and sighing appreciatively.

"Most welcome," I replied, and sat down and took a moment to savor the surrealism. I was having tea with Brighid, a goddess I'd worshipped since childhood, in a city that didn't exist when I was a child. And my wolfhound was joining us—I had made him a cup and cooled it down with ice, and he was now lapping it up from a dish on the floor.

Brighid appreciated it too, for she smiled and said, "This is very strange."

"I like strange things," I said. "At least the non-threatening kind of strange."

"Yes. Unfortunately, there has been plenty of the threatening kind of strange going on lately. You deserve an explanation, I think."

"That would be lovely," I allowed.

"Here, then, is the short version: My brother Aenghus Óg is moving against me. He seeks to supplant me as supreme amongst the Tuatha Dé Danann, but I suspect this is only a stepping-stone to something larger. To that end, whatever it may be, he has been collecting all the enchanted weapons and armor he can. He even got my fool of a husband to ask me to make a set of armor that would stop the blade of Fragarach. Not asking him why, I made some ridiculous-looking stuff and told him it would make him invincible. He promptly put it on and got himself killed, so well done, Druid."

"Um . . . " I didn't know what to say.

"I would have had to kill him myself if things had gone much farther. As it is, I would still like to avoid direct conflict with Aenghus Óg if I can. Descending to the level of battle is . . . distasteful, especially with one's own brother."

Descending to the level of death is also distasteful, and that's a distinct possibility once one is in a battle. I kept that thought to myself, however, and nodded sympathetically.

"Aenghus wants Fragarach because he believes it will penetrate my armor," she said, tapping her helmet.

"Won't it?"

"I don't know for sure," Brighid said. "This armor is an honest attempt to forge something immune to Fragarach, unlike what I gave to Bres. I'd rather not test it."

"I would never wield Fragarach against you."

Brighid laughed. It was like listening to a symphony that makes you shiver and cry for the joy of it.

"I know that, Atticus. And I would rather Aenghus not wield it against me either."

"I'd have to be dead first."

"Precisely. I think you are fit to wield it, and I would rather it remain in your possession. But Aenghus definitely wants it and he is manipulating events to make sure it falls to him. You may have noticed some of this already."

"You mean the Fir Bolgs who attacked me last night? I noticed that, yeah."

"I was speaking of other matters. For example, the mortal police pursuing your wolfhound."

"But that came about because of Flidais, and you said you sent her."

"I sent her to warn you, yes. But that park ranger was the work of my husband, doing Aenghus's bidding. The police are now tools of the love god."

"They're definitely tools," I agreed.

"They will try to find a way to take the sword from you, even if you resist. Aenghus hopes you will, because the police will pull their weapons and take the sword from you at the first sign of resistance. He will have no trouble taking it from them after that."

"I see. They will probably get that search warrant, then. I should warn my lawyer."

"There is more. Aenghus has recruited a coven of witches against you."

"What?" I said. "Which coven?"

"They call themselves the Sisters of the Three Auroras."

I felt the spike in my blood pressure immediately. "But they claim to want nothing to do with Aenghus Óg! One of them is bedding him, and she asked me to brew a tea to make him impotent!"

"Aenghus Óg arranged the entire thing with them. It is both a way to give him just cause to kill you and a way to get the witches close to you."

"But I have Radomila's blood!" I spluttered. My outrage was sloshing over and turning to spittle. "Her coven is pledged to do me a favor in return for my services!"

"They are counting on you not being around much longer to collect," Brighid said. "If you ask them to do anything that conflicts with Aenghus Óg's interests, this Radomila will be conveniently unavailable."

"What do the witches get out of the deal? Aenghus must have promised them something huge."

"I do not know for sure. My guess is that he has promised them free traveling privileges through Tír na nÓg."

I gave a low whistle. "That would allow them to become a very powerful coven."

"Yes. But they are not the only group he is making promises to. He has enlisted the help of the Fomorians, he has stirred up a large number of the Fae against me, and I suspect he has made some bargains with hell."

That could be a fairly huge problem. There were way more of them than I, and they wouldn't listen to my lawyer. "What about the rest of the Tuatha Dé Danann? Where do they stand?"

"Most of them are with me. The idea of Fomorians and demons in Tír na nÓg does not make a convincing sales pitch."

"What about the Morrigan?"

"No one knows, because no one has spoken to her." Brighid grinned wryly. "I think Aenghus was worried she would end his plotting prematurely. For my part, I would rather not be in her debt. She does not work well with others."

"She has spoken to me," I said. "She is already suspicious that something is going on and is incensed at being left out."

"She will get herself involved as she chooses. Are you willing to get involved, Druid?"

"I already am involved, it seems."

"I am asking you to choose sides. My side, specifically."

"Done," I said instantly. What moral dilemma was there? She wanted me to keep the sword; Aenghus wanted to take it. She liked me alive; Aenghus didn't. She was hot; Aenghus was not.

"My thanks." She smiled so warmly, I felt as if my kidneys had melted. "Kill Aenghus Óg for me and I shall reward you." I have to admit that some of the warm fuzzies flew away right there. It made me feel like a mercenary. "And should you run into some demons, I have a gift for you. Give me your right hand."

I placed my right hand in her left. Her palm was cool to the touch, calloused from the forge; her fingers were long and strong. She placed her right index finger onto the loop of my tattoo and tried to do . . . something. Uh-oh.

"I do not understand." She frowned. "Something is preventing me from giving you the power of Cold Fire."

I kept my face carefully neutral, while part of me was

screaming inside and another part was thinking, *Coooooool*. My amulet had just prevented her from performing magic on me. It might have even protected me from summary incineration, had the meeting gone differently—it was not the sort of thing I wanted to test. But now she would become aware of its existence, and things could get awkward.

"Your aura is strange, Druid," she said, sitting back in her chair, noticing it for the first time. "What have you done to it?"

"I have bound it with cold iron," I said, pulling my necklace out from underneath my shirt. "It protects me from most magic."

Brighid said nothing at first, just sat and stared at my necklace. Then she said, "It is also protecting you from my aid. I cannot give you Cold Fire. If you face any demons, you will be left to your own devices, and I cannot see how that will avail you if you cannot use magic."

"Oh, I can use magic."

"Does not the iron prevent it?"

"I have discovered a solution to the old problem."

"Remarkable that you have found one where I have not," said the goddess of the forge.

"Have you truly tried?"

"No," she admitted. "I thought it was impossible."

"Turns out it's only next to impossible."

"Have you tested it against demons?"

"It prevents succubi from casting their charms on me."

"But you have not had to deal with hellfire or any other hellish attacks?"

"Not yet."

"You will need to test it soon. You need a way to deal with demons. Lots of them, if I am right about who Aenghus has been talking to."

"What does this Cold Fire do?"

"It allows you to burn them from within, but it burns like ice burns. It takes a lot of energy and it drains you—even if you draw power from the earth, it will drain you—but it will save you from being overwhelmed in a fight. Alas, I cannot give it to you."

"Sure you can," I said, and I took the necklace off. It changed my aura immediately, and I became nervous. She could hurt me as easily as help me now if she liked.

"That is truly wondrous craft, Siodhachan," she said admiringly, noticing how my aura changed. She'd forgotten my chosen name already and used the one I was born with. "I would have you teach it to me."

I was afraid of this. "My apologies, Brighid, but I have sworn to keep it a secret." I left out the rest of the sentence, which said, "except from the Morrigan," and hurried on before she thought to ask to whom I had sworn. "But now that you know such a thing is possible, I have no doubt that you can figure it out on your own. I counsel patience. This craft took me seven hundred and fifty years."

She did not appear offended, thankfully. Disappointed, yes. But as she continued to stare at the necklace on the table next to her gauntlets, her expression slowly changed. She looked delighted.

"You have given me a new challenge, Druid, and a most worthy one," she said. "I will try to fashion my own in a shorter period of time. I know you cannot tell me how it was made without breaking your oath, but will you allow me to inspect it from time to time?"

"Of course," I said.

"Am I right in thinking this necklace will work for no one but you?"

"Yes. It is bound specifically to me. For anyone else it would simply be jewelry."

"I see now why you have survived so long."

I blushed at her compliment and she put out her left hand again, smiling. I placed my right hand in hers, and she held it as she touched her finger to the loop of my tattoo. This time I felt something, a rush of heat and ice through my veins and a spell of dizziness.

"Now you have the power of Cold Fire," Brighid said. "It works only on hellspawn, and both you and your targets must be touching the earth. Point at your targets with your right hand, collect your will, and say 'Dóigh,' and they will be destroyed—though I warn you again, it takes a tremendous amount of your energy, so use it sparingly, and remember it will also take a few moments for them to die."

"Thank you, Brighid."

"Don't thank me yet," she said, giving Oberon a last scratch before donning her gauntlets again. "Despite the advantages you have, you are all that is keeping Aenghus Óg and his allies from moving openly against me. They are legion and you are one man, and I am glad you are so willing to stand in front of them. But I half-expect you to be dead by the dawn."

On that cheery note, she leaned across the table and kissed me. She tasted of milk and honey and berries, and it was simply blissful.

<You've been kissed by three goddesses in as many days,> Oberon said once Brighid had left, <so I think you owe me three hundred French poodles. That should make us about even.>

Chapter 15

I thought Sundays were supposed to be relaxing. As a male citizen of America, I'm entitled on Sundays to watch athletic men in tight uniforms ritualistically invade one another's territory, and while they're resting I get to be bombarded with commercials about trucks, pizza, beer, and financial services. That's how it's supposed to be; that's the American dream.

I suppose I cannot complain, because I'm not really a citizen of America. Mr. Semerdjian called the INS on me once, in fact. I waved my hand in front of the agents' faces and said, "I'm not the Druid you're looking for." They were not amused. I waved my hand again and said, "Move along," and they got out their handcuffs. That's when I got out my slightly scuffed yet soigné illegal documents, prepared for me by Leif Helgarson, Bloodsucking Attorney-at-Law. And after the INS agents went away, that's when I sent Oberon over to poop on Mr. Semerdjian's lawn for the first time.

We have not been on good terms since then. We never were, of course, but at least for the first few years he cheerfully ignored me. When he began to harass me, I suspected him of being either abysmally stupid or a pawn of the Fae. Turned out he was just mean, and dog shit on his lawn turned him into Flibbertigibbet, a regular Lebanese Tom o' Bedlam.

Now I suspected I was a pawn of the Fae. I didn't know whose pawn I was, precisely. I felt somewhat like Korea, with the United States and China fighting a proxy war through me.

I didn't want to be a pawn. Or Korea. It would be better to be a knight. Or Denmark. The Danes used to kick everyone's ass—until their victims figured out where they came from.

And that was precisely my problem. People knew where to find me. Especially, it seemed, on this particular Sunday.

I was calling a contractor to do an emergency replacement of my melted shop door when I saw, through the window, a familiar Crown Victoria pull up. Detective Carlos Jimenez climbed out, and shortly afterward a couple more cars screeched into parking spaces, and cops with sunglasses lumbered out of them to adjust their waistbands and check that their shirts were still tucked in. Detective Darren Fagles, the one who fancied himself a Reservoir Dog, had an official-looking piece of paper flapping in his hand, the legal-size sort with lots of fine print.

I hung up the phone as the contractor was in mid-sentence and told Oberon to leap up on top of the far table by the wall. "Curl yourself on top and don't move a muscle. Not an ear twitch, not a tail wag, nothing until these guys leave."

<What guys?> he said, as he moved to obey.

"Those cops are coming. If any of them manages to see you somehow, I want you to run out of here and go straight to the widow's backyard and hide there, okay? Don't wait for me to tell you."

<You think they can see through the camouflage?>

"They might be able to. They've certainly had help getting this far." Oberon jumped gingerly onto the table, dwarfing it but just able to coil himself on its top. As soon as he settled down, all hints of his presence disappeared. I shot a quick glance at Fragarach, still resting on the shelf underneath my counter, and cast camouflage on it for insurance.

As the cops grouped together and began to walk toward the door, I wondered if they had decided to come here first or if they had visited my house. If they had visited my house first, where the hell were my lawyers?

A horn honked loudly, demanding attention, as a metallic blue BMW Z4 growled to a halt behind Fagles. Hal Hauk sprang out the door as if summoned.

"Pardon me, are you Detective Fagles?" Hal said, placing himself in the detective's way perhaps a bit faster than a normal human could. The other officers registered this and tensed. A couple of hands drifted toward holsters.

"Stand aside, sir, I'm on official police business," Fagles commanded. Hal wasn't intimidated in the least.

"If your business is with Third Eye Books or its owner, then your business is with me," he said. "I am the attorney of record for Mr. Atticus O'Sullivan."

"You're the attorney of record? Then who was the other guy at his house?"

"One of my associates. He called me and reported that your search of his house was not entirely legal, and I assure you that we will be making a complaint, perhaps filing suit."

That got the cops' attention. They glowered at Hal, and Fagles sneered, "We have a warrant signed by a Tempe judge." He held it in front of Hal's face to emphasize his point. "Our search was entirely legal."

"But that warrant gives you permission to search for an Irish wolfhound or similar dog, I believe, and nothing more. Is that correct, Detective?"

Fagles didn't want to answer with a flat-out yes, so he

tried to sound defiant as he replied, "That's what the warrant says."

"An Irish wolfhound is a very large breed of dog. I saw the specific dog you're looking for before he ran away, and I assure you he weighs almost as much as you. That being given, we can assume that the dog could not possibly be hiding in a drawer or a dresser or in kitchen cupboards or underneath a basil plant. Yet you and your colleagues searched through all those things at my client's house, in clear violation of his civil rights."

I didn't need to hear any more than that to know they weren't looking for just my dog. Aenghus Óg had sent these guys to find Fragarach. And they had torn up my basil in the kitchen—at least I hoped that was all. If they got my whole backyard herb garden, which I had left camouflaged, Oberon would have to make a run for it soon.

"We did no such thing," Fagles said.

"My associate will testify that you did."

"His word against ours."

"He took some video of your search procedure with his cell phone."

Fagles bit back his initial retort and ground his teeth for a moment. Then he said, "Look, whoever you are—"

"Hal Hauk."

"Whatever. We have a legal warrant to search these premises. You will stand aside now or we will arrest you."

"I will stand aside, Detective, but I warn you not to repeat the methods you used at my client's house. You are looking for a large dog, nothing more, and I will be recording your search. If you look in places where a large dog could not possibly be hiding, then the lawsuit we bring against you will be much, much worse."

"Fine."

"Fine," Hal said. "I'll take that," and he snatched the warrant out of Fagles's hand, faster than the eye could track, before stepping aside. Fagles was *pissed*. He had probably wanted to slap the warrant against Hal's chest or something like that, a not-too-subtle push or jab to establish his superiority, but Hal had not only robbed him of that, he had made Fagles look slow and stupid— which, compared to Hal, he was. In Fagles's defense, he didn't know he was trying to play dominance games with a werewolf.

Rather than say anything to deepen his humiliation, Fagles stalked forward, with Jimenez and the others close behind. He paused at the door, examining the broken glass around the edges and scattered on the floor inside. He peered through at me before stepping across the threshold. I was standing to his left, behind my counter, access to which was open and visible from the shop entrance.

"What happened here, O'Sullivan?" he said.

"A customer objected strenuously to my returns policy," I said.

"Yeah, right," Fagles muttered as he stepped through the door. As soon as he did, wards around my shop alerted me that he had a binding on him. I looked closely at his aura as he gestured for the others to file in and start searching, and I turned on my faerie specs. A band of green knotwork wreathed Fagles's skull, almost like one of those Roman laurels. That was the primary method by which he was being controlled. But interlaced with those strands, I saw, were very fine blue and red threads. I could not break the green binding without breaking those too, and I didn't know what those were for, though I assumed they weren't friendly by their design—fail-safes, perhaps, or magical booby traps, or merely something for me to waste my time on.

The other officers, I noted quickly, had nothing about

them beyond their normal human auras—all tinged with aggression and stress, but that was only to be expected after being schooled by a lawyer. Hal followed Jimenez and the other cops as they spread out through the store, which meant I could safely focus all my attention on Fagles. He remained by the door, transfixed by something he saw on my counter shelves.

"What's that?" Fagles said, jerking his chin vaguely in my direction.

"What's what?"

"That," he said, removing his sunglasses and pointing, "That looks like a scabbard. You have a sword behind your counter?" He folded his sunglasses and slipped them into his shirt pocket before looking at me expectantly.

"Nope."

"Don't lie to me, I can see it!" Right. That told me quite a bit. If he could see the sword and not Oberon, who truly was sitting in plain sight on a table across the room, then Aenghus had given him a very selective ability: It wasn't the ability to see through camouflage, which would have instantly revealed to him the purported target of his search; rather, it was the specific ability to see Fragarach, which was supposed to be magically cloaked. That cloak had worked very well on Bres, so it should work equally well on Fagles—except that he seemed attuned to it. How does one get attuned to a cloaked item? You need to have a lot of help from the person who cast the cloak in the first place. That meant Radomila, leader of the Sisters of the Three Auroras. Fagles was walking, talking evidence they were working against me with Aenghus Óg.

"Is it a dog, Detective?" Hal asked, swinging around from surveying Jimenez's progress to confront Fagles. He stopped a couple of paces away from the detective, far enough into the shop that he wouldn't see what

Fagles was looking at. "Because if it's not, then it's none of your business."

The detective ignored him and said to me, "That's a deadly weapon you're hiding, and you need a permit for that. Do you have a concealed-weapons permit?"

"Don't answer," Hal told me, and pointed his cell phone at Fagles. "I am recording this, Detective. According to Arizona Revised Statute 13-3102, Subsection G, a permit is not necessary for weapons carried in a belt holster that is wholly or partially visible, or carried in a scabbard or case designed for carrying weapons that is wholly or partially visible."

Whoa. That's why Hal gets $350 an hour. Quoting Arizona statutes, complete with their soul-destroying legalistic sentence structure? That's Druidic.

"That is not a concealed weapon," Hal continued, "nor is it a dog, which is all you are authorized to search for."

I tuned the two of them out as they continued to wrangle over whether the scabbard was concealed or not on my shelf and turned my attention to the bindings floating about Fagles's impeccably coiffed dome.

My hunch was that the blue knots represented the binding that allowed him to see the cloak—which was, in turn, allowing him to penetrate the camouflage—so if I unraveled that particular binding, the problem of my sword would quite literally disappear. The trouble was that breaking the blue knots would snap the red ones too, and while I could appreciate the craft that went into these particular bindings, I still had no way of telling precisely what Aenghus had wrought there. Perhaps the Morrigan or Brighid could tell me precisely what spells the knots represented and how to deal with them safely, but the best I could figure was that the red knots were bad juju. If I took time to deal with it, it might "go off" in response to my tampering anyway, and I would still need to deal with the blue knot afterward, because I could tell Fagles wouldn't give up until he tried taking the sword from me—Aenghus wouldn't have it any other way. And the green knot? That would be a direct magical battle with Aenghus Óg for control of Fagles, during the course of which he would learn quite a bit about my abilities, and I didn't want to tip my hand quite that much yet.

Here, then, would be a true test of my wards and bindings: I decided to activate all the magic dampening I could from my shop's wards, then go after the blue knots and let the red knots do whatever they were designed to do, damn the consequences. It was one of those decisions you make when you have too much testosterone bubbling around in your system, or when you've been raised in a culture of ridiculous machismo, as I was.

The blue knot was absurdly fragile—it snapped almost immediately with the gentlest of mental tugs, and the red one snapped along with it: definitely a trap, the concussive sort. I felt a *whump* against my face, like getting hit unexpectedly full force with a pillow, and I saw Hal's head snap back abruptly. He fell over backward, snarling in surprise. Fagles yelped and grabbed at his head, and then as Hal and I were recovering—Hal red-faced and eyes a bit yellow, his wolf close to the surface—Fagles went completely batshit and drew his gun on me.

"Hands up!" he yelled, and of course that brought all the other cops running over, Jimenez in the lead, drawing his gun out too. I raised my hands and wondered what would have happened if I hadn't activated the shop's wards first. Hal might have had his head taken off. He had taken a good shot as it was, and I got only a fraction of the power thanks to the stronger protections of my necklace. Fagles was reacting to some magical feedback, nothing more, and it looked like none of the other cops farther away had felt a thing—they were just backing Fagles's play.

<What happened?> Oberon asked.

It's okay. Don't move, I told him.

"Whoa, Detective, that's not necessary. You're pointing a gun at an unarmed man who's cooperating with a legal search!" Hal said, panting a bit.

"Bullshit! He assaulted me!" Fagles spat.

"What? That's nonsense, man. He's been standing there passively more than five feet away from you the entire time!"

"He just hit me upside the head!"

<Well, I'm sure he deserved it, Atticus.>

Hush, I didn't hit him.

"He most certainly did not, and that security camera right there will prove it!" Hal exclaimed, pointing at the camera. All eyes followed his finger and saw that it would most definitely prove whether or not I had moved to slap Detective Fagles upside the head. Fagles heard the certainty in Hal's voice, saw the doubt in his colleagues' faces, and practically stomped his foot as he cried, "Well, something hit my head, and it sure as hell wasn't me!"

"Something hit me too, Detective, but it wasn't my client, and there's no reason to keep pointing your gun at him. Let's all calm down now."

"I want to know what hit me!" Fagles insisted. "And hey! Where did the sword go? It's gone!"

It wasn't gone. But he couldn't see it now that I had snapped that blue knot—the camouflage was in effect.

"What sword?" I said, playing dumb.

"The sword that we were just talking about!" Fagles screamed. "The one that was on that shelf!" He pointed impotently at the spot where my sword still lay, hidden from his unaided vision.

<Now that's funny,> Oberon said. <I think his panties are getting twisted. If I had any sausage to spare, I would give you one for that right there.>

"You saw it too!" Fagles accused Hal, looking around at the other cops who were eyeing him a bit uncertainly.

"How could I have seen it, Detective? I'm on this side of the counter," Hal pointed out, the very picture of reason and affability.

"But you argued about it with me!"

"That's because I'm paid to argue about things. But I never saw this sword you're referring to. I merely objected to you taking anything not included in the warrant. Speaking of which, has anyone found the large dog yet?"

Detective Jimenez sighed and put away his gun, and all the other cops relaxed too, save for Fagles. They were beginning to look a bit embarrassed.

"I still don't know what hit me, and I want an answer," Fagles ground out, his chin lifted obstinately.

"I think it was a freak gust of wind, Detective," Hal said, "coming through the broken door. I felt it too."

That did it for Detective Jimenez. "The dog isn't here, Fagles," he said. "Let's go; put the gun away."

Fagles gritted his teeth in frustration, and the green wreath around his head flared menacingly. And that's when he shot me.

Chapter 16

You know that old saw about your life flashing before your eyes at the moment of death? Well, if you've lived more than two thousand years, it's going to take a while for your subconscious to put together a decent retrospective, and I imagined that there must be one of those "spinning beach balls of death" hovering over my head like when I asked my computer to do too many things at once. But that's not the first thing I thought about as I fell to the ground with a hole in my chest; it was the second.

The first thing I thought was, "Oh no! I've been shot!" in the immortal words of the golden protocol droid when he got lased with special effects in a mining colony.

As I waited for my life's highlight reel—much like those tributes they play at the Oscars every year—to play in my mind, quite a few people became excited in my shop.

All the cops, led by Jimenez, pulled their guns back out and pointed them at Fagles, shouting at him to put his gun down *now*. And Oberon wanted to start tearing into him right away.

<ATTICUS!>

It's okay, buddy, stay there. I'll be fine.

Poor Fagles. Even as I watched from flat on my back,

the green binding about his head dissolved. He came back to full conscious control of his mind to find himself standing over me with a smoking gun hanging from his hand and five cops pointing their guns at him.

His voice, thin and trembling, said, "It wasn't me."

"Drop the gun, Fagles!" Jimenez commanded. Fagles didn't seem to hear.

"There was someone in my mind. Telling me what to do. He wanted the sword."

"There is no sword!" Hal spoke up. "Only my unarmed client bleeding on the floor!"

That drew my attention back to my condition and how very, very much it hurt. Thanks a lot, Hal. I was bleeding out pretty good, and I had a punctured left lung that was filling up with blood as well. I reached for some power to begin healing . . . and didn't have any to tap. I'd used everything I had stored in my bear charm on casting camouflage and dealing with Aenghus Óg's bindings. I needed to get outside, where I could touch the earth, but Fagles was still standing there and the cops were still telling him to drop the gun, and no one was dialing 911 while they had an armed rogue cop to deal with. Owie.

"But I didn't shoot him. It wasn't me," Fagles pleaded. "You don't understand."

"There's a security camera and six witnesses who watched you pull the trigger on an unarmed, unresisting man," Jimenez said. "You know what that means. Drop the weapon now, Fagles."

Tears began leaking from Fagles's eyes, and his chin quivered. "I don't understand how this happened," he said. "I would never do something like this."

"We all saw you do it," Jimenez said. "Last warning. Drop the weapon or we will be forced to shoot you."

The direct threat jarred Fagles out of his self-pity. "Oh, you're going to shoot me, are you?" he sneered, and then he became unhinged. "Well, that's better than going to prison! And even better than that would be taking you with me!"

"Fagles, don't—"

And then there was a lot of noise. Fagles's inchoate roar of rage against what he knew to be injustice, his brief attempt to raise his weapon, and then the percussive explosions of five guns going off, sending Fagles howling backward through the door, and finally the curses of the cops who knew they'd all be sitting on their asses for days, pending investigation.

"Somebody get the paramedics here and some black-and-whites to block off the street," Jimenez said. "And we're going to need that security tape."

Hal rushed forward and knelt down to see how I was doing.

"I need to get outside to draw some power," I whispered at him. "Lung filling up with blood," and then I coughed some up for him by way of punctuation.

"How's he doing?" Jimenez asked, looking over Hal's shoulder.

"Help me move him. He needs air," Hal said, and the detective backed off.

"Whoa, we need to wait for the paramedics. We're not supposed to do anything."

"Fine, I'll do it myself," Hal said, and he hooked an arm under my shoulders and knees and scooped me up as effortlessly as he would an Italian runway model. Silly cop, I don't need your help; I have a werewolf on retainer.

"Hey, if he dies, it's going to be your fault."

"If he dies, he can sue me," Hal said. "Get out of the way." He sidestepped through the broken door, over the body of Detective Fagles, and then placed me down on the grass strip outside my shop. I gasped in relief as I immediately began to draw power from the earth.

Between bloody coughs, I spoke quietly so that only Hal would be able to hear me as I began closing my wounds.

"I need the sword. It's invisible, but you can feel it on the shelf. Bring it to me. And get someone over here to clean up all of my blood, completely sanitize the place, every drop. Including your clothes."

Hal looked down and saw my blood all over him. "This is a three-thousand-dollar suit."

"I'm good for it. Gotta get the door fixed too. And Oberon will need looking after."

"Ah, I thought I smelled him," Hal said.

I nodded. "He's in the shop. Camouflaged like the sword. I'll tell him to jump in your Beemer."

"Okay, I'll go open the door and leave it open. But tell him to be careful on the leather seats."

"Sybarite," I said.

"Ascetic," he retorted, and he got up to go open his car door.

I heard sirens wailing in an urban imitation of the *bean sidhe,* and as I poured everything I could into accelerating my healing, I reached out to Oberon.

Okay, Oberon, I'm healing up fine, but they're going to come take me to the hospital for a while and I need you to go with Hal for now. I should be back tomorrow.

<Why do you need to go at all?>

There's some fluid in my lungs and I can't get that out without some help. Hal has opened the door of his car for you. Try to get out of the store as quietly as you can and watch out for blood on the ground, because your paw prints will give you away. There's a dead body right outside the door, so be careful.

<There are a lot of people milling around by the door.>

There's going to be more of them soon. The longer

you wait, the more there will be. I'm outside on the ground to the right.

<Wait.>

What's wrong?

<Is that tiny little toy car Hal's?>

It's a very expensive toy. You're supposed to be careful with the leather seats.

<So I'm supposed to ninja past these cops, tread across the broken glass—you remember the broken glass, right?—avoid the buckets o' blood outside the door, and jump silently into that puny car without saying hello to the upholstery?>

An excellent summation. Make it quick.

<Not so fast. Promise you'll get me a date with a French poodle?>

Seriously? You're holding out on me right now? I've been shot and I'm coughing up blood and you're negotiating for some tail?

<Oh, all right. But I totally deserve one and you know it. I've been a good widdle doggie.>

It was at this moment that Perry, who had slunk out of the shop more than an hour ago under the glowing red eyes of the Morrigan, chose to return from lunch.

"Holy shit, boss!" he said. "Did that big fucking bird do all of this?"

Chapter 17

I beckoned Perry over. "I'll explain what happened later," I said as he squatted next to me in the grass. "The bird was just the beginning. But listen—" I paused to cough up some more blood.

"Damn, Atticus, I knew that bird was bad news. I'm sorry, man, I should have stayed to help you out."

"Don't worry about it. You can help me now. You're on the clock until you get a glass contractor out here to fix up the door. Once that's done, lock up and head home. Open up tomorrow for me and make a cup of Humili-Tea—there's some sachets already made—you know the one I'm talking about, the one that sorority girls ask for when they want to end a relationship?" Perry nodded and grinned wryly. "Good. Make it for a customer named Emily. Don't tell her anything about what you saw here or where I'm at or anything, is that clear? If she asks you what the weather's like outside, you shrug your shoulders and say you don't know, all right?"

"Got it, boss."

"That goes for everybody who asks anything. Tell them I'll be back in a few days. If you don't know how to make a certain kind of tea for someone, then don't even try. Just apologize and tell them I'll be back soon."

"Is that true?"

I tried to laugh but coughed instead. "What, that I'll be back? I certainly hope so."

"You're not going to be in the hospital for weeks? Because that looks like a bullet hole in your shirt."

"As the Black Knight famously said, that's just a flesh wound."

"The Black Knight always triumphs!" Perry beamed. Monty Python is like catnip for nerds. Once you get them started quoting it, they are constitutionally incapable of feeling depressed.

"That's right. It would greatly ease my mind if you took care of things, Perry. And if a guy named Hal tells you to do anything, you do it as if it came from my mouth, okay? He's my attorney. Speaking of whom, here he is."

Hal returned from the inside of the store, and he had Fragarach clutched invisibly in his left hand. He knelt down on the other side of me, seeming to use his left hand for support, but in truth laying the sword down in the grass against my side. As he did this, he held out his right hand to Perry to distract him. "Pleased to meet you. I'm Hal Hauk," he said.

"Perry Thomas," he said, taking Hal's hand and shaking it. "I work for Atticus."

"Excellent. Let's get you inside, then, past all the police. I'll be right back, Atticus," he said to me. They rose and left me there, and I took the opportunity to check on Oberon.

Where are you now?

<Where do you expect? I'm totally a ninja wolfhound. This car is ridiculous, though. He has a revolting citrus air freshener in here. Do you know when his birthday is? We should get him one that smells like steak or Italian sausage.>

I'm not sure they make them in those scents, Oberon.

<Why not? You'd think they'd sell like Milk-Bones,

especially to a werewolf who's trying to compensate for something with a slick sports car.>

Ow! Don't make me laugh right now!

After giving Oberon a mental scratch on the head, I went to work on Fragarach. I dispelled the camouflage as the ambulance arrived, because I didn't want anyone to accidentally touch it and freak out, then placed a binding on the scabbard that would prevent it from moving farther than five feet from me. I had wanted to do this in the shop in case Fagles ever got his hands on it, but the binding takes longer to cast than camouflage and requires more power, and I didn't have access to much of either earlier.

Jimenez came out to meet the paramedics and pointed them in my direction. Hal also came out and asked them to take me to Scottsdale Memorial Hospital, where my personal doctor could operate on me.

I didn't really have a personal doctor, but the Pack did. Dr. Snorri Jodursson was part of the Pack himself, and he was the go-to guy for the paranormal community in the Phoenix area. He didn't raise an eyebrow at unusually fast healing, for example, and he was rumored to be an excellent bonesetter and a quick surgeon. He was also willing to do things off the books; he had a whole surgical team who would work off record for obscene amounts of cash. I'd met him a couple of times when I ran with the Pack—he was probably sixth or seventh in their hierarchy—but I'd never had cause to use his professional services until now.

The reason people like me need people like Snorri is because of reactions like the paramedics had when they examined me.

"I thought you were supposed to have been shot," one of them said.

"I was. Fluid in my lungs," I gurgled. "I'm stable, but I need to see my doctor."

"Well, where's the bullet hole?"

Whoops. In my haste to prevent infection, I probably grew that skin over a bit too fast. It was still angry red, I'm sure, but not an open wound anymore. I'd put all my effort into closing up the skin and the lung, so the muscle tissue on either side was still pretty torn and would take some time to mend—and the skin and lung tissue needed time to strengthen too.

"Um, it was a rubber bullet. Hit me there and caused internal bleeding," I said.

"Detectives don't use rubber bullets. And even if they did and it caused some internal bleeding, you shouldn't have fluid in your lung from that."

"Tell you what, sport. Put me on a stretcher and get me to my doctor and let him worry about it." I was ready to go. I had done all I could here, including a recharge of my bear charm. Now I needed a surgeon and some time.

"You mean to tell me your bullet wound healed up that fast?"

"I mean to tell you to give me one of those oxygen masks and get me out of here. And this sword comes with me." I patted Fragarach and the paramedic looked down, noticing it for the first time. "Doesn't leave my side."

"What? We cannot allow weapons in the ambulance."

"It's sheathed and it's incredibly valuable. Look at my shop." I gestured toward the broken door. "I can't leave it here."

Hal, who had been hanging back silently watching the proceedings, loomed suddenly over the paramedic's shoulder. "Are you refusing to transport my client in a medical emergency?"

"No," the paramedic replied, squinting up at him. "I'm refusing to transport his weapon."

"You mean his priceless Celtic art? That's not a weapon, sir. It's a family heirloom of intense sentimental value, and the trauma he would suffer by being separated from it would be greater than any physical pain he currently feels. Which, I notice, you've done absolutely nothing about since you arrived."

The paramedic clenched his jaw and exhaled sharply through his nose as he turned back to me. "Effing lawyers," he muttered quietly, thinking perhaps Hal wouldn't hear it. But werewolves tend to hear things like that.

"That's right, sir, I am an effing lawyer, and I will effing file suit against you if you don't effing get my client and his art to Scottsdale Memorial right now!"

"All right, whatever!" huffed the paramedic, who could not stand to be bludgeoned with lawsuit threats for long. He and his partner went to get the stretcher, and shortly I was being loaded into the back of the ambulance, Fragarach clutched in my right hand. Jimenez and the other cops were so busy worrying about what the press would do when they found out that a Phoenix detective had shot a Tempe detective stone dead that they completely missed the fact that the sword Fagles had been hollering about actually existed.

"I'll see you there soon," Hal said with a wave. "Snorri will take good care of you; he knows you're coming. And don't worry about these guys," he said, indicating the paramedics. "Leif will pay them a visit tonight and they won't remember a thing." Since the paramedics had finally put an oxygen mask on me, I couldn't answer, so I just gave a weak nod.

<Hurry back, Atticus. I'm going to be bored. These werewolves can't talk to me. And this camouflage stuff still kinda tickles.>

I'll probably see you by lunchtime tomorrow, I said back to my dog.

<Will there be sausage?>

Only if Hal tells me you've been good.

<I'm going to hold you to that,> Oberon said, his mental voice fading as the ambulance put some distance between us.

Okay, be good, then, I projected, and hoped he heard it. We warbled up Mill Avenue and doubtless gave the stoners loitering on the corner outside Trippie Hippie a quick jolt of paranoia. Sirens just harsh on their mellow, man.

Drives in the back of an ambulance are simultaneously boring and stressful. I needed relief from both. Paramedic Man wasn't about to talk to me anymore, so I decided to mess with him a bit, since Leif would make sure he wouldn't remember anything later. Am I above immature trickery? No. It keeps me young.

Using a bit of power recently banked in my bear charm, I bound a few of the natural threads in the elastic band of his underwear to the fine hairs in the center of his back about five inches up. The result was an instant wedgie. Those have been funny for two thousand years, but they're even more hilarious when your victim is sanctimoniously trying to behave like he knows more than you.

I really shouldn't have done it, though, because his reaction—a girlish squeal followed by a high-octave "Ahh! What the fuck?!?" and an abrupt attempt to stand up, which cracked his head on the ceiling—got me laughing too hard, and that brought on a serious case of bloody hacking and a heaping spoonful of pain. Served me right, I suppose. I messed up the inside of the oxygen mask, then released the binding so he could calm down and help me.

He never saw me laughing, so the poor guy thought his antics had caused me to become upset, and he was very solicitous as soon as he was able to reestablish some room in his shorts. Best ambulance ride ever.

When we got to the hospital and his partner came around to help unload me from the back, he noticed that Mr. Wedgie had a flushed face.

"What happened?" he asked.

"He had a bit of distress during the ride, but he's stable for the moment," Wedgie said as they put my rolling stretcher on the ground and started pushing me toward the sterile electric doors of the emergency room.

"But you look like something happened to you," his partner replied. "Are you okay, man?"

"I'm fine," Wedgie snapped. "Nothing happened. I— ahh, Jesus Christ!"

Well, I couldn't resist when he was lying like that, could I? Besides, there's that saying about laughter being the best medicine. Whoever said that didn't have blood in their left lung, though, I feel certain.

Dr. Snorri Jodursson got his first look at me while I was in the midst of another hacking fit. He appeared to be in his forties, though of course he was older than that, like all the members of the Tempe Pack. He was dressed in blue scrubs, which drew attention to the startling blue ice of his eyes and the blond eyebrows furrowed above them. His sharp nose and chiseled jaw made him look like a thunder god, though considering his pack's antipathy for Thor, that wasn't a compliment I would think of paying him aloud. He had his blond hair cropped fairly close along the sides, but it was tousled and teased on the top after the fashion of frat-boy douche bags—and I wasn't going to tell him that either.

"Atticus, I've seen you looking better," he said, as he kept pace with the gurney being wheeled into pre-op by a couple of nurses. "Tell me what you can when you feel up to it."

"Am I able to talk freely?" I asked, tilting my eyes toward the nurses rolling my gurney.

"Oh yes, they're part of my team," Jodursson said.

"You can count on their discretion as long as you pay for it."

"All right, I need blood removed from my left lung, then," I said, "and use a local anesthetic. I can't afford to go under."

"If that's all you need, we don't need to cut you open at all. We'll insert a tube down your throat, charge the liquid, and then use magnets to draw it up out of there. We do it for pneumonia patients all the time. You'll still need a local, because it tends to hurt like hell, but you'll remain conscious. Good enough?"

"Perfect. Treat this whole thing as outpatient, because I need you to let me go right afterward, and you should bill full costs to Magnusson and Hauk, no insurance. Include in your records whatever tests and exams you'd do for a normal human. You know the drill, I'm sure. Make sure you mention the bullet hole and what a good job you did patching it up, because this is going to get looked at by the cops. No way around it."

"Am I removing a bullet?"

"No, it passed through me, and they're digging it out of my shop somewhere."

"So you're sure it traveled cleanly between your ribs? I don't have to worry about any bone chips floating around?"

"As certain as I can be. I'm just half drowned." We entered an elevator and paused until the doors closed.

"Would you mind if I did a chest X-ray to be sure? The cops are going to want to see one anyway. Kind of a standard procedure."

"Well, I've already plugged up the holes in my lung and the entry and exit wounds too, so it's going to look a bit odd."

Jodursson scowled for the first time. Until then, he'd been conversing with half a grin on his face. "That was probably more efficient than you should have been."

"Well, you're going to charge me thousands for chest bandages I'll never use, so I figure we're even. You and your team will just have to lie convincingly on the stand when you get called up." The elevator bell dinged and the doors opened, and the nurses rolled me into a busy hallway lined with surgical bays.

"You're going to sue the cops, then?" Jodursson asked.

"Sure, why not? Somebody has to pay for all this, and I'd rather it not be me."

"You've got a solid case?"

"As solid as Hal can make it. Five cops saw the other cop shoot me when I was standing dead still with my hands up, offering no resistance. Got it on security cam too. You write up a good story about your medical wizardry, and it's guaranteed."

"Excellent. I'll be sure to pad the bill."

"You're the reason we need health care reform, you know."

Jodursson's grin returned. "There's also going to be the matter of my team's hush money."

"Sure, no problem. This one's going to get a lot of attention, because the press can't leave something like this alone. Just let Hal know how much, and I'll make sure he gets it to you."

"Do we have to rush this?"

"The faster the better. You're going to have the police and press here sooner rather than later, and I'd prefer to disappear if I can before they get here."

And so Dr. Snorri Jodursson had me out of there by the time night fell, scooting out a side door in a wheelchair and conveniently missing all the people waiting for me in recovery.

We didn't miss the guy waiting by the side door, though. That would be Detective Carlos Jimenez. He was showing some annoying signs of sentience.

"You're looking pretty good for a guy who got shot in the chest," he said.

"Detective." I nodded at him. "How may I help you?"

"I need a statement."

"I got shot in Tempe. You're from Phoenix. There's a statement. Two, in fact."

"I know, Mr. O'Sullivan, I just need your version of events to put in my report. There's always a lot of scrutiny when a cop gets shot, and it gets insane when he gets shot by other cops. So oblige me, will you?"

"All right. Detective Fagles shot me for no good reason while I had my hands up and was making no threatening movements or statements. The brave and decisive action of Detective Carlos Jimenez prevented me from suffering further injury and possibly saved my life. I am going to sue Tempe for millions. How's that?"

"That was great. Thanks. Where are you off to in such a hurry?"

"Maybe I'm going to a titty bar. It's none of your business. Come on, Doctor, let's go." Snorri began to roll me forward, and as he did, Jimenez registered what was slung around the back of my wheelchair.

"Hey, is that a scabbard? Or a sword, rather?"

"Whoa. Déjà vu," I said, gesturing for Snorri to keep on pushing. "That sounds eerily like the line of questioning Detective Fagles used today when he was supposed to be searching for the dog I don't have."

"If that's the sword Detective Fagles was talking about, then you removed it from a crime scene," Jimenez replied, walking a pace or two behind us.

"If it is the same sword, Detective—and that's a big *if*, since nobody ever saw that imaginary sword but Fagles—then it's just as legally in my possession here as it was in my shop. Good evening, sir."

"Wait a second," Jimenez said. "Where can I find you if I need additional information?"

"You already know where I live and where I work,"
I said.

"You're going home, then?" He was a persistent bugger.

"Tell you what. If you cannot find me at home or at
work, you may contact me through Hal Hauk, my
attorney." My plan had been to be out of the chair and
walking north up Civic Center at this point, but
Jimenez was kind of putting a crimp in my plans. He
noticed this as we ran out of the parking lot and arrived
at the street, where Snorri stopped pushing my wheelchair.

"What, no ride?" Jimenez asked.

"Good night, Detective," I said pointedly.

He ignored me and addressed Snorri. "Has Mr.
O'Sullivan been checked out of the hospital, then?"

"Yes, on my authority."

"And you are?"

"Dr. Snorri Jodursson."

"What can you tell me about his condition, Doctor?"

"I can tell you nothing right now, as you know. But
once I receive a proper medical records request, you
may of course read his chart and my notes yourself.
And the sooner you leave me alone, the sooner I can get
the paperwork finished."

"Well, you're quite a pair," Jimenez said, folding his
arms across his chest and locking his knees. He said
nothing more, just stood there and stared at us. I kept
my gaze focused on Scottsdale Stadium across the
street, and I think Snorri was returning his gaze. I bet
Jimenez would blink first—werewolves, you know—
but Snorri didn't have the patience to stare him down
baldly. He employed a legal argument to save time.

"If you will excuse us, Detective, I need to consult
with my patient in private," Snorri said, and then I
could practically feel him turning on that werewolf vibe
that says back the hell off.

It took about two seconds for Jimenez to lower his eyes. He said, "Of course, Doctor. Good evening to you. And to you, Mr. O'Sullivan. I'll be in touch." We made no reply as he walked south along the sidewalk for about twenty-five yards. Then he stopped and pulled out a pack of cigarettes from his jacket and started slapping it against his palm. He looked back at us as he put one between his lips and lit up, clearly intending to wait around to see who gave me a ride. Annoying.

"Snorri, start walking me north toward Civic Center park," I whispered, confident that he could hear me, and he complied. "I'm going to cast camouflage on myself and the sword now that you're concealing me from his sight," I said, "and I'll get up while you're pushing me and walk along with you. I don't think he'll spot the movement, since it's dark. When we get up to the corner of Second Street, we'll lose him around the corner and you can walk back, saying I caught a ride in a waiting car."

"All right," he whispered. "He's following us. And he's just pulled out his cell phone."

"Can you hear who he's talking to?"

"Hold on." For a few moments there was nothing but the sound of the wheelchair thunking across cracks in the sidewalk. Then Snorri said, "He's asking the Scottsdale police to get a car over here to tail you."

"Ha! Won't get here in time." I cast camouflage on myself and on Fragarach once more and felt my energy stores dwindle down to Death Valley levels—that was the price I paid for playing wedgie games. Then I rocked myself forward onto the footrests, and hopped off into the street, so that Snorri could keep pushing the wheelchair as if I were still in it. I tried to take my first deep breath since getting shot and immediately discovered what a bad idea it was.

"Don't try to take a deep breath until you heal up

fully," Snorri advised me as I gasped and clutched at my throat. "That local is probably wearing off, and the tissue in your throat is scraped raw and extremely dry at this point."

"Thanks for the timely warning," I whispered, over what felt like a windpipe made of molten gravel.

"That's why I get paid the big bucks," he said lightly.

"Speaking of which," I wheezed, "you might want to have Hal take a look at your report before you hand it over to the cops, just to make sure it's consistent with what actually happened."

"Will do."

I turned to look over my shoulder at Jimenez trailing us. He was picking up his pace as he saw us nearing the corner. I reached out to the wheelchair and snagged Fragarach from the back and slung it over my shoulder.

"I'm going to jog up to the park now. Tell Hal I'll meet him for lunch at Rúla Búla tomorrow at noon and to bring Oberon with him."

"Okay. Get well and try not to worry. We have your back."

"Thanks, Snorri. You're worth every penny." I veered off to the right, crossing the deserted street to a wide median populated with old olive trees that gave Civic Center its peculiar character. After drawing some energy from a tree to allow me to breathe more freely, if not without pain, I left Snorri and Jimenez behind to play Where's the Druid? and jogged the last quarter mile to the Civic Center Plaza, an expansive grassy area dotted with some old oaks and the occasional bronze statue. It was a little too manicured for my taste, but it was a large enough source of natural power to take care of my healing needs.

I walked a few paces into the grass and sank my fingers into the soil, reaching out with my consciousness to get to know this carefully kept landscape of modern serenity. Five minutes of meditation revealed to me a place near an oak tree that was rarely trod upon, so I made my way there and shucked myself out of my clothes, folding them neatly and hiding them up in a crook of the tree's branches. I checked my cell phone for messages and had several texts—two from Hal and one from Perry—updating me that all was well for the moment, then turned it off to go completely incommunicado. Then, naked and camouflaged, I lay down on my right side so that my tattoos would have as much contact with the earth as possible and put Fragarach in front of me, nestled against my chest and belly. I placed some precautionary wards about myself, then instructed my body to heal and detoxify while I slept, drawing on the power of Civic Center's abundant (if somewhat chemically assisted) life energy.

I had escaped Aenghus Óg's machinations on this day, but at the cost of Fagles's life. If I continued to let Aenghus test my defenses and provide him with a stationary target, eventually he would find a way to break me—especially with a coven of witches backing him up. So it was time to change the game somehow, and I had two choices: run like hell or fight like hell.

Running wasn't attractive to me anymore, because I'd been there and done that for two millennia, and since I had basically pledged on my honor to Brighid that I would fight for her against Aenghus, it really wasn't a viable option. On top of that, there was the betrayal of the Sisters of the Three Auroras. My ego didn't want to let a bunch of Polish witches less than half my age get away with bearding me in my own den.

So it was going to be fight like hell, and about time too. I had managed to out-dither Hamlet, and the famous Dane's words now haunted me: "I do not know why yet I live to say 'This thing's to do,' sith I have cause and will and strength and means to do't." Hamlet promised himself he'd throw down afterward, but I think perhaps when he said, "From this time forth, my thoughts be bloody, or be nothing worth!" the limits of blank verse weakened his resolve somehow. If he'd been free to follow the dictates of his conscience rather than the pen of Shakespeare, perhaps he would have abandoned verse altogether, like me, and contented himself with this instead: "Bring it, muthafuckas. Bring it."

Chapter 18

I awoke in the morning remarkably refreshed but with urgent pressure on my bladder. After relieving myself on the oak tree—out of sight of the few people strolling through the park—I took a deep breath, and it felt remarkably good. I twirled my arms experimentally and felt no tightness in my chest, and I smiled. The earth was so good to me, so giving and so kind.

I retrieved my cell phone and powered it on, checking the time: It was ten a.m., plenty of time to make it to Rúla Búla. I pulled down my clothes, dressed, slung Fragarach across my back, and dispelled the camouflage, walking plainly in the world again. My bear charm was fully charged and I felt completely restored, albeit dreadfully thirsty and a bit esurient.

I had messages from the Tempe Police Department, at first requesting and then demanding that I contact them immediately, as well as messages from Hal, Snorri, and Perry.

Hal just wanted me to know that Oberon was a bottomless pit, and while my dog had been very careful with his car's upholstery and he appreciated it, the blasted canine had destroyed his citrus air freshener for some unknown reason and left it in shreds all over his interior. All business matters he would tell me at Rúla Búla.

Snorri told me Hal had approved his medical report and thanked me in advance for paying his very large bill.

In a message time-stamped at nine-thirty, Perry called to tell me that the shop door had been successfully replaced. More important, a "totally hawt" blond woman named Malina had shown up at the shop to say Emily would not require her tea or my services further; the contract was considered fulfilled. Whoa. Did that mean the adorable couple of Aenghus and Emily had broken up? Or did it mean something else? And he also said she asked about a letter from a friend of hers; she wanted it back really badly but Perry couldn't find it anywhere in the shop, though he looked.

Ah, Malina had tried to get Radomila's blood back. I bet she used that hair charm on Perry and he turned the store upside down trying to find it for her. And now I wondered if Fagles and the gang had gone through the books in my study when they searched my house. If they had, they might have found the scrap of paper with Radomila's blood on it . . . and that associate lawyer of Hal's easily could have missed it or not known its significance.

Better to save such questions for Hal at Rúla Búla, I thought. I assumed my house and the shop would be watched, so I took a taxi instead to the widow MacDonagh's house.

"Ah, Atticus, me lad!" The widow smiled a cheery greeting and raised her morning glass of whiskey at me from the porch. "What happened to yer bicycle that yer drivin' up to me door in a taxi?"

"Well, Mrs. MacDonagh, I had myself one of the most hectic Sundays you could possibly imagine," I said, seating myself in a rocking chair next to hers and sighing in satisfaction. That's always a good thing to do with the widow: She likes to think that her front porch is the most welcoming and relaxing spot in the city. She might be right.

"Did y'now? Do tell, me boy." She clinked the ice in her glass and eyed the level of liquid speculatively. "But first I'll be gettin' meself a refill, if y'wouldn't mind sittin' fer a spell." She pushed herself up out of the chair with a couple of creaks and said, "Ye'll be takin' a glass with me, won't ye? 'Tisn't Sunday anymore, and I can't imagine ye objectin' to a cold handful of Tullamore Dew."

"Ah, you're right, Mrs. MacDonagh, I have no need to refuse, nor would I want to. A cold glass would be lovely."

The widow's face shone and her eyes began to fill as she looked down at me gratefully, tousling my hair as she made her way to the door. "Yer a fine lad, Atticus, drinkin' whiskey with a widow on a Monday."

"Not at all, Mrs. MacDonagh, not at all." I really did enjoy her company. And I knew too well the loneliness that clamps around one's heart when loved ones have passed on before. To have that companionship, the comfort of someone being at home for you for years, and then suddenly *not* to have it anymore—well, every day can seem darker after that, and the vise clutches tighter in your chest every night you spend in a lonely bed. Unless you find someone to spend some time with (and that time is sunlight, golden minutes when you forget you're alone), that vise will eventually crush your heart. My deal with the Morrigan aside, it's other people who have kept me alive so long—and I include Oberon in that. Other people in my life right now, who help me forget all the other people I have buried or lost: They are truly magic for me.

The widow returned with two glasses of whiskey on the rocks, humming an old Irish tune as she jiggled the ice around. She was happy.

"Now tell me, lad," she said as she sank back into her chair, "what made yer Sunday so dreadful."

I took a sip of the whiskey and enjoyed the burn of the alcohol and the chill of the ice. "At this point, Mrs. MacDonagh, I'm thinking I should have taken you up on your offer and gone to get baptized. Was the service properly mellow yesterday?"

The widow cackled and grinned at me. "So mellow I can't even remember enough to tell ye what the father said. Right boring it was. But *you*," she said, pronouncing the word carefully like an American and grinning, "had an exciting day?"

"Oh, aye. Got myself shot."

"Shot?"

"Just a flesh wound."

"Attaboy. Who shot ye?"

"A Tempe police detective."

"Lord ha' mercy, I saw something about that in the paper this mornin'! TEMPE DETECTIVE SHOT DEAD BY POLICE, it said, and a subhead said, *Detective shot civilian without cause*. But I didn't read the whole thing."

"Yep, that was me."

"Well, I'll be! Why did the daft fool shoot ye? It wasn't because of y'killin' that worthless Brit bastard, was it?"

"No, not at all," I said. And so I whiled away a pleasant hour telling the widow just enough of the truth to entertain her yet keep her safe. Eventually I made my farewells, promised to trim that grapefruit tree soon, and walked over to Mill Avenue and thence north to Rúla Búla. I got some odd looks, and people gave me a wide berth when they saw the sword hilt peeking over my shoulder, but otherwise it was uneventful.

I got there a few minutes early and Hal wasn't there yet, so I took a seat at the bar and grinned charmingly at Granuaile. Gods Below, but she was a vision! Her red hair was still curly and damp from a shower she must have taken right before coming to work. Her teeth flashed white at me for a moment, and then she sauntered over to me with a lopsided smirk on her face.

"I knew I shouldn't have worried," she said. "When I saw that article in the newspaper, I was thinking I might not see you for weeks. And now here you are, a supposed shooting victim, looking downright thirsty."

"Oh, I'm a shooting victim all right," I said. "I just heal fast."

Granuaile's expression abruptly changed. Her eyes narrowed and she tilted her head to the side as she placed a bar napkin in front of me, and her voice became throatier as she spoke with a newfound accent: "Druids usually do." With only three words to work with, all I could do was hazard a guess that the accent was from somewhere on the Indian subcontinent. Then, without much of a pause, the old Granuaile—the perky and beguiling barmaid—was back. "What'll it be? A Smithwick's?"

"What? How can you change gears like that? What did you just say to me?"

"I asked if you wanted a Smithwick's," she said, her face bemused.

"No, what you said before that."

"I said you looked thirsty."

"No, what did you say after that and before the Smithwick's?"

"Um . . . " Granuaile's eyes boggled at me uncertainly for a moment, and then comprehension dawned—at least, it did for her. "Oh, I know what happened. *She* must have talked to you. It's about time. She's been wanting to talk for weeks now."

"What? Who? You can't throw around pronouns like that without their antecedents if you want people to follow you."

She smiled and then held up her hands. "Listen, you're going to need a drink and time for a long story."

"Well I'll have a Smithwick's, then, but I don't have much time. I'm meeting my lawyer here in a few minutes."

"Gonna sue them, eh?" She grinned as she went to pull a draught for me.

"Yes, I'm thinking that they deserve a nice lawsuit."

"Okay then, maybe you can hang out for a little while afterward and I'll let you talk to her again." She placed the dark beer down on my napkin and smiled again. I melted inside and began to wonder if it was Granuaile that had this effect on me or whoever it was she had hitchhiking in her brain.

"You'll let me? Seemed like whoever it was chose her own time to speak up and you didn't have much say in the matter."

"She doesn't do that often," Granuaile said, brushing off her temporary possession as a minor irritation, as if it were a mosquito bite. "Usually she's very polite about leaving me in control."

"A name. Give me a name. Who is she?"

Before she could answer, Hal and Oberon entered the pub, both of them greeting me loudly, though only Hal could be heard and seen by everyone else. Oberon was still in camouflage, but I could see flashes of color shimmering rapidly in the air—he must have been wagging his tail like mad. Someone was bound to notice if that kept up; it wasn't as if Rúla Búla was empty during the lunch hour.

<Atticus! I'm so happy to see you! Werewolves have no sense of humor!>

"Hi, Hal," I waved, then switched mental gears for Oberon's sake.

I'm glad to sort of see you too, buddy. Go hide under the table of an empty booth really quick before some-

one sees your tail wagging and wonders if they've had too much to drink. I'll come pet you and get some sausages for lunch. Be careful not to run into anyone.

<Okay! Wow, I've missed you!>

I told Granuaile we'd settle up later when I settled down for a nice long talk. She nodded and waved as I followed Hal to a booth where Oberon was waiting, his tail thumping loudly against the seat. People were looking around, wondering what was making the noise.

"By Odin's beard, get that hound to calm down," Hal growled.

"All right, I'm on it," I said as we slid into the booth. I found Oberon's head and began scratching him behind the ears.

Okay, buddy, you need to calm down. Your tail is giving you away.

<But I'm so excited to be with you again! You have no idea how bitchy werewolves can be!>

I have a pretty good idea, believe me. And I appreciate your being good all that time. That's why I'm getting you two orders of bangers and mash, but you need to chill out, because we're starting to get unwanted attention.

<OH! Okay! I'll try! But it's REALLY REALLY hard to chill! I want to play!>

I know, but we can't right now. Back up and trap your tail against the wall—there. Now, did you behave perfectly while you stayed with Hal?

<Yes, I didn't leave a single mark on his upholstery, and I didn't break anything in his house either.>

Aren't you leaving something out? Hal told me you ripped up his air freshener.

<I was doing him a favor! No self-respecting canine enjoys the smell of citrus!>

Heh! You have a point. Quiet now, here comes the waitress.

We ordered two plates of the finest fish and chips and two plates of bangers and mash for Oberon. The poor dog was about to go nuts—I really needed to let him run somewhere until he collapsed.

"Thanks for your patience, Hal," I said after the waitress left. "He's just happy I'm still alive and all that."

"Snorri fixed you up, then?"

"That and a night in the park worked wonders. I feel great."

"Try to feign some pain when the Tempe police see you, please. You have a bandage on your chest, I hope?"

"No, but I can put one on if I need to."

Hal nodded. "I think it would be wise. It will be tough to press our suit if they see no evidence of you being shot the day after."

Hal reviewed with me what the security camera revealed—namely, that we had the most airtight case possible against the Tempe police for shooting a citizen for no probable cause—and we spent some time hashing out how to deal with police questions, the nature of the suit, and how much we'd ask for.

"Look, I'm going to give you my instructions now," I said. "When the money is finally in your account, I want you to take your cut, then reimburse me for Snorri's fees for last night. The remainder should go to Fagles's family as an anonymous donation, all right? I don't want to profit from some binding of Aenghus Óg's on an innocent man."

Hal regarded me steadily for a moment as he chewed a succulent piece of beer-battered cod fillet. Then he said in a dry voice, "How very noble of you."

I nearly choked on a chip. "Noble?" I spluttered.

<Told you werewolves were bitchy,> Oberon said smugly as he inhaled a sausage. I ignored him and concentrated on Hal's gibe.

"Nobility has nothing to do with it. And I'm not knocking you for making a buck on the situation. All I'm saying is that I don't want to profit by it, not even by getting some dubious credit for my charity."

Hal apparently had some doubts but wasn't willing to say them aloud, so all he said was "Hmph," as he wiped his hands on a napkin.

"So listen," I said, changing the subject and trying to cover the slobbery licking noises Oberon was making, "I got a lead on our mysterious barmaid."

"The redhead who smells like two people?"

I blinked at him. "You never told me that," I said.

"As I recall that particular conversation, you asked me if she smelled like a goddess"—he began to tick off my queries on his fingers—"a demon, a lycanthrope, or some other kind of therianthrope." Hal smirked. "You were too smitten at the time to ask me what she actually smelled like."

Oberon? Is the werewolf telling me the truth?

<Don't know for sure. I never paid her much attention, and his nose might be a bit better than mine. If you would just let me go have a nice sniff of her ass, I could—>

Never mind.

"All right, Hal, what else does she smell like?"

"I've told you all I know, Atticus. You can shift to a hound and smell her yourself if you want." He placed his hands flat on the table and drummed his fingers, deliberately trying to goad me.

"Thanks, but I'm going to find out the old-fashioned way. She's going to tell me what's going on—after I'm through with you."

"Ah. Is that my cue to leave, then?"

"Almost. This might take a while, so I want you to take Oberon with you to the widow MacDonagh's house."

Hal winced and Oberon whined.

<Do I have to?>

"Must I really?"

"Yes," I said to both of them.

They left a bit disgruntled but quietly enough, leaving me to settle up with the waitress. She looked at the plates of bangers and mash, which looked like they had been licked disturbingly clean, and then at the plates of fish and chips, which had a few scraps of detritus and slaw on them as normal plates would—and then glanced at me uncertainly, knowing that something was very wrong but unable to imagine a satisfactory explanation.

I really enjoy moments like that. Thinking it would be amusing to create another, I dispelled Oberon's camouflage so that the sudden appearance of a huge dog would be sure to startle someone on Mill Avenue, and if that someone was Hal, so much the better.

The fine bar at Rúla Búla had a few more stools available as the slightly sauced lunch crowd returned to their jobs, and Granuaile had nothing to do but polish glasses when I sat down in front of her. Head slightly bowed, her green eyes locked on to mine as she seductively licked her upper lip, a coy smile playing at the edges of her mouth. Refusing to be toyed with, I looked up at the high shelves full of whiskey and knickknacks as if she were doing nothing more interesting than predicting another day of dry heat, and she chuckled at me.

"What'll it be, Atticus?" she said, placing a napkin in front of me.

"A name, I believe, was where we left off."

"You're going to need a drink first."

"Tullamore Dew, then, on the rocks."

"You got it. But you're going to have to be patient. I'm going to tell this my way."

"Your way? No one else's? Like, no one else in your head?"

"That's right. My way," she said, pouring me a generous shot over ice. She placed it squarely in front of me, then folded her arms under her bosom and leaned against the bar, her face only a foot away from mine. Perfect skin, a slight tilt to the end of her nose, strawberry gloss on her lips. It was difficult not to think about kissing her, especially as she pursed her lips for a moment before saying, "So. You're a Druid."

"If you say so. What are you?"

"I am a vessel," she replied, and then her eyes grew round. "Or maybe you should think of me as a Vessel with a capital V. That would be more impressive, more mysterious and Scooby-Doo, you know?"

"Okay. A vessel for what, or for whom?"

"For a very nice lady from southern India. Her name is Laksha Kulasekaran. You should not be alarmed at all by the fact that she's a witch."

Chapter 19

Gods Below, I hate witches.

Since one of them was probably listening to me through Granuaile's ears, however, I thought it more discreet to keep that observation to myself. But doubt would be permissible to express where outright disdain would not. I gave her my best Harrison Ford half grin o' cynicism, worn by every character from Deckard to Han Solo to Indiana Jones, and picked up my glass. "A nice lady, huh?"

"Very nice." Granuaile nodded slowly, ignoring my look of disbelief.

I took a luxurious sip from the glass and waited for her to continue, but apparently the ball was in my court. If doing things her way meant I had to ask more questions, so be it. "And how long has this nice lady had a timeshare in your noggin?"

"Since shortly after you came back from that trip to Mendocino."

"What?" Even though I had just taken a sip of fire water, I suddenly felt cold.

"You remember. You turned into a sea otter and removed a pretty golden necklace set with rubies from the hand of a skeleton that was—what?—only fifty feet below the surface and a couple of feet beneath the sand?"

Chills and thrills at the Irish pub. "How do you know about that?"

"How do you think? Laksha told me."

"Right, but how does she know?"

"She was originally the owner of that skeleton, but that particular mortal coil failed her in 1850. Since then, and up until recently, she resided in the largest ruby of that necklace."

I decided to save all my questions about turning rubies into soul catchers for later. "Then what happened?"

"Well, you can probably figure it out from there. Once you got the necklace, what did you do with it?"

"I gave it to a witch named Radomila—"

"Who is not as friendly as she likes to pretend and happens to live upstairs from me in a very stylish urban condo—"

"And she promptly exorcised Laksha from the necklace—"

"And that's how I got a roommate in my skull!" Granuaile pushed back from the bar and clapped manically for me as if I had just finished playing *Rhapsody in Blue* in a third-grade talent show.

"Well, okay, I understand now, but I think we skipped a few of the details." I downed the rest of my whiskey, and when I put the glass down, Granuaile was there with the bottle, ready to refill it.

"You're going to need a double," she said, pouring more than was probably advisable. "Nurse that for a bit while I get some work done." Then she slid out of my vision to attend to her few remaining customers.

I had plenty of thoughts to nurse along with the whiskey. Indian witches, in my limited experience, were capable of some really dark hoodoo, and any witch capable of jumping out of one body into a gemstone and then into another body after 160 years or so had some serious magical muscle. My main question was how I could get the witch out of Granuaile's head safely—and who else would have to suffer to make it happen.

The witch obviously wanted my help with something, and I could only assume that she wanted a new body to inhabit. But I didn't have any of those currently in stock, and bodies were one of the few things you couldn't buy (yet) on Amazon.

Whatever this Indian witch wanted from me, I knew it would mean quite a bit of trouble, and it didn't escape me that I owed the lot of it to Radomila, along with so many other recent woes. A confrontation with her—and, by extension, her entire coven—might soon be unavoidable. On this gloomy note, Granuaile returned.

"Right about now I bet you're wondering what Laksha wants," she said lightly.

"That thought had indeed crossed my mind."

"But what you should be wondering is what your favorite bartender wants."

"Is that so?" I grinned.

She nodded. "It is. You see, I kind of like having Laksha in my head. She's been teaching me all kinds of stuff."

"Such as?"

"Such as, all the monsters are real—the vampires and the ghouls and even the *chupacabra*."

"Really? How about Sasquatch?"

"She doesn't know about that one; it's too modern. But all the gods are real, and for some reason almost everyone who knows him thinks that Thor is a giant dick. But the most interesting thing she's told me so far is that there's still one honest-to-goodness Druid walking around after all the rest have died, and I've served him a whole lot of dark beer, bottles and bottles of whiskey, and occasionally flirted with him shamelessly."

"Well, if you're going to flirt, that's the only way to do it."

"Are you really older than Christianity?"

There was no use lying. The voice in her head had already told her everything. Besides, the whiskey was good, and I could blame everything I said on it if I had to. "Yep," I admitted.

"And how did you manage that? You aren't a god."

"Airmid," I said simply, thinking Granuaile would have no idea what I was talking about.

She narrowed her eyes. "Are you talking about Airmid, daughter of Dian Cecht, sister of Miach who was slain?" she asked.

That sobered me up some. "Wow. You'd win a shit-load of money on *Jeopardy!* with a brain like that. They teach Celtic mythology at the university here?"

Refusing to be distracted, Granuaile pressed, "You're telling me you know the herblore of Airmid? The three hundred sixty-five herbs grown from the grave of Miach?"

"Aye. All of it."

"And why would she have shared such priceless knowledge with you?"

That was a story for another day. "Can't tell you." I shook my head with seeming regret. "You're too young."

Granuaile snorted. "Whatever. So is this lore of Airmid's the secret to your eternal youth?"

I nodded. "I call it Immortali-Tea because I'm fond of puns. I drink it every week or so and I stay fresh and unspoiled."

"So this handsome face of yours isn't an illusion? It's really you?"

"Yes. Biologically, I'm still twenty-one."

"Out. Fucking. Standing. Wow." She leaned forward over the bar again, even closer than she had before. "So here is what I want, Atticus." I could smell her strawberry lip gloss, the peppermint of her breath, and that peculiar scent that I now knew was only half hers: redwine bouquet mixed with saffron and poppies. "I want to be your apprentice. Teach me."

"Truly? That is what you want?" I raised my eyebrows.

"Yes. I want to be a Druid."

I hadn't heard that one in more than a century; the last person to ask me to teach them was one of those silly Victorians who thought Druids wore white robes and grew beards like cumulonimbus clouds. "I see. And what do I get in return?"

"Laksha's help. Her gratitude. And mine."

"Hmm. Let's put some details with each of those, if we're bargaining."

"Laksha knows you have a problem with Radomila."

"Wait," I said, putting up a hand to forestall her speech. "How does she know that?"

"Two of the coven came in here yesterday while I was working, and she—or rather, I—overheard snatches of their conversation. When I heard your name I started paying attention. They were talking about taking something away from you, but I don't know what because they never called it by name."

I grimaced. "I know what they want. Did they say how they were going to manage it?"

"No, they were talking about how they'd be rewarded once they got it."

"Interesting. What did they say?"

"They mentioned Mag Mell."

"You're kidding. Mag Mell? He was going to give them passage through there?"

"That and a permanent estate."

"Unbelievable." My nostrils flared and my fingers tightened around my glass. "Do you know what Mag Mell is?"

"I had to look it up, but yes. It's one of the Fae planes. The really posh one."

"Aye, the really beautiful one. And it's being sold off to Polish witches. I wonder if Manannan Mac Lir knows anything about it." Manannan was supposed to be the ruler of Mag Mell. If he knew about Aenghus Óg's promise and had done nothing, then he was part of the collusion against Brighid; the more likely scenario was that Aenghus Óg was plotting against Manannan as well.

"I don't have an answer for that," Granuaile replied, "but I heard one say to the other that they had to leave because Radomila would be waiting for them. Obviously that piqued Laksha's interest, and that's how she knows your interests and hers coincide. She wants you to get her a shot at Radomila so she can get the necklace back."

"If you live below Radomila, why can't she just take a shot any night of the week?"

"Radomila's condo is highly protected, the same as your home is probably protected. Laksha needs you to get Radomila out of her safety zone and keep her distracted for about five minutes."

"That's it?"

"And maybe get something of Radomila's."

"Ah, I see. How about a drop of her blood?"

"That will do," Granuaile said.

"Does Laksha realize that besides the two you saw here, Radomila has eleven other witches in her coven, all of them magically accomplished? She's picking a pretty big fight."

"Laksha can take them all once she has her necklace back."

"Really?" If that wasn't overconfidence, then it was pretty scary. I'd be able to hold off a coven like theirs long enough to run away. Take them out all by myself? Not so much. "What's so special about the necklace?"

"I'll let her tell you soon." Granuaile waved away the question. "Don't get distracted. Laksha says that she is already grateful to you for rescuing her from the sea, but if you help her earn true freedom again, she will grant you any boon that is in her power to give."

"And how do I earn her true freedom?"

"Distract Radomila so that she can get the necklace back."

"There has to be more to it than that. For example, where is she going to go? Into Radomila, or back into the necklace? She's not staying in your head, is she?"

"No." Granuaile shook her head. "She's been a wonderful guest, but we are both ready to be alone with our thoughts again. I will let her explain that. Last but not least, you will have my gratitude. I'm not able to grant you magical favors, but considering that apprentices in the old days were worked pretty hard, I'm sure I'll be working off my debt to you."

"What if I don't want an apprentice?" I asked. "I've been doing just fine without one."

"Oh, I see. Getting shot is doing just fine, is it?"

"Why can't I help you get Laksha out of your head and call it a day?"

"No deal. Laksha won't go unless you agree to my apprenticeship."

"What?" I furrowed my brow. This was wholly unexpected. Typically, any being capable of possessing another cares very little about the wants and needs of those it possesses. "Why does she care?"

"She knows that I don't want to be pulling draughts all day for every Mike and Tom who comes in here. I want to do something fantastic with my life. I'm only twenty-two, you know," she said. "I want to learn."

"That's good, because there's not much else to being a

Druid's apprentice than learning. But if I don't agree, then what happens? Laksha stays in your head forever?"

Granuaile shrugged. "No, we'll figure out something else. Eventually we'll try to get the necklace back without your help. See if someone else in town would like to earn the gratitude of a sorceress."

"And what of you, then? Will you try to become something else?"

Granuaile nodded and held my eyes. Hers were emerald dappled with light, and they reminded me of home. "If you leave me no other option, I will become a witch like Laksha. But it's not my first choice."

"Oh? And why is that?" I asked the question casually, but it was a deadly serious one—perhaps the most serious question of all. If she took this opening to make a joke or to flirt or kiss my ass, I would tell her no right then. But she paused before answering—perhaps getting coached by Laksha?

"There are several reasons, actually," she began in a low voice. "Laksha knows a great deal about magic, because she has been around for a long time. But she knows you are older than she is. Much older than any other being she has ever met, aside from gods. If that is true, then it follows you would know even more than she does and would have seen things the rest of us can only read about—and that is why I want you to teach me. I want to know what truly happened in history from someone who was there. I want to know the things you know, especially the things humanity has forgotten or never knew in the first place. It's just the general principle that knowing is better than not knowing, knowledge is power, and so on."

I've heard worse. She walked up to the precipice of brownnosing, took a good look, but stepped back at the last moment.

"Another reason," she continued, "is that I think

Laksha's magic is a bit scary, and I say that hoping she isn't offended." She rolled her eyes up for a moment, apparently conducting some internal dialogue. Then she looked back at me. "I think that much of what she has told me about her magic, and much of what I have read about magic with true power behind it, is a bit alarming. It seems to involve trafficking with H. P. Lovecraft action figures, and there are some rituals that I would have a problem with morally and, like, digestively. Toenails and body fluids—ew!" She shuddered. "But your power, a Druid's power, comes from the earth, right?"

"That's correct."

She pointed at my right arm. "Laksha tells me those tattoos aren't just for show."

"She's right."

"That sounds like something I could live with."

"Are you sure? It limits you. A Druid cannot do all the things a witch can do. If it's power you're after, then witches can access far more of it far faster than a Druid can."

"There are different kinds of power," Granuaile shot back. "And witches have the power to dominate and destroy. Your power is to defend and build."

"Nah, no." I shook my head. "I think you're romanticizing quite a bit. My powers can also be used to dominate and destroy." Aenghus Óg had certainly dominated Fagles. And Bres had tried to destroy me using a glamour.

"Okay, granted," she conceded. "Anything can be twisted from its original intent. But the intent is what I'm talking about, Atticus. Laksha knows of rituals and spells that cannot possibly be, you know, benign. The difference is, your magic can be twisted to evil purposes, but some of the magic Laksha knows cannot ever be good. That is an important distinction for me."

"So what do you think a Druid is?" I asked. If she mentioned white robes and ZZ Top beards, I would scream.

"They are healers and wise people," she said. "Tellers of tales, repositories of culture, shape-shifters according to some stories, and able to exert a little influence over the weather."

"Hmm, not bad," I said. "Do they ever kick ass?"

I said it flippantly, but she knew this was a test. "Occasionally they kicked some ass in battles." Granuaile frowned. "I mean according to some of the old legends. But they used swords and axes to do that, not magic force. That's a nice sword you have there, by the way," she said, tilting her chin to the hilt of Fragarach peeking over my shoulder. "Are you planning on kicking some ass?"

I ignored her question and asked her another. "What did the Druids do in the old legends you read?"

"Mostly they advised kings and tried to predict the future—oh, I forgot that. Divination is kind of a Druid thing. Do you cut open animals and look at their guts?" She crinkled her nose at me and held her breath.

"No," I answered, shaking my head, and she relaxed. "I prefer to cast wands."

"There, see?" She tapped me teasingly on the arm. "You don't destroy things."

"Do you seriously want to become a Druid initiate? Before you answer, let me explain what that would involve, because Laksha could not possibly know, and if you've been reading any of that New Age crap that says you only need to take some plant life and pray to Brighid or the Morrigan, well, it's not like that. First, you get twelve years of memorizing things. No spells, nothing remotely cool or powerful. Just memorizing and regurgitating for twelve years. You might be able to knock off a year or so because you're starting later than most initiates and your brain is fully developed, but still, it's a long time. You have to seriously like books and learning and languages, because you'd have to learn a few, and that's all you'd do, full time, until you're in your thirties."

"Oh," she said in a tiny voice. "What about paying bills and things like that?"

"You'd have to quit your job here and come work for me in my bookstore. To relieve the tedium of reading books, I can occasionally allow you the tedium of selling them to other people. And maybe I'll teach you how to brew some special teas."

"Wow. Okay."

"After you pass all your tests, we can start teaching you some magic. But you have to be able to draw power for that, and that means getting yourself tattooed ritualistically with vegetable-based dyes. It takes five months."

"Five months?" Granuaile's eyes bugged.

"I just told you about twelve years of study up front and you didn't even blink, and now you're worried about five months?"

"Well, this is five months of getting stabbed with a needle, right?"

"Thorns, actually. This is very old-school. Doesn't get much older."

"Yeah, see, that's a bit different than curling up with a book and a mug of hot chocolate."

"But it's necessary if you want to perform Druidic magic. It's a ritual that binds you to the earth and allows you to tap its power. And once you're bound to it, you will never want to do anything to harm it. Aenghus Óg might be dealing with demons these days, if Brighid's right, but even he wouldn't dare mess with the earth." After I said that, it occurred to me that a man willing to deal with demons might do much worse, so I added, "I hope," sotto voce.

"You talked to Brighid? And who's Aenghus Óg? You mean the old Irish love god?"

"Yeah, him," I said, mildly surprised and impressed that she was able to place the name, though I shouldn't have been after she had correctly identified Airmid. "But forget I mentioned him. The point is, Granuaile, it will be more than a decade before you get to feel anything that can be called magical power. If you're anxious to start wielding magic, Laksha might know a ritual that can get you started tonight. What kind of patience do you have?"

"The right kind," she said. "And I have enough." She reached out and covered my hand with hers, giving it a gentle squeeze. "I truly want this."

"You said you're twenty-two. Don't you have a college degree already?"

She rolled her eyes at me. "Yeah, I graduated in May with a degree in philosophy. And now I tend bar because what the hell else am I going to do with a philosophy degree?"

All right," I said after studying her face. "I'll take your application seriously and consider it. But before I make a decision, I need to speak to Laksha."

"I figured as much." She twisted her lips in an expression of regret and let her hand slip back to her side. "I need to work a bit before I let her take over, though. She doesn't know jack about bartending. Hold on." She quickly revisited her lingering patrons, getting a refill here, closing out a check there, distributing smiles and thanks and drinks with equal facility.

Tullamore Dew trickled down my throat as I considered her and reviewed why I hadn't had an apprentice in more than a thousand years. Mostly it was because everyone thought the Druids had all died out, and they didn't know there was still someone around to ask for training. I was kind of like Yoda chilling out in the

Dagobah system. But even when people found me—as they occasionally did, as Granuaile just had—training someone had been impractical, because I had to remain mobile and I couldn't afford to stay in one place for so long. I had also been working on my necklace for much of that time, and you can't concentrate on a project like that with constant questions and the need to plan instruction for someone else.

My last apprentice had left this plane near the very end of the tenth century. He was a bright, earnest lad named Cibrán, who managed to play the role of an illiterate Catholic peasant convincingly while learning the mysteries of the earth from me. I was hiding underneath the skirts of the Holy Roman Empire at the time—a far-flung fold of its skirts, really, near the city of Compostela in the kingdom of Galicia. I had a modest farm a couple of miles from town, and everyone liked me because I gave all the credit for my crops to Jesus and paid the clergy generous tithes. Cibrán's father was a smith in town, and he sent his son out to my farm a few times a week to get fresh produce and eggs from the chickens I kept. He paid me with Cibrán's labor on the farm, and that's how we found time to conduct his education. He had nearly completed his studies, and we were about to travel into the woods to begin his tattoos, when Al-Mansur's forces swept up from the southern Caliphate and sacked the city in 997, killing him and his father before I could get there to protect him. That was when I gave up on trying to be a teacher. Neither I nor the Iberian Peninsula was stable enough to allow it to bear fruit. I packed my things and headed off to Asia, eventually coming back to Europe with Khan's hordes.

Since then I had from time to time toyed with the idea of starting a small Druidic grove somewhere, but the threat of Aenghus Óg on the one hand and persecution by monotheists on the other always made that an idle daydream. Perhaps now it would not be so far-fetched, though, if I was able to survive the Morrigan's divination.

My deal with her wasn't a universal get-out-of-death-free card. It applied only to the Morrigan, who had first dibs on my life, and that was grand, no doubt; but death gods are a staple of every pantheon, and if Aenghus Óg was truly making an alliance of some kind with hell, then death would come for me on a pale horse, according to Revelation 6:8.

The part of her divination that truly bothered me was the Heather wand, which suggested that the soon-to-be-dead warrior would be surprised before he bit the dust. I didn't think Aenghus could do much to surprise me at this point, but that coven of witches certainly could. They had already surprised me several times, first with the runaround about making Aenghus impotent, then lying to my face about their alliance with him, and even giving me their leader's blood with confidence that they could either steal it back or that I would never use it against them. And all of that was accomplished by only three of the witches in their coven: What would they surprise me with when the whole lot of them focused on me?

And now here, in Rúla Búla, in Granuaile's head, was another witch who claimed she could take on the whole Polish coven by herself, provided she had a certain ruby necklace—which obviously was a potent magical item or none of the cool witches would want to kill one another for it. Did I want to let someone that powerful off the leash?

Granuaile stopped in front of me and leaned over to get my attention before I could answer the question.

"Okay, Atticus, I'm going to let Laksha come out. Play nice." She grinned impishly at me, and then her head lolled to one side as she relinquished control. When her head came back up, her expression was inscrutable, though a sense of old age was conveyed by a tightening around the eyes and mouth. Her accented voice greeted me with clipped consonants and vowels and the lilting intonation of Tamil speakers. "I have been looking forward to our conversation, Druid," she said. "I am Laksha Kulasekaran, greeting you in peace."

The transformation from a young, sunny Irish American girl to an ancient Indian witch was absolutely creepy, no matter how many words of peace came flowing out of Granuaile's mouth. It gave me what Samuel Clemens used to call a shivering case of the fan-tods.

Chapter 20

"I hope we remain at peace," I said to the witch in Granuaile's head. "Why don't you tell me how you came to be talking to me here."

"I was born in 1277 in Madurai during the reign of the Pandyan king Maravaramban Kulasekaran, whose name I honor by taking it myself," Laksha said. "I met Marco Polo when I was sixteen and through him realized how large the world must be to contain people like him in it.

"I married a Brahmin and played the dutiful wife while he was at home. While he was away, I played with the demon kingdom. I saw no other way for a woman in a caste system to free herself from that system.

"The things I have learned are mostly horrible— *rakshasas* have nothing delightful to share. The trick of transferring one's spirit from place to place I learned from a *vetala*. You have heard of them?"

"Yes," I replied. "Vedic demons. They possess corpses."

"Precisely. I use the same principle to transfer my spirit into a gem or into a person."

"Can you transfer it into anything?"

Laksha seemed surprised by the question. "I suppose. The spirit can fit almost anywhere. But why would you want to put it into something that could be broken or something that is of small worth? Gems tend to endure."

"All right. Tell me how you wound up on the ocean floor inside a ruby."

Lasksha shrugged Granuaile's shoulders. "I wanted a new life—a new world. I decided to leave India. In 1850 I bought passage on a clipper ship that ran opium to China. Once there, the owners of this ship, called the *Frolic,* wanted to capitalize on the gold rush in California. So they loaded the ship in China with expensive silks, rugs, and other luxuries that would be sold in San Francisco and insured it heavily.

"This was an opportunity I could not pass up. America was much newer than China, a place where a woman could own a business if she chose, and so I bought passage there too, bribing the captain with promises of sexual favors to keep my name off the list.

"He was unimaginative in bed and smelled awful. Perhaps he sensed my dissatisfaction, for when the ship ran into some rocks off the coast of what is now Mendocino and the hull began to fill with water, he did not take me in his lifeboat.

"Everyone got into lifeboats, but I was sharing a boat with Chinese crewmen who had no loyalty to me and did not speak any language I knew. And on the water, without the time and space for ritual, I am not powerful.

"As we were making our way to shore, with four of the men rowing, I saw that the men were looking at my necklace and talking about me. They were probably thinking that I could simply disappear, a victim of the shipwreck, and no one would be the wiser. They probably planned to sell the necklace in San Francisco and split the money between them.

"Whatever their plan was, one of them suddenly

drew a knife behind me and plunged it into my back, while another tried to tear the necklace from my throat. In tremendous pain and trying to get away from the knife, I stood up abruptly and pitched myself overboard, taking the would-be thief with me, still fighting for the necklace.

"I could feel myself dying, and I could not swim anyway. Luckily, neither could my assailant. He succeeded in pulling the necklace from my throat, but not from my hands, and soon he gave up in a panic and left me to thrash his way to the surface, where his crewmates would rescue him.

"With my vision fading and not trusting the *vetala*'s methods in water, I had to choose between leaving this world or sending my spirit into the stone through direct contact. Obviously I chose the latter, and now here I am." She did not finish her story with a smile. She simply stopped and waited for my reaction.

"All right, what are your goals now?"

"To get my necklace back and then get a new body."

"Right, let's take those one at a time. Why is it important to get the necklace back? We can go to the jewelry store and buy you a ruby right now if that's what you want."

"No. That particular necklace is a magical focus, crafted by a demon. It amplifies my powers. Does your necklace not serve the same purpose for you?" She pointed a finger at it and tilted her head quizzically.

"It wasn't made by a demon, but, yes, it serves a similar function," I replied, trying my best to sound nonchalant. All this time my Scary Witch-O-Meter had been traveling further and further into the red. The phrase *crafted by a demon* sent it all the way over to the right so that the arrow was pointing only a degree or two above the x axis. But I asked myself, Why stop there? Let's ask her a *really* scary question. "Tell me about getting a new body. How do you propose to do that?"

"In the past I just took them, but now I adhere to a higher moral standard."

"Took them? I beg your pardon, did you mean live ones or dead ones?"

"Whatever was available and attractive at the time."

"So the body at the bottom of the sea—that wasn't the body you were born with?"

"Of course not! I am not knowing of a way to make bodies last for hundreds of years."

"Of course not." I smiled and shook my head. "Stupid question, sorry." The dial on the Scary Witch-O-Meter was now maxed out. If I told her I had figured out how to make my body last thousands of years with a special tea blend, would she eat my brain? Had she heard me tell Granuaile about my knowledge of Airmid's herblore? "But forgive my ignorance on this issue—when you took a living body, what happened to the soul that was in it at the time?"

"This is the question that has puzzled humanity for centuries."

"You mean you killed them?"

"I allowed them to move on in the cycle of birth and rebirth."

I struggled to contain my disgust at her actions and her callous rationale for them. I don't think I was entirely successful; I saw the beginnings of a frown on her face as she registered how I was taking it. "How do you know they moved on?" I asked. "If you shoved their souls out of their bodies rather than allowing them to die, they may still be wandering the earth as unhoused spirits."

"That may be true. And believe me, I now know it was terribly wrong of me. I have had plenty of time to dwell on my actions over the past 160 years, and I saw how I preyed on innocent people as I was preyed upon by those Chinese sailors. It was karma coming back to me, and I know it was only a fraction of the atonement I must make for my centuries of sin."

"Would you say that your time in the ruby was a large fraction of the atonement you need to make, or do you still have a long way to go?"

Laksha raised Granuaile's eyebrows in surprise and then frowned at the question. "I think you are doubting my good intentions," she said.

"Given the very brief history you've shared with me, I think I'm taking it remarkably well. You've achieved a kind of immortality through some really evil body-snatching process, and you consort with demons."

"Consort!" Laksha looked aggrieved at that accusation. Really evil body-snatching she was okay with, apparently. But then I remembered that Flidais had accused me of consorting with vampires not so long ago, and my reaction was similar to Laksha's. That's what I hate about the Vedic concept of karma: Once somebody starts talking about it, I start noticing it.

"All right, I take it back," I said, waving my hands in frustration. I didn't want to get sidetracked here. "That word has too much baggage and I shouldn't have used it, because I hate it too. My point is that your acquaintance with demons and evil magic makes it difficult for me to trust you now and somewhat reluctant to help you. I hope you will forgive my frankness, but I prefer speaking plainly."

Laksha gave a tight grin and nodded her head once. "I respect that very much. I, too, prefer to speak plainly. So let me make something very clear: I could have taken Granuaile's body forcibly, as I used to do in days past. It would have been easier to do it that way. And if I wanted to, I could leave her at any time and jump into the body of anyone on the street or anyone sitting at the bar. But I do not wish to behave that way any longer, and that is why I asked her permission to share her body for a time, and she agreed. That is why I am trying to get my necklace back through cooperation and mutual benefit, rather than aggressive and selfish means. I am trying now to enrich the world with my gifts rather than spread chaos and ruin."

"Truly? And what will happen to Radomila if I help you?"

"Karma. It happens to everyone eventually."

I let that one slide. "How will you find another body to live in?"

"Granuaile has suggested to me that we visit a hospital where there are people deep in comas or in persistent vegetative states. Bodies that are still alive but whose spirits have already left them. Perhaps I can make use of them, reawaken the brain to a functional level. I have learned much about brains over the years."

My cell phone beeped at me and I silenced it. "And what if these bodies have spirits still tethered to them, however tenuously?"

"I would ask those spirits if they wanted my help to return to consciousness. There will be many who wish for that. I will help them if I can, then return to Granuaile and try again. Eventually, I will find one without a spirit or one that wishes to pass on. Then I may occupy that body without further staining my soul."

"So the immediate future for you works like this—please correct me if I'm wrong: I agree to take on Granuaile as an apprentice and help you make karma happen to Radomila. Then, necklace in hand, you go to a hospital and find a new body to inhabit. Is that right?"

"That is correct."

"Well, it doesn't seem to me that I'm getting much out of this scenario."

"I am ridding you of Radomila. She is a thorn in your side, yes?"

"But she is also a thorn in yours. Counting something you want to do for yourself as something you're doing for me is an accounting trick decidedly skewed in your favor."

"All right." She grinned. "I will concede that. What do you want?"

"You see this sword I have strapped to my back? It's a very powerful magical item."

"Is it? I had not noticed. May I see it?"

I carefully pulled the scabbard over my head and laid it down on the bar. I withdrew the hilt just enough to show a handbreadth of steel. Laksha studied it, Granuaile's eyebrows furrowing, and after a moment looked up at me quizzically.

"There is a spell on this that will prevent it from being removed from your person, but otherwise it appears to be a normal sword to me."

That was pretty good. She could not only sense my bindings but also determine their intent. "Precisely. That is because Radomila has placed a magical cloak on it. I want you to remove it, if you can." I could remove it at any time with my tears—or so Radomila claimed, but I didn't really trust her word anymore—and I wanted to see what Laksha could do. Those last three words guaranteed she would do it if she could. She didn't want to admit that Radomila was a better witch than she was.

"Ah, now I know what to look for. Just a minute." She bent to study the sword again, stretched out a hand toward the hilt, then stopped and looked up. "May I?" I nodded and she continued. She lifted up the hilt from the bar and peered closely at the base of it. That evidently was not enough; she closed her eyes and then drew it toward her forehead, resting it there for about five seconds. Then the mask of concentration broke and she smiled, placing the hilt back on the bar.

"Magical cloaks have to be fastened to the object, just like a normal cloak must be fastened about one's neck. The most logical place to do that on a sword would be at the base of the hilt, and that is what she has done. She did a very good job; the cloak overlaps and there is almost no magical leakage at all. What did you have to pay her for such a service?"

"Well, I went to Mendocino to fetch her a certain necklace."

Laksha threw Granuaile's head back and laughed. It was not a reassuring one.

"You gave her my necklace in exchange for this cloak! I think she got the better of you in that bargain!"

"Well, she is going to get her karma soon, isn't she?"

Laksha nodded. "Yes, she will."

"Can you remove her cloak?"

"Yes. It is the work of ten minutes."

"Excellent. There is one more small service I shall require of you to feel myself duly compensated in our exchange of favors."

The amused countenance on Granuaile's face turned suddenly businesslike. "One more. Name it."

"When this is over—when you have your necklace back and a new body to live in—you will live east of the Mississippi and never enter Arizona again without informing me first."

She narrowed Granuaile's eyes at me. "May I ask why?"

"Certainly," I said. "I have a healthy respect for your abilities, Laksha Kulasekaran. And I applaud your resolution to live cleanly and even do good works from this day forth. I especially appreciate the consideration you have shown to Granuaile to this point—and to me. But in the unlikely event you should again . . . traffic . . . with demons, I would prefer that it be someone else's problem, far, far away."

She regarded me steadily, and I thought briefly it was going to become an Ancient Geezer Staring Contest, but she dropped her eyes and nodded before it could be construed as a challenge. "Done," she said. "Contact Granuaile when you wish to dispel this cloak. It will require some preparation and some privacy. Contact her also when it is time to go after Radomila."

"I will. Thank you."

Granuaile's head lolled to the side as if she were chronically narcoleptic, and then it bobbed back up again with the native owner's personality back in charge.

"Hi, Atticus!" she said, beaming. "Need another drink yet?"

I looked at my glass, still half full, and quickly downed it. "Yep," I said, plopping the glass down a bit sloppily. "Good to have you back. I missed you." I took a deep breath and exhaled as the whiskey did its work, burning the tension away. She filled me up again and told me she'd be back after another round of visits to the rest of her customers.

I never got to enjoy that last whiskey, because that's when Gunnar Magnusson, alpha male of the Tempe Pack, came barging into Rúla Búla with most of his werewolves behind him—including Dr. Snorri Jodursson.

"Where's Hal?" he snarled at me.

"He left almost an hour ago," I said.

"Something's wrong," Magnusson said. "Have you checked your phone lately?"

"No," I admitted, then remembered it beeping at me in the middle of my conversation with Laksha. I pulled it out of my pocket and checked the display. It was from Emily, the youngest of the Sisters of the Three

Auroras. The text read, "I have your lawyer and your little dog, too! Bring the sword to me or they both die. Emily."

It had been a long time since I'd felt any desire to truly inflict pain upon another person. I tend to take the long view on dealing with irritating people—as in, I'm going to outlive whoever irritates me, so the problem will eventually go away. I had privately changed "This, too, shall pass" into "You, too, shall die," and it helped me avoid all sorts of conflict. I can honestly say I had not felt such anger thrumming in my bones since World War II, but that text managed to bring all the old rage rushing back.

She dognaps my friend, holds him for ransom, and makes *Wizard of Oz* jokes?

Gods Below, I hate witches.

Chapter 21

I showed the text to Magnusson, unable to summon anything coherent to say. He grunted at the message, and passed the phone back to me. I could see the other werewolves bristle as he communicated the message to them through their mental link.

"Will you call her for me, please," Magnusson said, struggling mightily to control his anger, "and discover where they are holding Hal? He was unconscious for a time, and now he's awake but they have him blindfolded and he cannot say where he is."

"Absolutely," I said. "Please remain quiet during the call so she will not know you are listening." Werewolves would have no trouble hearing everything she said.

Magnusson confined himself to a curt nod, and I punched in the number indicated from the text.

"It took you long enough," Emily purred at me after a single ring. "Maybe your dog doesn't mean as much to you as we thought."

"Prove to me he is still alive," I ground out. "I will not talk to you any further without that."

"I will have your lawyer confirm it," she said. "Hold on." There was a pause, some rustling and snarling, and then I heard Emily telling Hal to tell me he was okay.

"Atticus," he gasped at me, strain evident in his voice. "I see half the coven in the woods somewhere." There was a thud and a snarl, and I heard Emily in the distance shouting at him to just tell me the dog was fine, nothing more. "We're tied up to trees. Silver chains. Oberon is unharmed so far."

"That's enough!" Emily yelled. She returned the phone to her mouth and I heard a couple of whines from Oberon. He was still alive.

"In the eastern Superstition Mountains, take the Haunted Canyon trail to Tony Cabin," she said. "On some maps it's called Tony Ranch—same thing. Come alone after dark. Bring the sword. We will bring the dog and the wolf."

"If either of them is harmed, I will bring the sword into contact with your neck, and damn the consequences," my voice rasped into the phone. "Do you understand me, witch? You are bound to me by your own blood. If you kill them, you can be sure that I— along with Hal's pack—will hunt you down. You have no idea what is coming after you now."

"Don't I? I suppose I will just have to ask my friend Aenghus Óg. I'm sure he'll let me know what manner of worm you are."

"Ask yourself this, witch: If I am a worm to him, why hasn't he crushed me in the last two thousand years? And why does he feel the need to ally himself with your coven if I am so easily dealt with?"

"Two thousand years?" Emily said.

"Two thousand years?" Magnusson said.

Whoops! This is why I don't like to get angry. It makes you reveal things you would rather keep secret. Still, I couldn't let Emily know that she had scored any kind of coup by getting a fairly accurate estimate of my age, so I used it as a hammer.

"That's right, lassie, you're completely fucked. The

only chance you have of surviving this night is bringing me my friends healthy and happy." I hung up before she could reply.

"You're not going out there alone," Magnusson said immediately. He had of course heard every word.

"I was rather counting on you to come along," I replied.

"They've put the sack back over his head," Magnusson said, "but we saw six witches through the link before they did. Your hound is with them. And Hal smelled someone else there too, but didn't see who it was."

"What did it smell like?"

Magnusson's eyes rolled up as he recalled it and put words to it. "Oak and bear fur and . . . wet feathers. Some kind of bird."

"That would be a swan," I said. "It's one of Aenghus Óg's animal forms."

"Who is this Aenghus Óg?"

"Long story," I said. "The short version is this: He's a god, and he'll have some demons with him on top of the witches. I'll tell you more on the drive out there. Bottom line is we're in for one hell of a scrap. But we might be able to bring along someone they're not expecting."

"Who?"

I turned my head to find the redheaded siren pulling a pint of Guinness for an older gentleman down the bar. "Granuaile!" I called as I pulled out my wallet to pay the bill. "I will accept you as my apprentice if you will have me as your master. Do you still wish to become an initiate?"

"Very much!" She nodded and grinned at me as she placed the pint in front of the customer.

"Then tell your manager you quit, effective immediately," I said. "I will be your employer from now on. We need to leave now, though, so make it quick."

Her eyes flicked to the werewolves standing around behind me, crowded into the foyer of the pub.

"Something has happened, hasn't it?"

"Yes, it has, and we need your friend right away," I said, tapping the side of my head to make it clear I was speaking of Laksha. "This is both her chance and yours, but we have to go now."

"Okay," she said, beaming as she jogged back to the kitchen entrance to slap open the swinging door. "Hey, Liam! I quit!" Then she vaulted herself onto the bar, swung her legs around, and hopped off between a couple of stools.

"Attagirl," an elderly gentleman said, raising his pint in salute.

We left the place en masse before Liam, whoever he was, could properly register that he had just lost a damn fine bartender.

The lot of us piled into various souped-up werewolf cars parked across from the light rail station, and then we drove south on Mill to University. We took a right, and from there took a left on Roosevelt, winding up in front of the widow's house.

I promptly set them all, except Granuaile and Gunnar, to trimming the widow's grapefruit tree and weeding her flower bed. Since the Tempe police were still staking out my house and I had a pack of werewolves on the verge of going all hairy, it seemed like the best way to keep my promise to the widow and keep the Pack walking around on two legs.

While the widow was happily occupied admiring impossibly fit men and women grooming her landscape, I retired to the backyard with Gunnar and Granuaile.

"Please have Laksha remove the cloak on this now," I said to Granuaile as I placed Fragarach in her hands and dispelled the binding that kept it close to me. "And you," I said to Gunnar, "make sure she doesn't take off with my sword."

Granuaile's eyes bugged. "You think Laksha would do that?"

"No," I said. "But I've been wrong before, and I'm just paranoid, okay?"

The alpha male scowled at me. "Where are you going?"

"I'm going to get something out of my house," I said. "I'll probably be back in less than ten minutes. If I'm not, send someone to check."

Magnusson nodded, and I began stripping off my clothes.

"What are you doing?" Granuaile asked uncertainly.

"Same thing you'll be able to do in about twenty years or so," I said, pulling my keys out of my pocket and carefully laying them down on top of my jeans.

"You mean get naked? I can do that now. Wow," she sniggered, "you need to get some sun."

"Shut up. I'm Irish." I drew power from the earth through my tattoos and enjoyed Granuaile's gasp of astonishment as I turned into a great horned owl. I snapped up my key ring in my beak before launching myself into the sky on silent wings.

"Show-off," Gunnar called after me. He was just jealous. People don't gasp appreciatively when he changes form in front of them; they scream.

It was less than a minute's flight, as the owl flies, to my house from the widow's. The police sitting in the patrol car outside my house looked supremely bored. I spiraled down into my backyard for a landing and took a nice long look around before changing back into human form. My wards were still in place, and no one was watching, so I grew myself some opposable thumbs and entered through my back door. The slip of paper with Radomila's blood on it was still locked up in my bookcase, precisely where I had left it. I punched a hole through one corner and threaded it onto my key ring, then returned to my backyard. There I bound myself back to an owl, picked up the keys in my beak, and enjoyed the short flight back to the widow's house.

Granuaile was seated in the lotus position inside a circle she had traced in the dirt, Fragarach laying across her lap, cradled at either end by her hands. She was chanting something in Tamil, so I was fairly certain that Laksha was in charge.

Gunnar Magnusson was still in human form, but his hackles were up, if you know what I mean. He looked mightily relieved to see me.

"How long has she been at it?" I asked in a low voice once I had the use of my vocal cords again. My clothes were still laying where I had left them, but I didn't feel especially anxious to put them back on yet. Switching forms so quickly left me feeling a bit twitchy and sensitive, and I didn't want the abrasion or confinement until I absolutely had to have it. The widow rarely came out to her backyard, and I could see no reason why she would with all of that fine beefcake parading before her.

"Only a couple of minutes," Magnusson grumbled, almost a whisper. "But it feels like an eternity. That witch creeps me out, Atticus. Do you trust her?"

"No, I never trust witches," I said. "But I do trust her to do this job. It's an ego trip, or rather a professional pride sort of thing. If she can undo the cloak Radomila set on my sword, she proves she's better than Radomila."

"Do you need her to prove that, or is this just for her?"

"It's for me," I replied. "Radomila, not Emily, is the witch who's really holding Hal and Oberon. If we're going to take on her whole coven, we're going to need a serious witch of our own who's at least the equal of Radomila."

"Is that the entire point of this exercise? Didn't you want that cloak on there?"

I shook my head. "Not anymore. Yesterday Radomila proved that she still has a connection to this sword that she can use against me; she was able to show Aenghus Óg how to bind Detective Fagles in such a way that he could sense the cloak, and thus see my sword, even through my camouflage spell. What if she could do more to the sword through that link? Turn it against me as I wield it, perhaps? I cannot take that risk."

"No, you can't," Magnusson agreed.

"Besides, the entire reason I was cloaking it was to keep it hidden from Aenghus Óg and his allies. Since he knows where I am now and Brighid told me she wants me to keep it, there's no more reason to hide. It's actually going to help having its magic in the open, Gunnar. Because that means Aenghus Óg and the coven will be focused on me and the threat I represent. They won't be worrying about you and the Pack circling around behind them . . ."

Magnusson allowed himself a feral grin.

" . . . but they will know you are most likely coming," I continued. "They would be stupid not to prepare themselves. So you, in turn, must be prepared. They will have silver, Gunnar. Guaranteed."

The alpha male's grin melted into a snarl, and his features began to ripple as his eyes flashed bright yellow.

"Whoa, whoa! Calm yourself. Now is not the time, my friend." I placed a steadying hand on his shoulder and continued to make reassuring noises until his face stopped running like hot wax and the lights in his eyes faded to their normal brown. I heard some howls and barking in the front yard, though. Not all the Pack members had as much control as Gunnar, and he had almost lost it as the alpha.

"I am sorry," he gasped, short of breath and sweating. "But we have been provoked past all endurance."

"I know. But tell the ones who changed in the front to come back here and leave the widow alone."

"It is done," he said. Shortly thereafter, three agitated werewolves were circling the two of us but studiously keeping their eyes lowered.

I moved carefully to my clothes and started putting them on, explaining as I did so. "The widow is going to need to see a familiar face at this point," I said, "because she just watched three of your pack make the change, if I'm not mistaken."

"That she did," Magnusson confirmed. "Can she be trusted?"

"Absolutely," I replied. "Two days ago she watched me kill someone, and she offered me her backyard as a place to hide the body."

"Truly?" Magnusson raised his eyebrows in surprise. "That's a fine woman."

"The very finest." I grinned as I pulled on my pants and dropped my keys, along with the scrap of paper, into my pocket. "But she's probably a bit scared right now. When the witch is finished," I nodded over to Laksha–Granuaile, still chanting away in a trancelike state, "ask her from me to step away from the sword and allow you to take possession by my request. If she refuses, send a wolf to let me know immediately, but do not attack her. Just keep her from leaving."

"You want me to send a werewolf to bark at you like Lassie?" Magnusson looked outraged.

"Fine, come tell me yourself, then." I rolled my eyes as I pulled on my shirt. "Hopefully I'll be back in time to make the point moot."

I sprinted around the side of the house to the front

porch, where the widow was yelling at the remaining werewolves, including Dr. Snorri Jodursson, to get their damn spooky selves off her lawn.

"Mrs. MacDonagh, it's okay, they're perfectly safe—"

"Gah! Atticus, yer not one of them, are ye?" The widow raised her arm in front of her throat.

"No," I assured her. "I'm not."

"Some of yer friends turned into bloody big dogs right before me eyes!" She took a couple of deep breaths and clutched at the railing for support.

"I know. They won't hurt you, though."

"G'wan, now!" she scolded me. "Yer not goin' ter tell me it's the drink talkin'?"

"No, what you saw was real. But it's okay."

"Why? Are they Irish?"

"They're Icelandic, for the most part. The younger ones are Americans."

"Wait, wasn't Iceland a British colony?"

"No, it was a Nordic colony. Listen, Mrs. MacDonagh, I apologize, but I have some strange friends. None of them are British, though, and they won't hurt you."

"I think ye owe me an explanation, Atticus."

As a rule I don't tell the truth about the world, because shattered illusions are no fun to clean up. But if the widow had a strong enough constitution to shoo werewolves off her lawn, I figured she could handle it. We sat down in her rockers as the remainder of the Pack hurriedly cleaned up the trimmings and drifted one by one to the backyard, and I gave her the short version: There are more things under heaven and earth than are dreamt of in our philosophy—including Druids like me and werewolves like the Tempe Pack.

"Yer a real Druid? Aren't y'supposed to be dead?"

"Lots of people sure think so."

"All of it's real, then? There's no make-believe?"

"There's plenty of make-believe in the details. This

vampire I know actually likes garlic quite a bit. And werewolves, as you just saw, can change anytime, though they do try to confine it to the full moons when they have to change, because it's a pretty painful transformation."

"So God really exists?"

"All the gods exist, or at least did exist at one time."

"But I mean Jesus and Mary and all that lot."

"Sure, they existed. Still do. Nice people."

"And Lucifer?"

"I've never personally met him, but I have no doubt he's around somewhere. Allah is doing his thing too, and so are Buddha and Shiva and the Morrigan and so on. The point is, Mrs. MacDonagh, that the universe is exactly the size that your soul can encompass. Some people live in extremely small worlds, and some live in a world of infinite possibility. You have just received some sensory input that suggests it's bigger than you previously thought. What are you going to do with that information? Will you deny it or embrace it?"

She grinned fondly. "Ah, me dear boy, how can I deny anything y'say? If ye haven't killed me yet for seein' more than I ought ter, I figger ye mus' like me and ye wouldn't steer an old widow wrong. And besides that, I saw those bloody werewolves with me own eyes."

I smiled at her and patted her hand, small and wrinkled and spotted with age. "I do like you, Mrs. MacDonagh, quite a bit. I trust you and know that you're the really good sort of friend who would help me move a body, as your Sean would say. I know you must have a bushel of questions for me, but right now there's a crisis to deal with. Oberon's been kidnapped along with one of the werewolves, and that's why we're all so upset. We'll talk more tomorrow, and I promise to answer all your questions if I survive the night," I said.

The widow's eyebrows raised. "Ye've got all these nasty pooches to run around with and ye still might die?"

"I'm going to go fight with a god, some demons, and a coven of witches who all want to kill me," I said, "so it's a distinct possibility."

"Are y'goin' t'kill 'em back?"

"I'd certainly like to."

"Attaboy," the widow chuckled. "Off y'go, then. Kill every last one o' the bastards and call me in the mornin'."

"An excellent suggestion," said Gunnar Magnusson, coming around the corner and stepping onto the porch with Fragarach in his hand. His pack followed him— both in human form and wolf—along with Granuaile. Just by the way she carried herself, I could see she was still controlled by Laksha.

Radomila's cloak had most definitely been sloughed off. Fragarach practically hummed with ancient Irish juju, and as I grasped the proffered hilt and felt the magic pulse through my forearm, I was reminded of its deadly purpose and of the deadly purpose I also had now.

"Right," I said, pulling the sword out and admiring its blade. "I've waited long enough. If Aenghus Óg wants this sword, then he can have it—for just as long as it takes me to eviscerate him."

Chapter 22

The Haunted Canyon trail Emily spoke of is in the Superstition wilderness, which spans the infamous range of mountains where over one hundred stupid people have died trying to find gold. Some of the most treacherous country anywhere, it's a rocky, thorny nightmare, spotted here and there with pleasant chaparral meadows.

We drove east on U.S. 60 out past Superior and took a left on Pinto Valley Road. That led us right to a copper mine, but a public access road through that property allowed us to get to the trailhead. This was the eastern edge of the Superstitions, little traveled and fairly remote. Most people went to the Peralta trailhead, where the hiking was a bit easier and the scenery more in keeping with their preconceived notions of what Arizona was supposed to be like—majestic saguaros, ocotillo, horned toads, and Gila monsters.

The eastern side of the Superstitions was less lush high desert and more chaparral, with little cactus beyond some prickly pear and several species of agave. Still, it did not lack for spiny obstacles: There was scrub oak, manzanita, and catclaw, chokeberry bushes and whitethorn. But there were also cottonwood trees and sycamores, able to survive on the seasonal rains and flash-flooded washes winding through the canyon.

Our caravan of cars arrived at the trailhead, and

Gunnar had apparently told the Pack they could let their wolves out as soon as they got there. The lot of them leapt out of their sports models and half-tore off their clothes in their eagerness to let the rage inside them loose. Gunnar Magnusson changed as well, for we had spoken of our plans thoroughly on the ride over. Only Granuaile and I were left standing on two legs, but Laksha was in control and showed little curiosity at the spectacle of twenty werewolves changing in front of us. I beckoned her over to me.

"Let Granuaile see this, will you?" I said. "I need to speak with her anyway before we go."

"Very well," Laksha said, and then her head lolled to one side for a moment as she went to wake Granuaile. The head snapped back up and Granuaile smiled at me for a nanosecond before she registered the contorting, howling animals around us and said, "What the hell?"

"Shhh," I said. "You're safe, but I wanted you to see this. This is the Tempe Pack, and you've probably served most of them at one time or another at Rúla Búla."

"Where are we and what are we doing here?"

I explained the situation briefly, and she was relieved to hear that Laksha would soon have her chance at Radomila.

"I'm going to put a couple of bindings on you now before we go," I said, "because we're going to run through this country, not take a leisurely hike. I've been on this trail before; it climbs more than a thousand feet in the first couple of miles. So I'm going to bind you to me so that you can draw on my energy, which I pull from the earth—that means basically you can run all night without getting tired. That's the first thing you'll be able to do once you get your tattoos.

"And the other thing I'm going to do for you is give you night vision, because the sun is setting. We're going to run behind the wolves, because you really don't want to be running in front of them when they're this angry. After a couple of miles I'm going to have Laksha come back and do her thing, but I want you to have this experience."

Granuaile was a bit overwhelmed, and she confined herself to a nod and a meek little "Okay."

It was at this point that my cell phone rang.

"Wow, you get service out here?" Granuaile said.

"We're only six miles from the freeway." I didn't recognize the number, but I couldn't afford to ignore it.

"Mr. O'Sullivan," said a familiar Polish accent, "I have some important information for you."

"It's sure to be a lie, Malina," I replied, "because that's all I've heard from you up to now."

"I never knowingly lied to you," Malina said. "I believed everything I said to be true. It was only this afternoon that I found out that Radomila and Emily have made me seem to be a liar, that they have been plotting with Aenghus Óg and deliberately deceiving me and others. I have been lied to and manipulated just like you. I confronted them about it, but they refused to leave this foolish path they are on. So now our coven is split."

"Split how?"

"There are six of them waiting for you in the Superstition Mountains. They have no doubt contacted you by now."

I pretended not to hear her last sentence. "So where are the other seven?"

"We are currently at my home, and that is where we will stay while we consider what to do. We are forming a new coven and we have much to discuss."

"Which six are in the Superstitions?"

"That ungrateful snot Emily, and Radomila of course, as well as Jadwiga, Ludmila, Miroslawa, and Zdzislawa."

"And the witches with you are?"

"Bogumila, Berta, Kazimiera, Klaudia, Roksana, and Waclawa."

None of the names meant anything to me, but I filed them away for future reference. "How do I know any of this is true?"

Malina huffed in exasperation. "I suppose I can prove nothing over the phone. However, when you confront my former sisters tonight, I trust you will note my absence."

"It occurs to me that you would not be calling me if you expected me to die tonight. You're trying to prevent me from coming after you tomorrow."

"No, I fully expect you to die."

"Oh. How charming."

"I simply didn't want you to think I betrayed you. Unlike my former sisters, I have a sense of honor."

"We shall see," I said, and hung up. I'd make a point of calling her tomorrow. I shucked off my shoes as the werewolves finished their changes and milled around impatiently, waiting for me to signal them to go. "Have patience, please," I told them. "I have a couple of bindings to do."

I gave Granuaile the bindings I had promised, then told the wolves we were ready. I had to stay in human form to carry the sword and communicate with Granuaile. "We're going to sprint," I told her. "Go as fast as you can; don't worry about pacing yourself. You won't run out of breath. Just make sure you don't twist an ankle."

And with that we were off, with nothing more than a couple of excited yips from the Pack. Gunnar had strictly forbidden howling and barks by prearrangement, in hopes of keeping our numbers and our distance hidden from Aenghus Óg and the witches. The werewolves could communicate via their pack link, anyway. Our enemies might have heard the painful cries of the Pack turning wolf, but then again they might not have: Tony Cabin was a good six miles away, and the hill between us might have absorbed the sound.

Something I was curious about was whether I could shield my mind from Oberon once we got in range. I had never had any occasion to wish for such a thing before, but if he sensed me nearby, his tail would start to wag as sure as a princess waves in a parade, and that would alert our enemies to our proximity. I really didn't want to give them any warning if I could help it.

After about a half mile of running uphill at a full sprint—across rocky, treacherous terrain on a moonless night—I heard Granuaile giggle delightedly. "This is unbelievable!" she crowed. "What a trip, running with a pack of werewolves!"

"Remember this," I said, "when you get bogged down in your studies and wonder if it's all worth it. This is only a taste of what you will be able to do."

"Will I be able to turn into an owl too?"

"Perhaps. You can take four different animal forms, but those are determined by a ritual and not by whim. Everyone has slightly different forms."

"What are yours?"

"I can be an owl, wolfhound, otter, or stag. They are not forms I chose but rather forms that chose me in the ritual."

"Wow," she said, suitably awed. "That's pretty fucking cool."

I laughed and agreed with her. We crested the hill and, by prearrangement with Gunnar, we paused there at the entrance to Haunted Canyon. I had spoken with him extensively about our plans, because I could not communicate with him effectively when he was in wolf form. Communicating with Oberon was my magic, but communication amongst the Pack was their magic; I was not part of the Pack, no matter how friendly we were. And werewolves are, for the most part, immune to any magic that isn't theirs, even the benign sort that would allow me to talk to them mind-to-mind in wolf form.

"This, unfortunately," I said to Granuaile, "is where we need to part ways for some time. Laksha is going to need to rejoin us from here on out."

"Oh, okay, um, master, or sensei, or whatever. What should I call you?"

I laughed. "Archdruid would be the correct term, I suppose," I said. "But that doesn't fall trippingly off the tongue, does it? And it would turn heads in public, and we don't want that. So let's stick with sensei."

"Kick some ass, sensei." She clasped her hands together mantis style and bowed to me, and when she rose back up Laksha was in charge.

"Why was she bowing to you?" she asked in her Tamil accent.

"I'm her sensei now."

"I am not knowing this word."

"It's an honorific we've settled on. Listen, we're four miles, give or take, from Tony Cabin. How close do you need to get to Radomila?"

"To take the necklace back, I'll need to be right next to her."

"I mean how close do you need to be to, you know, make karma happen? Do you need line of sight?"

She shook her head. "I need only this drop of blood I have heard about."

I pulled Radomila's note from my pocket and handed it to her. She examined it the way a normal human being would for a couple of moments, but then she pulled some creepy witch stuff and made Granuaile's eyes roll back in their sockets so all I saw was the whites of her eyes. I knew it was something akin to my faerie specs—

the Vedic third eye that allowed them to see visible traces of magic—but it was still creepy. When she had seen what she needed to see, her eyes rolled back down like slot machine tumblers to give me double pupils. They focused on me and she said, "I can kill her from as far away as a mile with this. But I cannot kill the other witches without my necklace—unless you have their blood too?"

"No, I don't."

"I was not thinking so. You will have to get me the necklace, then, if you want me to be helping with them."

"I'll probably be busy at that point," I said dryly, thinking of Aenghus Óg. Suddenly I felt a tug at my feet, a subtle indication that someone nearby was drawing power from the earth. The only beings capable of doing that, besides me, were a few Old World dryads, Pan, and the Tuatha Dé Danann. Paranoia made me think of Aenghus Óg immediately, since I doubted Pan would be chasing any dryads in the Superstition Mountains. "Someone's coming," I said, drawing Fragarach from its sheath. The werewolves' hackles rose and they spread themselves before me, facing the direction I was facing and straining with snout and ear to sense what I had sensed. Nice doggies.

I wondered if the magic of the Tuatha Dé Danann would work on the werewolves; my own didn't seem to work very well, and it was the same as the Tuatha Dé's, albeit somewhat weaker. Laksha, I saw peripherally, had coiled Granuaile's body into a defensive stance that was probably some form of varma kalai, an Indian martial art based on attacking pressure points. She wasn't dependent entirely on magic, then, like most witches, for her offense and defense—good to know. In case, you know, we weren't on the same side someday.

The tug at my heels felt nearer—whoever it was, they

were definitely coming this way. I looked down the slope into Haunted Canyon but could not spy anything moving. The choked overgrowth of scrub oak and manzanita along the trail had quite a bit to do with that; someone determined to remain concealed could do so until they were practically on top of us. As it was almost certainly one of the Tuatha Dé Danaan, they would have camouflage cast on them in any case.

I saw a couple of werewolves snarl and leap slightly off to my left, and I shifted my stance to meet whatever threat might materialize there. The werewolves oddly tried to change course in midair, but apparently they could not avoid whatever alarmed them. Instead, they collided broadside with something that sent them whirling to the ground with dismayed whimpers.

Werewolves, in my considerable experience, simply do not *do* that. The things that werewolves attack are usually the ones whimpering in dismay—shortly before they expire from an acute case of missing jugular.

I expected Magnusson to completely lose his shit at this point and teach that thin air a lesson, or at least give his whimpering pack members a mental bitch slap. But he and the rest of the Pack all flopped down, rolled over, and presented their throats to the air.

Werewolves *never* do that. I was very glad I wasn't in hound form—and then understanding broke upon me as Flidais, goddess of the hunt, dispelled her invisibility and addressed me with a pack of submissive werewolves at her feet.

"Atticus, I must speak with you before you confront Aenghus Óg," she said. "If you proceed as is, this magnificent pack will be destroyed."

Chapter 23

I was doubly resolved never to shape-shift around Flidais again. I had already experienced the danger before, but this object lesson positively cowed me. Her control over the animal form was absolute; I had not thought it possible to subdue a pack of werewolves through magic, but she had just made it look effortless. It provided me with a new perspective on our earlier encounter: My amulet had indeed saved me from the brunt of her power, where I had thought it had failed somehow—and Oberon had been as helpless to disobey her as earth is helpless to remain dry in the presence of rain.

"Flidais." I nodded to her and lowered my sword but did not relax my grip. I could bring it up with a snap of the wrist if necessary. "What news?"

"The coven of witches with Aenghus Óg is tasked with taking out the Pack so that you arrive without help. They have rigged traps around the cabin with magical triggers that will deliver silver in several ways."

"Physical traps with magic triggers?" I said.

"Aye. And even were the Pack to get past them, the witches all have silver daggers."

"Have you chosen sides, then?" I asked.

The red-haired goddess gave me an enigmatic shrug. "I will not fight for you or with you. Nor will I walk the path you walk."

"Because you may not be seen to take sides against the Tuatha Dé Danann."

One corner of her mouth quirked up, and she gave the barest of sardonic nods. No, Flidais would never be seen taking sides, but she could certainly give one side an intelligence bombshell on the sly. It was then I remembered she had sworn to be revenged upon Aenghus for interrupting her hunt in Papago Park. I was glad we had no quarrel; I think I would have had an arrow in my gob long ago. She had her bow and quiver with her now, I noticed; the protective rawhide strips on her left arm were new and fresh.

"Might you have any suggestions for us as to how we should avoid those traps?" I asked. Laksha had stepped behind me and was trying to be inconspicuous. If she was hoping Flidais wouldn't notice her, it was too late. Flidais had already registered her presence and decided she was nothing to worry about.

"You can't avoid them," she said to me. "You'll have to trip one. But they've only set up a circular perimeter, thinking the Pack will come from all directions."

"That's probably what they would have done."

"Aye. But if you attack one point and make a sacrifice, the rest will be able to get through. Then they will have only the daggers to deal with and whatever magic the witches can muster with werewolves at their throats."

"And I will have to deal with Aenghus Óg."

"Aye, he's there. He is doing something in the fire pit, drawing large amounts of power." Great.

"And what of my hound and my lawyer?"

"They are fine, bound to a tree but otherwise unharmed."

"That is good news. Thank you. But what about the Pack here?" I said, gesturing to the werewolves lying passively on the ground. "What have you done to them?"

"I have subdued them, of course. They were agitated and two of them leapt at me. We could hardly have a conversation while they were attacking me, and since you were doing nothing about it, I took the duty for myself."

"I have no power to subdue werewolves," I said, "and I would not use it even if I did."

"Oh?" She raised her eyebrows. "Then you are going to face an interesting situation when I leave, Druid."

"That's right," I said. "If they were agitated before, they will be pissed beyond reason when you release them. They will turn on me merely to vent their spleen."

"Vent their spleen? Are you trying to quote Master Shakespeare to me again?" She smiled at me, and I began to think of things I really shouldn't before going into battle. "Because no one in this age speaks of spleen venting."

"No, you're right," I said. "I get my idioms mixed up sometimes. It would be more contemporary to say they're going to go apeshit on my ass. So what would you suggest?"

"Communicate with them. Explain what I did and refocus them on their goal. They should vent—I mean, go apeshit—on the witches' asses, not yours."

"I cannot do that," I said. "I fall far short of your skills in these matters, Flidais."

She frowned at me but said nothing. Then she considered the werewolves splayed on the ground, and I felt her draw a bit more power as she spoke to them through their pack link. After about half a minute, the werewolves leapt to their feet as one and snarled at her. It became one long, threatening growl, and if I had that many burning eyes glowering at me, I'd probably have issues with a squirming colon. But Flidais appeared unconcerned. She said aloud, "Go and free your second. If your sacrifice survives the witches' traps, I will render what aid I can to remove the silver. You are a strong pack. Fight well, feast well, and be whole again."

Gunnar Magnusson barked a last note of defiance before turning around and launching himself down the path into the canyon. His pack quickly followed, and I had no time to do anything except mutter a clipped "Bye!" before taking off after them, Laksha close behind.

The werewolves were not bothering to keep their pace down for the slow bipeds anymore. They quickly outran us, and Laksha and I were left running alone. Some of them—perhaps many of them—would be severely injured or even killed tonight to rescue one of their own. But for Gunnar and the rest of them, this wasn't about saving a pack member so much as saving face. No one could be allowed to mess with the Pack and not suffer retribution—with, perhaps, the exception of Flidais.

I was glad not all the Tuatha Dé Danann had her gifts. Clearly Aenghus Óg did not, or he would not have given the coven the task of taking out the Pack. He had other gifts, though, and I could only hope mine were a match.

We ran in silence for a while, but by and by Laksha observed that Flidais's interference might turn out to be a good thing.

"I have never seen a pack so angry," she said. "It makes them stronger. They might survive the silver."

"Let's hope we all survive."

We ran six-minute miles over rough terrain in the unforgiving Superstitions, so we approached the Tony Cabin area in a little over twenty minutes. We heard the werewolves ahead of us going apeshit on someone, and that's when Laksha pulled up and told me she would attack Radomila from where she stood. Her eyes were rolled up in her head again, and I wondered if Granuaile would get a headache later.

"We are closer than we need to be now, and the werewolves could use my help. It will be only a few minutes."

I wasn't sure how she knew they needed her help. They sounded pissed off, but that didn't necessarily mean they required aid. "All right," I said. "I'll see you there."

Laksha was already drawing a circle in the dirt. "I am counting on it," she said.

I continued on in solitude.

Tony Cabin isn't situated in a bowl, nor on a hill, but rather in the middle of a meadow graced by little beyond dried grasses and weeds. Around it, sycamores and scrub oaks as well as mesquite and palo verde provide ample cover for stalkers. There are a few trees near the cabin itself, including a couple of sycamores, and it was to these that Hal and Oberon were chained. Oberon had not yet realized I was near, and for that I was grateful and continued to shield my thoughts as best as I could.

I saw where the werewolves had set off the witches' trap: It was hard to miss, because there was a werewolf moaning pitiably on the ground, with silver needles sticking out of him like S & M acupuncture. It was a bit difficult to tell for sure, but I thought it might be Dr. Snorri Jodursson's wolf, and I wondered how he had managed to draw the shortest straw. He wasn't at the bottom of the Pack but rather near the top—and as the Pack's doctor in both human and wolf form, they could ill afford to lose him. I would never understand pack politics.

There was a large fire pit giving off quite a bit of light in front of the cabin, but none of that light came from burning wood. It was orange and white and swirled around the pit in a torus like a hellish Creamsicle. It lit up the meadow fairly well, so I paused in the darkness about twenty yards north of Snorri's prone form and scouted the scenario.

The werewolves had already taken out three of the witches and dropped a fourth even as I watched, but they had taken some casualties as well; I saw three werewolves bleeding on the ground near the bodies of the witches. They were alive but in very bad shape. The witches were awfully fast with those knives, perhaps using the speed spell that Malina had offered to use on me. There were only two witches left—Emily and Radomila. (Malina and the other witches were nowhere in sight, which meant that she had been telling the truth on the phone.) Radomila would indeed prove a challenge to the werewolves: She was chanting a spell from within a cage settled on the opposite side of the cabin from the prisoners, the bars of which were no doubt lined with silver. The werewolves wouldn't be able to touch her.

Emily, however, had no such protection, and I saw her Barbie-doll eyes grow even wider than usual as she realized she was next up to become a chew toy. She was on the far side of the meadow, just visible between the sycamores next to the cabin, and she did not seem likely to stand her ground and die fighting like her sisters. Even as I thought this, she turned and ran into the woods, which would only encourage the werewolves to pursue her, frenzied as they were.

But then I saw it was cleverness as much as cowardice; she would lead them out to the perimeter of traps, which was still active, and the werewolves would trigger it again. Gunnar, whose wolf form was leading the chase, apparently realized this just in time, and he pulled up and commanded the Pack to stop too. They stood and snarled at the darkness Emily had disappeared into, frustrated to be denied her flesh but reluctant to leave the meadow when they were so close to freeing their pack mate.

It was time for me to act. There was nothing more they could do—I sincerely doubted they would be able to take on Aenghus Óg and last long. I doubted I could either, but I had some hope.

My nemesis was standing in the orange glow of that hellish fire he had summoned, facing the west, armored head to toe in silver plate. That wasn't for my benefit: He knew that if I could get past his guard, Fragarach would slice through the armor as if it were tissue paper. It was proof against the werewolves, in case they got past the witches—which they practically had, with Emily run off into the woods and Radomila still chanting something but having no visible effect.

Aenghus wore a Greek Corinthian helmet, so it was all of one piece and required no visor plate. It afforded him maximum visibility and breathability, but it would be extraordinarily difficult for a werewolf to get a lucky claw in there or underneath the long cheek guards to get at his throat. Even if one did, his neck was well protected with a solid gorget over silver chain, and he also had a chain skirt falling past his knees; there would be no quick swipes at his hamstrings from behind. Ankles are usually tough to protect from a rear attack, but he knew that if he was dealing with a pack of werewolves, they'd go after his Achilles tendon, so in a surreal mash-up of medieval armor and American spaghetti westerns, he actually wore silver spurs, and there were spikes thrusting from the backs of his calves.

Given all of this, it was clear he'd never expected me to arrive alone, and neither had the witches. He'd planned to involve the Tempe Pack all along—for many months, it would seem, because that suit of armor had to be a fairly recent commission. Werewolves were never a problem in Tír na nÓg, and one doesn't find custom suits of silver armor on Blue Light Special at Kmart. It spoke to me of a level of connivance that chilled the marrow of my bones—when he found out where I was, he had known I would involve the Pack through my lawyers—and I shuddered as I crouched behind the trunk of a cottonwood. It seemed to me as if we were playing a game of chess and he had thought many more moves ahead than I had. He had outplayed me with the witches from the beginning, had two different police departments playing fetch for him, and had anticipated or even counted on a pack of werewolves showing up tonight: What else had he thought of ahead of time? What was he doing with that fire pit, and what was Radomila up to? What would happen once I stepped out there and revealed myself?

As if in answer to my thoughts, something began to coalesce out of the fire pit and take shape to the right of Aenghus Óg. It remained somewhat insubstantial, with just enough translucence to show me the outlines of the cabin behind it, but its physical presence was undeniable: It was a tall, hooded figure on a pale horse, and its name was Death.

If I fell tonight, Death would come for me without delay. Somehow, Aenghus Óg knew of my bargain with the Morrigan. The simplest explanation, of course, was that she had told him. She would not betray her word to me—she'd never take my life—but I had never required her to keep our bargain secret. I had stupidly assumed she would keep it to herself so that Brighid would never know, but now it occurred to me that perhaps the Morrigan had decided to ally herself with Aenghus Óg, since Brighid had pointedly not asked for her help. If victorious, she would eliminate her biggest rival amongst the Tuatha Dé Danann and rid herself of a troublesome Druid who had lived long past his expiration date.

Something else disturbed me: Flidais had not been joking when she said Aenghus was drawing large amounts of power. It was dangerously high—so high that he was flirting with killing the earth for miles around, creating a blighted zone. If he went much further, it would take years of coaxing and care from a grove of Druids to bring it back to life again.

That sincerely chapped my hide and pulled me out of the whirlpool of doubt in which I had been flailing. Up to the point where I realized the threat he represented to the earth, I could have turned around and run. I could have gone to Greenland, where nothing was green, and hidden for a century or two. But now I could not. Aenghus Óg could betray me all he wanted, kidnap and even kill my beloved wolfhound, kill the whole Tempe Pack, even usurp Brighid's throne to become First among the Fae, and I could have chalked it all up to the steep price one pays sometimes for living another day. But killing the earth, to which he himself was bound with the same tattoos I wore, bespoke an evil I could not countenance—it was solid proof that his priorities had widely diverged from the old faith, and he had bound himself to darkness. That's what made me stand up and draw Fragarach from its sheath and charge into the circle of hellish light, leaping over the whimpering form of Dr. Jodursson. If I were to die tonight, then it would be a death any Druid would be proud of—not fighting on behalf of some petty Irish king's wounded pride or his yearning for power over a small island in the great wide world, but fighting on behalf of the earth, from which all our power derives and from which all our blessings spring.

I made no battle cry as I charged. Battle cries are for intimidation, and I could not intimidate Aenghus Óg. I

thought instead I could surprise him. But drawing
Fragarach from its sheath was apparently what they
were waiting for, because Radomila's eyes snapped
open and she cried from her silver cage, "He comes!"

If I could have paused again, I would have taken the
opportunity. Why would Radomila know of my
approach once I drew Fragarach from its sheath? But I
was committed: I had to press on.

Oberon spied me instantly once I charged into the
light, and he howled his relief and anxiety in my mind.

<ATTICUS!> he cried.

*I'm coming, buddy. I love you. But hush and let me
concentrate.* Dear lad that he was, I heard nothing
more from him.

What I heard instead was an unholy screech as
Aenghus Óg waved at the fire pit and caused it to erupt
with demons.

Chapter 24

People in this part of the world like to envision demons as fiery red creatures with horns sprouting from their foreheads and barbed, whiplike tails. If they really want to vent their spleens about the evil of heck and sin, they add on goats' legs and invariably point out the cloven hooves, in case you missed them. I'm not sure who came up with that—I think it was some feverish, sex-starved monk in Europe during the Crusades, and I tried to miss as much of that as I could by passing the time in Asia—but it's obviously been an enduring and compelling image for several centuries. I saw quite a few of them coming out of the hell pit, because it was nearly a contractual obligation by now that some of them appear in that form. But most of them were nightmares out of a painting by Hieronymus Bosch, or maybe Pieter Brueghel the Elder. Some of them flew on leathery wings into the desert night air, with fingerlike talons outstretched to rip into something soft; some of them bubbled across the ground in uneven gaits, owing to the uneven number of legs they had and differing lengths of their limbs; a few of them galloped on those infamous cloven hooves; but all of them, without exception, had lots of sharp, pointy parts, and they stank like ass.

Aenghus Óg didn't waste time with introductions or

even a respectable archvillain laugh. He didn't taunt me or inform me I was about to die; he just pointed at me and uttered the Irish equivalent of "Sic 'im, boys!"

Almost all of them did, but a couple of the bigger ones didn't—I distinctly saw one of the cloven-hoofed lads take off for the hills, and the largest thing on wings disappeared into the sky somewhere.

Aenghus had the gall to be surprised at their defection— he actually shouted at them to come back, and I supposed he must have been counting on them to finish me off after the smaller ones roughed me up a bit. I saw the Pack move to protect Hal and Oberon, who were chained up and unable to defend themselves from rogues or run away, and that gave me a brief moment's relief.

"What did you expect, Aenghus?" I mocked him as I beheaded the vanguard. "They're bloody *demons*." And then there was no time for me to talk, because they were upon me and all I could do was concentrate on what to kill next and on keeping down the contents of my stomach.

After about three seconds it occurred to me that I would be overwhelmed by sheer numbers or violent illness. An awful lot of the buggers had come out of that pit, and they were still coming. Luckily they were still in front of me—they hadn't had time to try flanking me—so I drew a little of the remaining precious power from the earth, pointed at them with my index finger off the hilt, and shouted, "*Dóigh!*" as Brighid had instructed, hoping that would take care of a few of them and bracing for the wave of weakness she warned me about.

It turns out you can't brace for that kind of weakness. There was a thing with stork legs propelling a huge mouth full of teeth coming at my throat from my left, what looked like the Iron Maiden mascot coming at me from the center, and a horrific cross between a

California girl and a Komodo dragon on my right. Every single one of them overshot me and even tripped over me as I abruptly dropped to the ground like a baby giraffe, my muscles utterly unable to function.

Aenghus Óg crowed in victory and yelled to Radomila, "I'm closing the portal now! He's dropped the sword! Do it!"

Oh yes. The sword. The one my fingers were incapable of holding now. The one that was keeping me from becoming demon food. I needed power, and I tried to draw some, but when I reached for it, it went dead beneath me. Aenghus Óg had drained it all to bring hell on earth. There was no telling how far I would have to go to draw enough strength to stand again; as it was, I could not move an inch. My night vision faded, and all I had to see by was the orange light of the fire pit. The skinless Iron Maiden demon scrambled back quickly and took the opportunity to snack on my ear, and the pain was unspeakable, worse than reading the collected works of Edith Wharton, but I couldn't muster the strength to pull away or even say ouch. Likewise for the armored mosquito the size of a schnauzer that landed on my chest and stuck its proboscis into my shoulder: I wanted to swat him, but I couldn't. Something with blue scales and a steroid habit hauled me up by my leg high into the air, and I saw a giant mouth of gleaming teeth and assumed I would be heading in there momentarily. The bloodsucking schnauzer–mosquito assumed that as well, because it pulled out with a wet pop and flew away. But then I was dropped unceremoniously to the ground, breaking my left wrist in the fall. I had fallen facing the hell pit, so I had a view of the horde and of Aenghus Óg berating Death.

"Well, he's obviously dead by now, so what are you waiting for?"

Not dead yet, Aenghus. Dead in short order, perhaps,

like the wasted land beneath me, but perhaps not. The horde of demons wailed and gnashed their teeth from an epic case of fiery (yet somehow cold) heartburn, forgetting about me, for the most part. The flying ones hadn't been affected by the Cold Fire, so the giant mosquito found me again and began to suck me dry. Unlike normal mosquitoes, it didn't inject a local anesthetic to deaden the pain when it stabbed me. But I bet its saliva would leave a much nastier mark afterward—if I lived to deal with it.

The demons I'd hit expired in several ways from the Cold Fire: Some of them melted into a puddle of goo, some of them exploded, and some of them flamed up briefly before scattering as ashes. The one who had eaten my ear ended that way—I'd never hear from him again, nor would I ever be able to appreciate Iron Maiden properly.

"What's happening?" Aenghus asked rhetorically, then answered it like the insufferable ass he was. "Oh, I see. Cold Fire. But that means he must be weak as a kitten. Where is the sword, Radomila?" Buried under demon goo a few yards away from me. Why would she know anything about that? And what was it he had commanded her to do earlier? And hey, Aenghus, are you going to do anything about the rest of the demons that didn't get hit with Cold Fire, like the flying one on my chest and the ones that came out of the pit after I used the spell but before you closed it? He'd probably let them all go, and they'd wind up blending in with the population of Apache Junction.

The werewolves were tearing into anything that came near Hal or Oberon—good. But they would need my help to break those silver chains, and I couldn't even help myself right now.

Radomila sounded apoplectic: "I can't find it. I know it's here, but I can't pinpoint it!"

"Then explain what good you are to me!" Aenghus spat. "The one thing you guaranteed me is that you would be able to find the sword and bring it to me even if he removed the cloak you put on it. Now you tell me you cannot?"

Ha-ha. I didn't remove the cloak. Laksha did, and when she removed it, she must have dispelled whatever tracer Radomila was trying to find. Laksha hadn't tried to hide Fragarach's natural magical signature, though, so that was why Radomila knew when I'd drawn it—she just couldn't get a fix on its location. Speaking of Laksha, shouldn't she have made some progress by now?

Radomila was about to offer Aenghus a snarky retort when her eyes flew wide open and lost their focus. Ah, yes, here we go. That look meant that Radomila sensed someone had a target lock on her ass. But this was one tail she couldn't shake: It was her own blood, after all.

"Answer me, witch!" For a god of love, Aenghus was remarkably blind to nonverbal cues. Radomila wasn't worried about him or any promises she had made right then. She was feverishly trying to figure out a way to ward off whatever was coming for her.

Too late. Her skull caved in from four directions, as if four railroad workers had swung their hammers perfectly in sync from the cardinal directions. Bits of brain and blood splattered the inside of the cage and even sullied the pristine armor of Aenghus Óg.

Now *that* is why I am paranoid about witches getting hold of my blood. Druid's Log, October 11: "Never make Laksha mad."

The giant sucker popped his proboscis out abruptly and took off—he wasn't full, so I assumed that something bigger and badder was coming to take a bite out of me.

It wasn't bigger, but it was definitely badder. As the

talons sank into my chest, I recognized the battle crow, the Morrigan as a Chooser of the Slain. Her eyes were red. Not a good sign.

Aenghus Óg recognized her too, and he finally spied me lying there amongst all the ruins of his demon army as he whirled around, trying to figure out how his pet witch had gotten smooshed. He looked uncertainly at Death, who had passively watched all the proceedings, but the hooded figure shook its head at him and then pointed in my general direction. He was pointing at Laksha in the woods behind me, of course, not at me, but Aenghus made the logical conclusion given his lack of information.

"Ah! Did you do that, Druid? Didn't know you had it in you. Well, it won't help you at all. There's the battle crow on you now, just like old Cúchulainn, and she will be supping on your eyeballs soon. I bet you can't move a muscle right now."

I entertained the possibility that he was right and that the Morrigan would betray me after all, but the crow's eyes flashed even redder and I knew that Aenghus had made a fatal error. The Morrigan does not like to be taken for granted. I think he realized it too, for he had taken a step toward me but halted at the flash in her eyes. I heard her voice in my mind.

He has killed this land for his dreams of power. He thinks the sword will let him stage a coup in Tír na nÓg, and for that he has betrayed his most sacred bond. He is corrupt. She shifted her talons painfully in my chest as she thought aloud, piercing me anew and either careless or unconscious of what she was doing. *I should not directly help you, but I will if you keep it secret from all. Agreed?*

I didn't have to think very hard. I agreed.

I am lending you my own power to fight him on equal terms. I began to feel my muscles again. *If you live, I will require it back. If you die, it will return to me in any case. Agreed?*

Again I agreed with her, and I began to feel much better—my left wrist healed, the weakness disappeared, and the wound where my ear had been at least closed up, though the ear didn't grow back. *Would you mind hunting down that mosquito demon and obliterating it for me, please, while I take care of Aenghus? It has an awful lot of my blood.*

The battle crow squawked in irritation and shook its wings. Aenghus Óg took a cautious step forward, and the crow's eyes blazed again in warning. Aenghus halted.

"Morrigan? What's going on?" he asked. She squawked at him threateningly and he held up his hands and said, "All right, take your time."

Very well, she said to me. *You know he is carrying Moralltach?*

I did not, but thank you for telling me. Moralltach was a magical sword like Fragarach; in English it would be called Great Fury. It had an interesting power: Its first blow was supposed to also be the coup de grâce. One hit and you'd be done. Under the fine magical print, it had to be one solid hit, not a glancing blow, and it was definitely not activated by simply clashing with an opponent's sword or shield.

You are aware of its power, then, and how you must attack?

Well aware, thank you. I'd have to put him on the defensive and prevent that blow from ever falling, especially since I had nothing on but one hundred percent cotton. And he, for his part, would have to guard his entire body just like me, because my sword's ability meant his armor was about as protective as my jeans and T-shirt.

Fragarach—in English, the Answerer—also had a

couple of other abilities: It gave me control of the winds, but I didn't need that so much, living in a desert. And if I held it at someone's throat and asked them a question, they'd have to tell the truth—hence, the Answerer. Perhaps I'd ask Aenghus, if I got the chance, why he wanted my sword so badly when he already had a neato-schmeato sword of his own. It was going to be an interesting duel.

You should be ready now. Fragarach is behind you and to the right, underneath the melted body of that lizard creature. The Morrigan withdrew her talons from me and launched herself on a course for Aenghus Óg. That sort of thing would worry anyone, and his eyes were fully upon her as she approached. While his attention was thus diverted, I sprang up, feeling remarkably well, and retrieved a gooey Fragarach from underneath the liquefied bosom of the California girl/Komodo dragon. I recast night vision on myself and turned my head just in time to see the Morrigan let loose with what may politely be called a "white blossom," square in the visor of Aenghus Óg's helmet. He cursed and clawed at his face, and the Morrigan croaked her laughter.

I kept silent with effort and stripped off my shirt to clean the blade and hilt of Fragarach, smiling as I did so. Then I realized that amusement was not the proper frame of mind for me to cultivate right now. Forty yards away from me stood the man who had done me—and the earth—more wrong than any other.

He removed his helmeet, wiped the crow shit from his eyes, and checked to be sure he still had his captives and that the werewolves were staying put. They were defending Hal and Oberon from the attack of stray demons but showed no signs of taking the offensive. He checked on Death, who remained astride the pale horse, unmoving. Satisfied, he turned to where he thought I was lying on the ground and instead saw me standing up with Fragarach in hand.

"Siodhachan Ó Suileabháin," he sneered, drawing Moralltach out of its sheath. "You've led me a right merry chase, and if there were any bards left to sing of it, they'd probably write a ballad about you. A proper one where the hero dies at the end, and the moral is don't *ever* fuck with Aenghus Óg!" Spittle flew from his mouth at the end, and his face turned purple as he shook with rage. I didn't respond. I just glowered at him and let him realize he had lost his self-control. He ground his teeth together and took a deep breath to re-collect his composure. "That sword," he said, pointing at me with his own, "is the rightful property of the Tuatha Dé Danann. You cannot escape me now except by begging for mercy. Drop the sword and fall to your knees."

<This guy is an epic douche. Kick his shiny ass, Atticus,> Oberon said.

I compartmentalized his comment and resolved to enjoy it later. I glared at this would-be usurper and said in my most authoritative voice, "Aenghus Óg, you have broken Druidic law by killing the land around us and opening a gate to hell, unleashing demons on this plane. I judge you guilty and sentence you to death."

<Amen, Atticus! Testify!>

Aenghus snorted in derision. "Druidic law doesn't apply here."

"Druidic law applies wherever I walk, and you know this."

"You have no authority to enforce your law upon me."

"My authority is here." I waved Fragarach and tapped its power to send a gust of wind at Aenghus. I only meant to intimidate him with its creepiness, but I must have put too much of my anger behind it, because the gust was so powerful it blew him backward onto his silver-plated derrière.

<You will respect my authori-*tah*!> Oberon said, in a passable imitation of Eric Cartman. I reminded him that I needed to concentrate. Sometimes dogs forget; they just get too excited.

I noticed that I had lost some energy by performing that little trick; the power to control winds may be inherent to Fragarach, but the will and force had to come from somewhere, and since I couldn't tap the earth here, it came directly from me—that is, it came from the energy Morrigan had lent me. That changed everything: If I was going to get tired, I couldn't fight him the same way. He was in the same situation, of course, so instead of charging him, I remained where I was and laughed. Go ahead, Aenghus, get angry. Throw some magic at me and spend yourself, and see what happens.

I put my left hand up to my necklace to reassure myself that it was still there and undamaged, as Aenghus struggled to get up. The spikes on the backs of his calves and the spurs on his ankles were giving him trouble, and I laughed all the harder. The werewolves started yipping at him too; most of the little demons had either cleared off or been killed, so they were able to watch the spectacle a bit and enjoy the silver man's difficulty.

His face red and flushed, he gave me one of those "You will pay!" looks and whipped his left hand at me as if he were throwing a Frisbee. But what came at me wasn't a pleasantly spinning plastic disc—it was a bright orange ball of hellfire, the sort that you get to fling around only if you've made a deal you really shouldn't have.

I'm not going to pretend my sphincter didn't clench— my survival instinct is too well developed—but other than that I gave no outward sign that I was concerned about the hellfire as I stood my ground. Now I'd find out how good my amulet was.

You know how it feels when you've nuked a Hot Pocket and you touch it too fast before it cools down? Well, the hellfire was like that: a flash of intense heat that was gone in less than a second, leaving nary a mark but setting my entire body to sweating.

Aenghus couldn't believe it. He thought he'd see a crispy critter clutching a glowing sword, but instead he saw an annoyed, very live Druid staring back at him, clutching a glowing sword.

"How is that possible?" he erupted. "Druids have no defense against hellfire! You should be dead!"

I said nothing but began to circle around to my right, trying to get to some ground that wasn't covered with slippery demon leftovers.

It was at this point that the figure on the pale horse began to laugh. Everything in the meadow stopped breathing, listened to the cloaked figure's hoarse, raspy chuckle, and wondered what it thought was so funny.

Taking advantage of the pause, Aenghus Óg's uncertainty, and the dry ground, I charged. What more was there to say? I'd sentenced him to death, and he'd demonstrated he wouldn't submit meekly, so there was nothing left but to go to't.

I wanted one of those fabulous anime moments where the hero sticks the sword into the bad guy's guts and everything quivers, even the sweat droplets, and the bad guy vomits blood and says something in a tiny surprised voice, like, "That really was a Hattori Hanzo sword," right before he dies. Alas, it was not to be.

Aenghus had been something of a swordsman in his earlier days; he'd helped the Fianna out of a tight spot or two—he had serious battlefield cred, unlike Bres. He parried my first flurry of blows, cursing all the while and promising to mutilate my body and then dig up the bones of all my descendants and turn them into glue, blah blah blah. He tried to back up, disengage, and give himself some space to begin a counterattack. That was precisely what I could not afford, so I pressed the attack and realized we were both fighting in the old Irish patterns—which was perhaps all he knew. But it certainly wasn't all I knew. I hadn't spent centuries in Asia and the last ten years sparring with a vampire to fall into old ruts like that. I switched my attack pattern to a Chinese series of forms that incorporated some deceptive wrist movements, and that brought me some success: He crossed his sword above him to parry a blow from above, only to find that it was coming from the side instead. The blade bit deep into his left arm above the elbow, and I snapped it out when I felt it hit bone. He yowled his pain and I think he tried to say something, but it was so mangled with spittle and inchoate rage that I didn't process a word. His left arm was useless now, hanging there like a mesquite branch damaged in a monsoon, and his balance would be skewed. I could gamble a wee bit—people with poor balance rarely win sword fights.

I backed off and let him bleed, allowing him to weaken with every passing second. He'd use some power to stop the bleeding, and that was fine with me; he'd still be weakened, and there was no way he could knit the muscle tissue in time. It was his turn to attack. I knew he'd do it; at this point we hated each other as much as it was possible for two Irishmen to do—and that's quite a bit.

"You've hounded me for centuries," I growled. "And you might have hounded me for many more, but your petty jealousy of Brighid has brought you to this end."

"Your end, you mean!" Aenghus roared, completely unhinged by my reducing all his elaborate schemes to a case of sibling rivalry. He lunged at me with a long diagonal hack, with all his strength behind it. But I knew how he fought now—the same old way. I saw it coming, and I knew I was faster, and stronger too. I parried his blade by sweeping mine in a rainbow move to my right, so that his sword was underneath mine when I brought it down and his sword arm was crossed in front of him. I stepped forward quickly and whipped Fragarach through his neck before he could regain his balance and try a backhand. His head tumbled backward, eyes wide in surprise, and wound up bouncing off his back as he fell to the ground.

"No, I meant your end," I said.

Death laughed again and goaded his horse toward us. I stood aside as the rider reached down and scooped Aenghus Óg's head from the ground, then began to tack his horse back around to the fire pit, laughing maniacally all the while.

The love god's mouth did not move, but still I heard him protest, *No! The Morrigan is supposed to take me! Not you! Morrigan! Take me to Tír na nÓg! Morrigaaaaan!*

The pale horse of Death leapt with its rider and cargo into the fire pit and descended back to hell, and I was finally free of Aenghus Óg.

Chapter 25

<All right, that's over. Now get me off this chain and buy me a steak,> Oberon said.

You got it, buddy. Let me get the werewolf free first so the Pack doesn't think I'm insulting them. You understand the need for diplomacy here, right?

<Yeah, but, jeez, they have such fragile egos. You wouldn't think they'd be so sensitive.>

The werewolves gave me some appreciative yips as I approached Hal and took the black bag off his head. His eyes were yellow and his wolf wanted out, but the silver wrapped around him was preventing it. His chest was heaving, and he was just barely able to hold on to his language faculties.

"Thanks . . . Atticus," he managed. "Saw through pack link . . . you know red-haired woman . . . who warned about silver traps."

"Yes, I do. That was Flidais." I frowned as I bent to examine his chains. They were locked with a padlock, and I wasn't a locksmith. Trying to dissolve the chains magically would take too much time. Someone had to have the key. "Why do you ask?"

"She was the one . . . who kidnapped us!"

"What? I thought that was Emily."

"No." He shook his head. "No. She drove car. Flidais talked us into . . . backseat."

I looked over at Oberon. "Why didn't you mention this before?" I asked aloud so all could hear.

<I was going to, but you haven't exactly let me talk very much. Hush, Oberon, quiet, Oberon, not now, Oberon—>

"Fair enough," I said. "Hal, I need a key. Any idea who has it?"

He jerked his chin in the direction of Radomila's remains. "Dead witch."

"Yuck. That's going to be messy." I walked over to the other side of the cabin where the cage was and grimaced at Laksha's handiwork. Radomila had been wearing a fine leather jacket, and once I dragged her corpse to the edge of the cage where I could reach her pockets, I found several keys in her right one. There was a lock on the cage she was in, and I unlocked that first to go inside and retrieve the necklace for Laksha. It was a bloody mess—the phrase "o'ersized with coagulate gore" came to mind—but since she had caused it, I figured she couldn't complain.

I went over to Hal next, who was panting heavily in anticipation. "Are you going to go wolf as soon as I unlock this?"

He nodded, too wound up to answer.

"All right. Tell the Pack this for me: If they see Flidais, leave her alone. She has promised to come back and help with your wounded. What I need you to do is go after Emily and bring me her head."

That got his attention. "Her . . . head?"

"Yes, I need it. Do what you want with the rest. But don't tear after her until we make sure those traps are disabled. Either Flidais can tell us or Laksha might be able to, when she gets here."

"There is no need, Druid," said the Morrigan, who had flown down and taken her human form beside me. She was naked again—must be feeling randy after watching an ancient rival get decapitated. "The traps expired when that witch did," she said, gesturing at Radomila's leftovers. "They were not permanent enchantments."

"Thank you, Morrigan," I said, and turned to Hal and began unlocking him. "There you go. Hunt well. I'll wait here and take care of your wounded as best I can."

The chains smoked a bit where they had come into contact with Hal's flesh, peeling some of the skin away with them. He hissed and snarled and changed form as soon as the silver chains were off him, ripping right through his nice three-thousand-dollar suit, for which I had no doubt I would be billed. The Pack surrounded him and welcomed him back, then he took his place next to Gunnar as they ran to the spot where Emily had left the meadow, to begin their hunt.

"Did you ever find that bloodsucking demon, Morrigan?" I asked as I unlocked Oberon. He gave me some sloppy kisses and I hugged him.

"Found and destroyed," she said. "Did you notice that my casting came true?"

"Aye, I noticed that," I replied, smiling. "Though it applied to Aenghus Óg, as I'd rather hoped. May I ask you something?"

"Certainly."

"Did you tell Aenghus Óg of our arrangement? That you would never take me?"

She slunk up next to me and overwhelmed my libido with that peculiar magic of hers, which my amulet could mute but not negate. She ran a fingernail down my bare chest and I forgot to breathe.

"Oh, but I *am* going to take you, Druid," she said, "many times, when you have recovered your strength." She snaked her tongue into my remaining ear.

<Aw, jeez, here we go again.> Oberon mentally rolled his eyes.

"That's not what I meant," I managed to say, pulling away. I determinedly began to think of baseball. Randy Johnson pitching. Great player, but not sexy. No sex. Stay focused. "Did you tell him you would never come for me?"

She laughed throatily and latched on to my left side again, her breath tickling my neck, and I reddened.

"I mean, did you tell him that you'd never take my life?"

"Yesssss," she whispered in my ear, and I had to close my eyes. Two outs, nobody on, bottom of the first. Completely unsexy.

"Why?"

She dug her nails into my pecs and I gasped, remembering when they were talons.

"I wanted him to summon Death," she said, "so that when you killed him, I would never have to see him again. I knew he would do it when I told him of our agreement, and he did. Thus I am eternally revenged for millennia of petty annoyances. He is now in a hell he never imagined for himself, denied his rest in Tír na nÓg. Am I not a fearsome enemy?"

"You frighten me primally."

The Morrigan sighed and ground her pelvis against my leg. What do you know? She liked to be told she was scary. Kinky.

"Why did he want Fragarach so badly?" I wondered. "I never got to ask him."

"There is a faction in Faerie—a rather large one— that thinks you should not wield it, since you are neither Fae nor of the Tuatha Dé Danann. They think Brighid has let too many of the old ways go, and allowing you to keep Fragarach is something they point to as evidence of their claims."

"So I'm a political football in Tír na nÓg."

"I don't know what a football is," she breathed in my

ear. "But I know you are aroused." Her left hand caressed the flat of my stomach and started to trail south to my jeans. "You cannot hide this from me."

She abruptly whipped her head to the northeast, and fun time was over. "Flidais approaches. We will speak later. You have some power to return to me. Spend the night regenerating your own, and I will return in the morning." The Morrigan turned back into a crow and flew off to the southwest even as Flidais entered the meadow from the opposite direction.

The goddess of the hunt gave me a cursory wave and ran over to Dr. Snorri Jodursson, who looked like a silver pincushion. Of the three other wolves who had fallen, two were turned back to human form, which meant they were dead. No wonder Hal and the Pack were so eager to catch up with Emily.

<I don't know what to think about that red-haired lady,> Oberon said, as I ran to help the other surviving werewolf. He loped easily alongside me, happy to stretch his legs. <She seemed so nice at first, but then she made me kill that guy and helped kidnap us—and now she's trying to heal that poor wolf. Do you think maybe she has a split personality?>

In a sense. She serves two masters.

<Really? Who?>

Herself and Brighid.

<So the nice half of her personality must be when she serves Brighid! I liked Brighid. She called me impressive, which showed great judgment, and she also gave me a belly rub. If you see her again, remember she likes milk and honey in her tea.>

I smiled. *I missed you, Oberon. Let's see what we can do for this werewolf.*

It was a female I didn't recognize. She growled and snarled when she first saw us come into view, but she subsided abruptly after she recalled we had been with the Pack. She had been stabbed under the left front leg and had a gash across the tendons of her right. They didn't look life-threatening, but she couldn't walk and the wounds wouldn't heal because of the silver traces in them.

My magic wouldn't work on her—werewolf immunity—but if I could get her wounds cleaned up she would heal herself. Easier said than done.

"Oberon, do you smell water anywhere nearby?"

He raised his snout to the air and took a few good long snuffles—he sneezed a couple of times—but he sounded sorry when he replied, <I can't smell anything over the blood and demon stench. Why don't you just bring some up from the earth? I've seen you do it before.>

"Aenghus Óg killed the land here. It won't obey me now."

"Do not trouble yourself, Druid," Flidais said from twenty yards and closing, running over to help. "I can clean the wounds without water and get her healing started."

"You can? You're already finished with Snorri?" I looked over at Snorri, who was still lying on the ground as before but without all the needles in him.

"I am. He is healing now. And soon this one will do the same," she said, kneeling down on her haunches and placing her tattooed hand on the werewolf's cut leg. "Her name is Greta."

"Why are you doing this?"

"I told you I would come back to heal the Pack."

"But you were the one who kidnapped Hal and Oberon and put them in a position to be harmed."

Flidais hissed with impatience. "I did so only at the instruction of Brighid."

I felt the blood drain from my face. "What?"

"Do not pretend you cannot follow me," she

snapped. "You know us well, and we know you even better. Admit it, Druid: Without your friends being held hostage, there was a significant chance you would have simply fled the confrontation. Brighid did not want that to happen, so I provided Aenghus Óg with a lever to make sure you showed up to be attacked. Thus Brighid got what she wanted—the removal of a rival—and Aenghus got what he deserved."

During this conversation, I missed what exactly Flidais did to remove the silver—I wanted to learn the trick, because it could come in handy later—but when I looked back down, the werewolf's wounds were already beginning to close, and the last thing I wanted was to be in Flidais's debt. I supposed I would have to find a lever against her.

I was flabbergasted by the extent to which I had been manipulated by various members of the Tuatha Dé Danann. I had indeed been a pawn for Brighid, Flidais, and the Morrigan—a pawn who took down two very troublesome gods. Still, there were clear blessings to be thankful for: I was still alive, and my worst enemy was in hell instead of angling to become First among the Fae. I could think of nothing else to say to Flidais that would not get me in trouble, so I took refuge in good manners.

"Thank you for healing the Pack, Flidais."

"It was my pleasure," she said, rising. "And now I get an even greater pleasure. Did you see that one of the large demon rams escaped?"

"Yes, I saw that. Big lad, he was."

"I'm going after him now." She grinned. "He's had a decent head start. Rams like him are casters, you know. It's going to be a fine chase, a finer battle, and he'll be a choice trophy on the wall of my lodge."

"Happy hunting."

"Fare you well, Druid," she said, and then she sprinted

toward Haunted Canyon, using who knew what for energy in this wasted land. The Tuatha Dé Danann obviously had access to a power source that I did not—but I could see now that they had labored for millennia to preserve the fiction that they were as limited as Druids were. Perhaps it did not matter anymore to keep it a secret: Who was I going to tell?

<You know what she's like, Atticus?>

What's that, buddy?

<A piece of steak you get caught in your teeth and you can't get out. I love me some steak, you know, but sometimes it can be supremely annoying and then I don't want steak again for a while.>

That's exactly what I feel too, Oberon.

He turned his head toward Snorri and pricked up his ears. <Hey, I think your crush from the bar is coming.>

She's my new apprentice. Well, half of her is, anyway.

<Wow, really? What's the other half going to do?>

Not sure about that yet. Let's go meet her. I waved good-bye to Greta the werewolf, who was out of danger now, and Oberon barked a farewell. We loped over to where Dr. Jodursson was healing—he looked as if he wanted to sleep, but that was doubtless impossible with the pack link overflowing with bloodlust at the moment.

"Thanks for taking one for the team, Snorri," I said. Oberon chimed in with a sort of rolling bark—*roo-woo-wooof.*

Snorri snorted his acknowledgment but otherwise didn't move.

Laksha walked up behind Snorri, holding her nose. "Smells like demons," she complained.

"Nice job on Radomila," I said.

"Did she have the necklace?"

"Yes, she did." I held it up so she could see her bloody treasure. "The rest of the coven is just about finished off, so you won't need to use its power on them. Here you go, as promised."

She took the necklace from me and smiled. "Thank you. It is a pleasure to work with a man who keeps his word."

"I am actually going to help you keep the remaining part of your bargain," I said.

"Oh?" Her eyes narrowed. "How so?"

"I'm giving Granuaile thirty thousand dollars to fly back east and find you a suitable host. Once you wake up in your new body, she'll give you the rest to get yourself set up somewhere, minus her airfare home."

"You have this kind of money to give away?"

I shrugged. "Ten grand just came from the coven. As for the rest, I live simply and I make a killing on long-term investments. Send me a postcard when you get settled; let me know how the karma rehab is going."

Laksha chuckled and shoved the bloody necklace into Granuaile's pocket. "I have no problem with this. Thank you for your consideration."

"Thank you for taking care of Granuaile."

"She is a sweet child, and very bright. She will make a good Druid."

"I agree. May I speak with her now?"

"Certainly. Farewell." Granuaile's head drooped, and when it came back up she staggered backward and covered her face with her hands.

"Fauggh! What is that fucking smell? Oh my God, it reeks! I can't—can't—" She couldn't finish her sentence because she was too busy vomiting on the side of the trail.

"Oh, yeah, I forgot about that," I said. "Sorry. You kind of get used to it after a while." Granuaile vomited again by way of reply, and it occurred to me that I hadn't actually answered her question, and she might jump to the wrong conclusion if I didn't say something soon. "It wasn't me," I assured her. "I swear it wasn't me. That's demons you're smelling."

"Whatever it is," she gasped, "do we have to stay here for long? Because I don't think—" She retched again, but now it was dry heaves. Part of me was finding this very interesting. Laksha had obviously been using the same nose as Granuaile, so the two had been exposed to the exact same stimuli, but Laksha had shown no urge to vomit so violently. It suggested that the physical reaction was even more psychologically based than I had previously supposed.

"Well, I have to stay and wait for the pack to return, but you could go back up the trail a little way until you can stand it. There's nothing pretty to see here."

"Then why did you have me come back here?"

"Precisely because there's nothing pretty to see here. I wanted to give you a last chance to back out of our arrangement. You're about to become an initiate in the world of magic, and that world can sometimes be brutally violent and smell as evil as it actually is. Breathe through your mouth and look around."

"It's all dark."

Oh, duh. My binding had snapped when I lost my energy and Aenghus Óg had drained the earth. Laksha clearly had used her own methods of seeing in the dark to get here. Using some more of the Morrigan's power, I gave Granuaile night vision again, and she looked at the meadow full of corpses.

"My God," she said. "Did you do all of this?"

"Everything except the witches and the two werewolves. But I had lots of help staying alive tonight. By rights I should be dead. And you should know that magic users rarely die peacefully in their sleep. So I want you to think about what you're looking at and what you smelled as you take Laksha back east. I don't want you entering into this with any romanticized ideals. And if you'd rather not be my apprentice when you come back, I will understand, no hard feelings, and I'll make sure you get a good job to replace the one you quit today."

"But what happened here? How did you manage this?"

"Whoa, hold that thought," I said, hearing yips from the opposite side of the meadow and seeing Snorri lift his head off the ground. "It sounds like the Pack is returning. We may be able to leave sooner than I thought."

Their arrival punctuated my point perfectly: Granuaile clutched my shoulder when she saw Emily's head dangling from Gunnar's jaws, and when he dropped it at my feet faceup, she hid behind my back.

"No, Granuaile, what are you hiding from? You need to see this too. This is part of it. This woman here looked about twenty before she died, and now we see her true age was closer to ninety. There are seven more witches who are older than she was and who think they're wiser, so they might get ideas about trying to succeed where this one failed. Maybe seeing the head of their youngest will drive home the point that it's not wise to tangle with me. When you cannot reason with people, you have to try scaring them. If that doesn't work, then you either run or you kill them. Or set your lawyers on them."

"Is that what you're doing? Trying to scare me?"

"Think of it as full disclosure."

"Okay. Thank you. I will think about it." She turned and started back up the trail. "I'm just going to go far enough ahead to where I can breathe normally again."

Gunnar and Hal sloughed off their fur and put their human skin on so they could carry their two fallen pack mates out of the wilderness. They didn't want to talk, and I figured they were probably calculating the costs of having me as a client. Snorri moved slowly and Greta trotted on three legs, but they were able to make it out without help now that the silver was out of their system.

Before I left, I made sure to pick up Aenghus Óg's sword, Moralltach, since it now belonged to me by virtue of my victory. The hike out took much longer than the trip in, and we were a weary, silent lot, but we were back to the cars well before dawn. About two miles away from the trailhead, I could feel the earth again, and I wept as I walked.

Hal and I dropped Granuaile off at her apartment, and I told her to pack her bags for the trip east the next day. I didn't know if I would see her again or not.

We made a call to Leif, who had woken up too late to join in the fun, and asked him to get his ghoul friends out there to clean up the mess.

Hal took me to a twenty-four-hour Walmart, and we bought gauze and tape to wrap around my chest where Fagles's bullet hole used to be. We covered up my missing ear while we were at it and fabricated a story to tell the police when I got home. I had been so traumatized by the attempt on my life by a police detective that I spent a couple of days incommunicado at my girl-friend's house—and that would be Granuaile, for the purposes of the story. But during my stay I'd been attacked and had my ear damaged by a feral cat. Not the best story, but better than the truth. Hal said he'd straighten it out with Granuaile, then he drove me to my house and delivered me to the Tempe police, who were still staked out there, awaiting my statement. Hal was going to keep Oberon—and Emily's head—until they left.

When they were finally satisfied with my story of a nervous breakdown coupled with unchecked feline aggression, I called Hal to bring Oberon (and Emily) over, and then every other thought was of collapsing into the backyard to begin my true recovery from using Cold Fire.

That had to wait: too many things to do first.

I made a special point of calling Malina Sokolowski to tell her I had seen the sunrise but Radomila had most definitely not.

"I know you fully expected me to die, Malina, but don't you think perhaps you underestimated me?"

"Perhaps I did," she admitted. "There is so little available literature about the powers of Druids, and it is difficult to judge. But I hope you recognize that you underestimated me as well, Mr. O'Sullivan."

"How so?" A thrill of panic shot down my spine. Did she get something of mine after all? Was I about to get magically squished?

"You thought me a liar and that I was somehow involved in this abhorrent plot to make bargains with hell and the Tuatha Dé Danann. I can understand why, because members of a coven tend to get painted with the same brush, often justifiably so. But looking back now, can you not see that I had only the best intentions?"

"You told me the truth about there being only six witches at Tony Cabin, and for that I thank you," I said. "But when I asked you at my shop how many of your coven were plotting to take the sword from me, you refused to answer."

"That is because I had no answer. At the time I had only suspicions, not confirmed evidence, and I could not share those with you and turn you against certain members of my coven without firm proof. Surely you understand this."

She was pretty smooth, and I found myself flirting with the idea that she might actually be an honest witch—as rare as an honest politician, if not more so.

My prejudice would not allow me to trust her, but perhaps I did not need to send her Emily's head in a box as I had planned. Despite what I had told Granuaile at the meadow, frightening people only pushes back the date of an inevitable fight. Cooperation makes fighting unnecessary—or, as Abraham Lincoln once said, "I destroy my enemies when I make them my friends."

"What has your coven decided to do now?" I asked. "Hunt down the Druid that killed your sisters?"

"Of course not," Malina scolded. "They clearly gave you just cause, and they got their just deserts. I told them it might not turn out well."

"What are your plans, then?"

Malina sighed. "That actually depends quite a bit on your plans, Mr. O'Sullivan. If you are planning some sort of pogrom against Polish witches, then I suppose we would prefer to flee rather than fight. But if I can convince you that we mean you no harm, then we would much rather stay in Tempe in a state of mutual nonaggression."

"Having you leave town sounds pretty good to me. Not much of a downside there, in my view."

"I respectfully suggest there might be. Our coven has kept undesirables out of the East Valley for many years now. We have chased off innumerable *brujas* over the years and a spate of voodoo priests after Katrina hit New Orleans. Last year we quietly took care of a Kali death cult. I also know that there is a group of Bacchants in Vegas that would love to expand here, but we have repulsed every foray into our territory. If you would like to deal with these problems in our absence, so be it."

"No, I had no idea that you were so active or so territorial."

"This is a nice place to live. We would like to keep it that way."

"I like it here too," I admitted. "Very well. Convince me that you mean me no harm."

"Are you willing to give us equal assurance?"

"I suppose that depends on what sort of assurance you seek."

"Let us have your lawyer draw up a treaty. We can spend as much time on the wording as you wish. When all parties are satisfied, we will sign in blood and the lawyer will keep it."

A nonaggression treaty signed in blood? Something about that struck me as oxymoronic. "I will begin the process with you in good faith," I said, "and see where negotiations lead us. What I want you to understand— what Emily and Radomila did not understand—is that though I avoid conflict where I can, it should never be misinterpreted as weakness. You expressed disbelief earlier that a member of the Tuatha Dé Danann should be afraid of me. But last night I killed him, and on top of that I took care of a horde of demons and your former sisters." I left out all the help I had. I didn't actually kill a single member of her coven, but she didn't need to know that. "It should be clear to you that Wikipedia knows nothing about what a real Druid can do."

"Crystal clear, Mr. O'Sullivan."

"Very well. My lawyer will contact you in a week or so."

That left me with a wizened witch's head to dispose of, but I was glad that I wouldn't need to use it after all. I knew precisely what to do with it. I cast camouflage on it and myself and crossed the street to Mr. Semerdjian's house. With some patient coaxing, the earth underneath his eucalyptus tree opened up and I tumbled her head into a hole beneath its roots, then closed the earth over it and dispelled the camouflage.

After that, I sent a courier over to Granuaile's place

with a check for the money I'd promised and wished her a safe journey.

Perry got an early-morning call asking him to keep the store running, and in return he'd get a week's paid vacation in a few days. The widow MacDonagh also received a call, reassuring her that her favorite Irish lad was still alive and planned to have that long talk with her soon. And then, finally, I went to take my rest.

I shucked my clothes and lay down on my right side so that my tattoos got maximum contact with the earth. I sighed in relief as I felt the first comforting wave of energy fill my cells. I must have fallen asleep inside of ten seconds, only to be rudely awakened ten seconds after that. The Morrigan flew into the yard, cawing loudly, and changed into her human form.

"Now that you are in a position to recharge yourself, Druid, I would like my energy returned to me."

Well, hello to you too, Morrigan. Yeesh.

"Thank you very much for the use of it," I told her diplomatically, and offered her my left hand. "Please take it back."

She grasped my hand, and when she was finished draining what was hers, my arm dropped to my side like a dead fish. I couldn't move again.

"You used way too much Cold Fire," the Morrigan said. "You should plan on being immobile for a couple of days. I hope you put on some of that lotion the mortals are so infatuated with. Can't have you dying of skin cancer."

The Morrigan laughed mockingly and then squawked harshly as she changed into a crow and flew away. And she wondered why she didn't have any friends.

Epilogue

The Chiricahua Mountains in southeastern Arizona have a sere beauty to them. One of the things I enjoy about the desert is the hardiness of the plants and animals that live there. Rains are unpredictable and the Arizona sun can be extraordinarily harsh, yet life thrives in the Chiricahuas, albeit without the lush display you find in wetter climes.

The Chiricahuas are unusual in that there are several "sky islands"—old volcanic ranges that jut nine thousand feet above the desert grasslands—featuring diverse ecosystems.

Oberon and I hunted mule deer and javelina there, and we also terrorized a couple of coatimundis just to hear them chitter at us. We didn't find any bighorn sheep but refused to let that small disappointment mar an idyllic outing.

<This place is great, Atticus,> he said as we rested by a canyon stream, enjoying the gurgle of the water as it tumbled over rocks and eddied around the stalks of cattails. <How long can we stay here?>

I wished I could tell him we could stay until he tired of it. This was what I'd fought and lived for—a world without Aenghus Óg in it. There wasn't a place in Tír na nÓg finer than that spot by the creek, and I couldn't remember a time in recent centuries when I'd felt more at peace than there with my friend at that particular moment. It reminded me that Oberon had magic of his own: He could focus my attention on how perfectly sublime life can be at times. Such moments are ephemeral, and without his guidance I might have missed many of them, working so hard to get somewhere that I would fail to recognize when I had arrived.

Just another couple of days, I said. *Then I have to get back to the shop and let Perry take his vacation.* There was also the matter of the dead land around Tony Cabin to heal, and I needed to figure out how to grow back a convincing right ear. All I'd been able to do so far was grow a disfigured lump of cartilage, and it had yet to earn me a single admiring glance. I might have to resort to plastic surgery.

<Aw. Too bad. I'll enjoy it while it lasts, then.>

I have a surprise for you to enjoy when we get back home.

<Did you get me that movie about Genghis Khan?>

It's in the Netflix queue, but that's not the surprise. You don't need to worry, it'll be something good. I just don't want you to feel depressed about going home.

<Oh, I won't. But it would be cool to have a stream like this in the backyard. Can you make one?>

Umm . . . no.

<I figured. Can't blame a hound for trying.>

Oberon was indeed surprised when we got back home to Tempe. Hal had made the arrangements for me, and Oberon perked up as soon as we were dropped off by the shuttle from the car rental company.

<Hey, smells like someone's in my territory,> he said.

Nobody could be here without my permission, you know that.

<Flidais did it.>

That isn't Flidais you smell, believe me.

I opened the front door, and Oberon immediately ran

to the kitchen window that gazed upon the backyard. He barked joyously when he saw what was waiting for him there.

<French poodles! All black and curly with poofy little tails!>

And every one of them in heat.

<Oh, WOW! Thanks, Atticus! I can't wait to sniff their asses!> He bounded over to the door and pawed at it because the doggie door was closed to prevent the poodles from entering.

You earned it, buddy. Hold on, get down off the door so I can open it for you, and be careful, don't hurt any of them.

I opened the door, expecting him to bolt through it and dive into his own personal canine harem, but instead he took one step and stopped, looking up at me with a mournful expression, his ears drooping and a tiny whine escaping his snout.

<Only five?>

Acknowledgments

My pint glass runneth over.

Though it's only my name that appears on the cover, novels truly don't happen without the collaboration of others. My parents have always been supportive of my creative endeavors, from music to art to writing, and if they hadn't convinced me that yes, I *could* do whatever I wanted creatively, I might have never started this project in the first place. My loving wife, Kimberly, has been watching me write one thing or another for close to twenty years now, and her iron conviction that I would get it right someday kept me going when I wanted to give up.

Several people provided valuable feedback in the early stages of the novel. Dr. Kim Hensley Owens, assistant professor of rhetoric at the University of Rhode Island, demanded consistency in the widow MacDonagh's accent and occasionally suggested economies of phrasing, for which I am grateful. Alan O'Bryan provided insight into the simple truth of sword fights—they don't last long—and introduced me to the Society for Creative Anachronism. Andrea Taylor had much to say on the subject of witches; I would tell you more except that I am under a spell.

I am convinced that my agent, Evan Goldfried, is a Magical Being. He said yes when others said no, and he sold the series so quickly that I'm still recovering from the whiplash. Cheers, Magic E.

Tricia Pasternak, my frabjous editor at Del Rey, is *sans pareil* in my esteem, and her enthusiasm for Atticus and Oberon is the reason you hold this book in your hand today. Her assistant editor, Mike Braff, tolerated my puerile shenanigans with great good humor and proved to be a font of wisdom regarding all things Nordic.

While the characters and events in *Hounded* are entirely fictional, one could, if one were so inclined, visit parts of the setting in Arizona. Third Eye Books and Herbs rests where the real-life comic shop of my cousin, Drew Sullivan, lies on Ash Avenue in Tempe; Tony Cabin is still out there in the Superstition Mountains, and the land around it is thankfully not dead; Rúla Búla on Mill Avenue is indeed one of the finest Irish pubs anywhere, and I have yet to find a plate of fish and chips that comes close to theirs.

Linguistics aficionados may notice that while the Sisters of the Three Auroras are Polish, they use a decidedly Russian name—the Zoryas—for the star goddesses from which they derive their powers. The Zoryas are known throughout the Slavic world by one name or another (such as Zvezda, Zwezda, Zorza, etc.), but since most of the coven was born in the nineteenth century, when the eastern portion of Poland was occupied by Russia, it made sense (to me) to have them use the Russian name. No one is required to agree that this makes sense; I explain this merely to give the impression that my backstory is remarkably thorough and well-researched.

Read on for a preview of the next thrilling
Atticus O'Sullivan adventure,

HEXED

Coming soon from Del Rey Books!

Chapter 1

Turns out that when you kill a god, people want to talk to you. Paranormal insurance salesmen with special "godslayer" term life policies. Charlatans with "godproof" armor and extraplanar safe houses for rent. But, most notably, other gods, who want to first congratulate you on your achievement, second warn you not to try such shenanigans on them, and finally suggest that you try to slay one of their rivals—purely as a shenanigan, of course.

Ever since word got around to the various pantheons that I had snuffed not one but two of the Tuatha Dé Danann—and sent the more powerful of the two to the Christian hell—I had been visited by various potentates, heralds, and ambassadors from most of the world's belief systems. All of them wanted me to leave them alone but pick a fight with someone else, and if I successfully lanced the immortal boil that vexed them, I'd be rewarded beyond my wildest dreams, blah blah barf yak.

That reward business was a giant load of shite, as they'd say in the U.K. Brighid, Celtic goddess of poetry, fire, and the forge, had promised to reward me if I killed Aenghus Óg, but I hadn't heard a word from her in the three weeks since Death carried him off to hell. I'd heard plenty from the rest of the world's gods, but from my own? Nothing but the chirping of crickets.

The Japanese wanted me to mess with the Chinese, and vice versa. The old Russian gods wanted me to stick it to the Hungarians. The Greeks wanted me to knock off their Roman copycats in a bizarre manifestation of self-loathing and internecine jealousy. The weirdest by far were those Easter Island guys, who wanted me to mess around with some rotting totem poles in the Seattle area. But everyone—at least, it sure seemed like everyone—wanted me to slay Thor as soon as I had a free moment. The whole world was tired of his shenanigans, I guess.

Foremost among these was my own attorney, Leif Helgarson. He was an old Icelandic vampire who had presumably worshipped Thor at some point in ancient history, but he'd never told me why he now harbored such hatred for him. Leif did some legal work for me, sparred with me regularly to keep my sword arm sharp, and occasionally drank a goblet full of my blood by way of payment.

I found him waiting for me on my porch the night after Samhain. It was a cool evening in Tempe, and I was in a good mood after having much to give thanks for. While the American children had busied themselves the night before by trick-or-treating on Halloween, I had paid plenty of attention to the Morrigan and Brighid in my own private ceremonies, and I was thrilled to have an apprentice to teach and to share the night with. Granuaile had returned from North Carolina in time for Samhain, and though the two of us were not much of a Druid's grove, it was still a better holy night than I had enjoyed in centuries. I was the only real Druid left, and the idea of starting a new grove after such a long time of going it alone had filled me with hope. So when Leif greeted me formally from my front porch as I came home from work, I was perhaps more exuberant in my response than I should have been.

"Leif, you spooky bastard, how the hell are ya?" I grinned widely as I braked my bike to a stop. He raised his eyebrows and peered at me down his long Nordic nose, and I realized that he was probably unused to such cavalier address.

"I am not a bastard," he replied archly. "Spooky I will grant you. And while I am well"—a corner of his mouth quirked upward a fraction—"I confess not so jocund as yourself."

"Jocund?" I raised my brows. Leif had asked me in the past to call him on behaviors that broadcast how much older he was than he looked.

Apparently he didn't want to be corrected right then. He exhaled noisily to express his exasperation. I thought it amusing that he employed that, since he had no need to breathe. "Fine," he said. "Not so jovial, then."

"No one uses those words anymore, Leif, except for old farts like us." I leaned my bike against the porch rails and mounted the three steps to take a seat next to him. "You really should spend some decent time learning how to blend in. Make it a project. Popular culture is mutating at a much faster rate these days. It's not like the Middle Ages, when you had the Church and the aristocracy keeping everything nice and stagnant."

"Very well, since you are the verbal acrobat who walks the tightrope of the zeitgeist, educate me. How should I have responded?"

"First, get rid of 'well.' Nobody uses that anymore either. Now they always say, 'I'm good.' "

Leif frowned. "But that is grammatically improper."

"These people don't care about proper. You can tell them they're trying to use an adjective as an adverb and they'll just stare at you like you're a toad."

"Their educational system has suffered serious setbacks, I see."

"Tell me about it. So what you should have said was, 'I'm not stoked like you, Atticus, but I'm chill.' "

"I'm 'chill'? That means I am well—or good, as you say?"

"Correct."

"But that's nonsense!" Leif protested.

"It's modern vernacular." I shrugged. "Date yourself if you want, but if you keep using nineteenth-century diction, people will start to think you're a spooky bastard."

"They already think that."

"You mean because you only come out at night and you suck their blood?" I said in a tiny, innocent voice.

"Precisely," Leif said, unaffected by my teasing.

"No, Leif." I shook my head in all seriousness. "They don't figure that out until much later, if they ever figure it out at all. These people think you're spooky because of the way you talk and the way you behave. They can tell you don't belong. Believe me, it's not that you have skin like two-percent milk. Lots of people are scared of skin cancer out here in the Valley of the Sun. It's once you start talking that people get creeped out. They know you're old then."

"But I *am* old, Atticus!"

"And I've got at least a thousand years on you, or have you forgotten?"

He sighed, the weary ancient vampire who had no need for respiration. "No, I have not forgotten."

"Fine. Don't complain to me about being old. I hang out with these college kids and they have no clue that I'm not one of them. They think my money comes from an inheritance or a trust fund, and they want to have a drink with me."

"I find the college children delightful. I would like to have a drink with them too."

"No, Leif, you want to drink *of* them, and they can sense that subconsciously because you radiate this predatory aura."

His affectation of a henpecked husband sloughed away and he looked at me sharply. "You told me they can't sense my aura as you do."

"No, they can't consciously sense it. But they pick up on your *otherness*, mostly because you don't respond like you should or act like a man of your cosmetic age."

"How old do I look?"

"Ehh," I appraised him, looking for wrinkles. You look like you're in your late thirties."

"I look that old? I was turned in my late twenties."

"Times were tougher back then." I shrugged again.

"I suppose. I have come to talk to you about those times, if you are free for the span of an hour or so."

"Right, I replied, rolling my eyes. Just let me go get my hourglass and my freakin' smoking jacket. Listen to yourself, Leif! Do you want to blend in or not? The span of an hour? Who says shit like that anymore?"

"What's wrong with that?"

"No one is so formal! You could just say 'if you're free' and end it there, though it would have been better to say 'if you ain't doin' nothing.' "

"But I enjoyed the anapestic meter of 'for the span of an hour' followed by the iamb—"

"Gods Below, you compose your sentences in blank verse? No wonder you can't carry on a half hour's conversation with a sorority girl! They're used to talking with frat boys, not Shakespearean scholars!"

<Atticus? You're home?> It was my Irish wolfhound, Oberon, speaking directly to my mind through the connection we share. He was probably on the other side of the door, listening to us talk. I told Leif to hold on a second as I spoke with him.

Yes, Oberon, I'm home. Leif's out here on the front porch, acting his age.

<I know, I smelled him earlier. It's like Eau de Death or something. I didn't bark, though, like you said.>

You're a good hound. Want to come hang out with us?
<Sure!>

I have to warn you, it might be boring. He wants to talk about something for a while, and he's looking particularly grim and Nordic. It might be epic.

<That's okay. You can rub my belly the whole time. I promise to be still.>

Thanks, buddy. I promise we'll go for a run when he leaves. I opened the front door and Oberon came bounding out, oblivious to the fact that his wagging tail was delivering steady blows to Leif's upper arm.

<Let's go down to Town Lake after the dead guy says good-bye. And then Rúla Búla.> He named our favorite Irish pub, from which I'd recently been banned.

The management of Rúla Búla is still mad at me for stealing Granuaile away from them. She was their best bartender.

<Still? But that was ages ago.>

It's been only three weeks, I reminded him. Dogs aren't all that great with time. *I'll let you run around the golf course and you can keep any rabbits you catch. Flop down for your belly rub. I have to talk to Leif now.* Oberon promptly obeyed, rattling the timbers of the porch as he thudded heavily onto his back between my seat and Leif's.

<This is the best! There's nothing better than belly rubs. Except maybe for French poodles. Remember Fifi? Good times, good times.>

"All right, Leif, he's a happy hound now," I said as I scratched Oberon's ribs. "What did you want to talk about?"

"It is fairly simple," he began, "but as with all simple things, vastly complicated."

"Wait. You sound too accomplished with adverbs. Use *really* and *very* for everything," I advised him.

"I would rather not, if you will forgive me. Since I am

not trying to disguise my true nature with you, may I speak as I wish?"

"Of course," I said, biting back the observation that he should use contractions more often. "I'm sorry, Leif, I'm just trying to help, you know."

"Yes, and I appreciate it. But this is going to be difficult enough without running my words through a filter of illiteracy." He took a deep, unnecessary breath and closed his eyes as he slowly exhaled. He looked like he was trying to center himself and find a chakra point. "There are many reasons why I require your aid, and many reasons why you should agree to help me, but those can wait a few moments. Here is the short version," he said, opening his eyes and turning to look at me. "I want you to help me kill Thor."

<Ha! Tell him to get in line!> Oberon said. He chuffed as he always did when he found something particularly funny. Thankfully, Leif did not recognize that my dog was laughing at him.

"Hmm," I said. "Thor certainly tends to inspire murderous thoughts. You're not the first person to suggest that to me these past couple of weeks."

Leif pounced. "One of the many reasons you should agree to help. You would have ample allies to secure whatever aid you needed and plenty of grateful admirers should you succeed."

"And plenty of mourners should I fail? If he's so universally hated, why hasn't someone else done the deed?"

"Because of Ragnarok," Leif replied, obviously anticipating the question. "That prophecy has everyone afraid of him, and it has made him insufferably arrogant. Their line of reasoning says that if he is going to be around for the end of the world, then obviously nothing can be done about him now. But that is poppycock."

I smiled. "Did you just say Ragnarok is poppycock?" Oberon chuffed some more.

Leif ignored me and plowed on. "Not all of the prophesied apocalypses can come true, just as only one of the creations can possibly be true, if any of them are. We cannot be tied down by some ancient tale dreamed up in the frozen brains of my ancestors. We can change it right now."

"Look, Leif, I know you have a saga full of reasons why I should do this, but I really can't internalize any of it. I simply don't think it's my duty to do this. Aenghus Óg and Bres both came to me and picked a fight, and all I did was finish it. And, you know, it could have easily gone the other way. You weren't there: I nearly didn't make it. You've seen this, I imagine?" I pointed to my disfigured right ear. A demon that looked like the Iron Maiden mascot had chewed it off, and I hadn't been able to regenerate anything except a mangled mass of cartilage. (I'd already caught myself singing, "Don't spend your time always searching for those wasted ears.")

"Of course I've seen it," Leif replied.

"I'm lucky I got away with so little damage. Even though I haven't paid a huge price for killing Aenghus, I've had several unpleasant visits from other gods as a result. And that's only because I'm still small potatoes. Can you imagine what the rest of the gods would do if I managed to knock off someone big like Thor? They'd all take me out collectively just to remove the threat. Besides, I don't think it's possible to kill him."

"Oh, but it is possible," Leif said, raising a finger and shaking it at me. "The Norse gods are like your Tuatha Dé Danann. They have eternal youth, but they can be killed."

"Originally, yeah," I agreed. "I've read the old stuff, and I know that you're after Thor version 1.0. But you know, there's more than one version of Thor out there now, just like there are multiple Coyotes and various versions of Jesus and Buddha and Elvis. We can invade Asgard, kill Thor 1.0, and then, if we manage to avoid getting creamed by the rest of the Norse, we could come back here to Midgard only to have the comic book Thor smite the hell out of us like the naughty varlets we are. Did you think about that?"

Leif looked utterly bewildered. "Thor has a comic book?"

"Yeah, how did you miss this? There's a movie about him based on the comic too. He's a heroic kind of guy here in the States, not nearly so much of a dick as the original. He'll ignore you unless you draw attention to yourself, and storming Asgard will probably get his attention pretty fast."

"Hmm. Say that I can put together a coalition of beings willing to participate in the physical assault on Asgard and accompany us back to Midgard. Could I count on your aid in such a scenario?"

I slowly shook my head. "No, Leif, I'm sorry. One reason I'm still alive is that I've never gone toe-to-toe with a thunder god. It's a good survival strategy, and I'm going to stick with it. But if you're going to do something like that, I recommend avoiding Loki. He'll pretend to be on your side, but he'll spill his guts to Odin first chance he gets, and then you'll have that entire pantheon coming after you with a wooden stake."

"That might be preferable to me, at this point, than continuing to coexist with him. I want revenge."

"Revenge for what, exactly?" Normally I don't pry into vampiric psychology, because it's so predictable: The only things they tend to get exercised about are power and territory. They enjoy being asked questions, though, so that they can ignore you and appear mysterious when they don't answer.

Leif never got the chance to answer me, though he looked ready enough to do so for a half second. As he opened his mouth to speak, his eyes flicked down to the base of my throat where my cold iron amulet rested, just as I began to feel the space between my clavicles heat up—even burn.

"Um," Leif said in perhaps his most inarticulate moment ever, "why is your amulet glowing?"

I felt the heat surge like mercury on an August morning, sweat popped out on my scalp, and the sickening sound of sizzling in my ears was a little piece of me frying like bacon. And even though I instinctively wanted to peel off the necklace and chuck it onto the lawn, I fought back the urge, because the smoldering lump of cold iron—the antithesis of magic—was the only thing keeping me alive.

"I'm under magical attack!" I hissed through clenched teeth as I clutched the chair arms, white-knuckled and concentrating on blocking the pain. I wasn't working on that only to silence my screaming nerves; if I let the pain get to me, I was finished. Pain is the fastest way to stir up the reptilian brain, and once awakened, it tends to shut off the higher functions of the cerebral cortex, leaving one witless and unable to function beyond the instinctive fight-or-flight level—and that would have left me unable to communicate coherently and connect the dots for Leif, in case he was missing out on the salient point: "Someone's trying to kill me!"